Andrew Lang

The Companions of Pickle

Being a Sequel to Pickle the Spy

Andrew Lang

The Companions of Pickle
Being a Sequel to Pickle the Spy

ISBN/EAN: 9783337295936

Printed in Europe, USA, Canada, Australia, Japan

Cover: Foto ©Andreas Hilbeck / pixelio.de

More available books at **www.hansebooks.com**

'The Earl's Marischal'
1717.

THE

COMPANIONS OF PICKLE

BEING A SEQUEL TO 'PICKLE THE SPY'

BY

ANDREW LANG

WITH FOUR ILLUSTRATIONS

LONGMANS, GREEN, AND CO.
39 PATERNOSTER ROW, LONDON
NEW YORK AND BOMBAY
1898

PREFACE

THE appearance of 'Pickle the Spy' was welcomed
by a good deal of clamour on the part of some Highland critics. It was said that I had brought a
disgraceful charge, without proof, against a Chief of
unstained honour. Scarcely any arguments were
adduced in favour of Glengarry. What could be
said in suspense of judgment was said in the *Scottish
Review*, by Mr. A. H. Millar. That gentleman, however, was brought round to my view, as I understand, when he compared the handwriting of Pickle
with that of Glengarry. Mr. Millar's letter on the
subject will be found in this book (pp. 247, 248).

The doubts and opposition which my theory
encountered made it desirable to examine fresh
documents in the Record Office, the British Museum,
and the Royal Library at Windsor Castle, while
General Alastair Macdonald (whose family recently
owned Lochgarry) has kindly permitted me to read
Glengarry's MS. Letter Book, in his possession. The
results will be found in the following pages.

Being engaged on the subject, I made a series of

studies of persons connected with Prince Charles,
and with the Jacobite movement. Of these the Earl
Marischal was the most important, and, by reason of
his long life and charming character—a compound
of 'Aberdeen and Valencia'—the most interesting.
As a foil to the good Earl, who finally abandoned the
Jacobite party, I chose Murray of Broughton, who,
though he turned informer, remained true in sentiment, I believe, to his old love.   His character may,
perhaps, be read otherwise, but such is the impression
left on me by his 'Memorials,' documents edited
recently for the Scottish History Society by Mr.
Fitzroy Bell.

In Barisdale, whose treachery was perfectly well
known at the time, and was punished by both parties,
we have a picture of the Highlander at his worst.
Culloden made such a career as that of Barisdale for
ever impossible.

In the chapters on 'Cluny's Treasure' and 'The
Troubles of the Camerons' I have, I hope, redeemed
the characters of Cluny and Dr. Archibald Cameron
from the charges of flagrant dishonesty brought
against them by young Glengarry.   Both gentlemen
were reduced to destitution, which by itself is incompatible with the allegations of their common enemy.

'The Uprooting of Fassifern' illustrates the
unscrupulous nature of judicial proceedings in Scotland after Culloden.   A part of Fassifern's conduct
is not easily explained in a favourable sense, but he
was persecuted in a strangely unjust and intolerable

manner. Incidentally it appears that public indignation against this sort of procedure, rather than
distrust of 'what the soldier said' in his ghostly
apparitions, procured the acquittal of the murderers
of Sergeant Davies.

'The Last Days of Glengarry' is based on a study
of his MS. Letter Book, while 'The Case against
Glengarry' sums up the old and re-states the new
evidence that identifies him with Pickle the Spy.

The last chapter is an attempt to estimate the
social situation created in the Highlands by the
collapse of the Clan system.

I have inserted, in 'A Gentleman of Knoydart,'
an account of a foil to Barisdale, derived from the
Memoirs of a young member of his clan, John
Macdonell, of the Scotus family. The editor of
Macmillan's Magazine has kindly permitted me to
reprint this article from his serial for June 1898.

A note on 'Mlle. Luci' corrects an error about
Montesquieu into which I had fallen when writing
'Pickle the Spy,' and throws fresh light on Mlle.
Ferrand.

It is, or should be, superfluous to disclaim an
enmity to the Celtic race, and rebut the charge of
'not leaving unraked a dunghill in search for a
'cudgel wherewith to maltreat the Highlanders, particularly those who rose in the Forty-five.' This
elegant extract is from a Gaelic address by a minister
to the Gaelic Society of Inverness.[1] I have not

¹ *Literature*, July 30, 1898, p. 93.

raked dunghills in search of cudgels, nor are my
sympathies hostile to the brave men, Highland or
Lowland, who died on the field or scaffold in 1745-53.
The perfidy of which so many proofs come to light
was in no sense peculiarly Celtic. The history of
Scotland, till after the Reformation, is full of
examples in which Lowlanders unscrupulously used
the worst weapons of the weak. Historical conditions, not race, gave birth to the Douglases and
Brunstons whom Barisdale, Glengarry, and others
imitated on a smaller scale. These men were the
exceptions, the rare exceptions, in a race illustrious
for loyalty. I have tried to show the historical and
social sources of their demoralisation, so extraordinary when found among the countrymen of
Keppoch, Clanranald, Glenaladale, Scotus, and
Lochiel.

I must apologise for occasional repetitions which
I have been unable to avoid in a set of separate
studies of characters engaged in the same set of
circumstances.

My most respectful thanks are due to Her
Majesty for her gracious permission to study the
collection of Cumberland Papers in her library at
Windsor Castle. Only a small portion of these
valuable documents has been examined for the
present purpose. Mr. Richard Holmes, Her Majesty's
Librarian, lent his kind advice, and Miss Violet
Simpson aided me in examining and copying these
and other papers referred to in their proper places.

Indeed I cannot overestimate my debt to the research and acuteness of this lady.

To General Macdonald I have to repeat my thanks for the use of his papers, and the Duke of Atholl has kindly permitted me to cite his privately printed collections, where they illustrate the matter in hand.

Sir Thomas Gibson Carmichael was good enough to lend me, for reproduction, his miniature of the Duke of York and Prince Charles.

The earlier portrait of the Earl Marischal is from the Scottish National Museum, the later (of 1752?) is from the National Portrait Gallery. It gives a likeness of one of the good Earl's menagerie of young heathens. The miniature of Prince Charles (p. 110) is a copy or replica of one given by him to a Macleod of the Raasay house in September, 1746. The Royal Society of Edinburgh kindly permitted me to have copies made of several of the Earl Marischal's letters to David Hume, in their possession. In some of these (unprinted) the Earl touches on a theme for which *le bon David* frankly expresses his affection in a letter to the Lord Advocate.

CORRIGENDA

P. 12, note, *for* twenty-two in 1716, *read* twenty-three

P. 17, note, *for* 33,900 *read* 33,950

CONTENTS

ILLUSTRATIONS

COMPANIONS OF PICKLE

..

I

THE LAST EARL MARISCHAL

In a work where we must make the acquaintance of some very unfortunate characters, it is well to begin with a *preux chevalier*. If there was a conspicuously honest man in the eighteenth century, one 'whose conscience might gild the walls of a dungeon,' as an observer of his conduct declared, that man was the Earl Marischal, George Keith. The name of the last Earl Marischal of Scotland haunts the reader of the history of the eighteenth century. He appears in battles for the Stuart cause in 1715 and 1719, he figures dimly in the records of 1745, and of Charles Edward, after the ruin of Culloden. We find him in the correspondence of Voltaire, Rousseau, Hume, and Frederick the Great, and even in Casanova. He is obscurely felt in the diplomacy which ended in Pitt's resignation of office. Many travellers describe his old age at Potzdam, and d'Alembert wrote his *Éloge*.

B

He was the last direct representative of that historical house of Keith whose laurels were first won in the decisive charge of Bruce's handful of cavalry on the English archers at Bannockburn. Though the Earl Marischal of the confused times after the death of James V. was a pensioner of Henry VIII., like so many of the Scottish *noblesse*, the House was Royalist, and national as a rule. Yet, after a long life of exile as a Jacobite, the last Earl Marischal, always at heart a Republican, reconciled himself to the House of Hanover. The biography of the Earl has never been written, though few Scottish worthies have better deserved this far from uncommon honour.

Materials for a complete life of the Earl do not exist. We are obliged to follow him by aid of slight traces in historical manuscripts, biographies, memoirs, and letters, published or unpublished. Even in this unsatisfactory way, the Earl is worth pursuing ; for if he left slight traces on history, and was never successful in action, he was a man, and a humourist, of singular merit and charm, a person almost universally honoured and beloved through three generations. This last of the Earls Marischal of Scotland was certainly one of the most original and one of the most typical characters of the eighteenth century. Losing home, lands, and rank for the cause of Legitimism, the Earl was the reverse of a fanatical Royalist ; indeed he seems to have become a Jacobite from Republican principles. These were strengthened, no doubt, by his great experience of kings; but even when he was a young man his bookplate bore the motto *Manus hæc inimica tyrannis*. Then probably, as certainly in later life, he loved to praise Sidney, and others who (in his opinion) died for freedom. Yet the Earl was 'out,' for no Liberal cause, in 1715, and in 1719 : while he was plotting against King George and for King James, till 1745. He was admitted to the secret of the rather Fenian Elibank Plot in 1752, and only reconciled himself with the English Government in 1759. On his death-bed he called himself ' an old Jacobite,' while, for twenty years at least, his favourite companions had been the advanced thinkers, prelusive to the Revolution, Rousseau, Hume, d'Alembert, Voltaire, Helvetius.

All this appears the reverse of consistent. The Earl gave up everything, and risked his life often, for the White Rose, while his opinions, religious and political, tended in the direction of the Red Cap of Liberty and the Rights of Man. The explanation is that the Earl, when young, a patriotic Scot, and a persecuted Episcopalian, saw ' freedom ' in the emancipation of Scotland from a foreign tyrant, the Elector of Hanover ; in the Repeal of the Union, and in the relief of his religious body from the tyranny of the Kirk. Till his death he was all for liberty, and could not bear to see even a caged bird. These were the unusual motives (these, and the influence of his mother, a Jacobite by family and sentiment) which converted a born Liberal into a partisan of the King over the Water. Thus this representative

of traditional and romantic Scottish loyalty to the
Stuarts was essentially a child of the advanced, and
emancipated, and enlightened century which succeeded that into which he was born.

Original in his political conduct, the Earl was no
less unusual in personal character. He was one of
those who, as Plato says, are 'naturally good,' naturally examples of righteousness in a naughty world.
Nature made him temperate, contented, kind, charitable, brave, and humorous—one who, as Montaigne
advises, never 'made a marvel of his own fortunes.'
His virtue, as far as can be learned, owed nothing to
religion. He was 'born to be so,' as another man is
born to be a poet. He had a native genius for excellence.

He was ruined without rancour, and all the
buffets of unhappy fortune, all the political and
social vicissitudes of nearly a century, could not
cloud his content, or diminish his pleasure in life
and the sun. He was true to his exiled Princes,
till they, or one of them at least, ceased to be true
to themselves. He was perhaps the only friend
whom Rousseau could not drag into a quarrel or
estrange, and the only companion whom Frederick
the Great loved so well that he never made experi-
ments on him in the art of tyrannical tormenting.
Familiar, rather than respectful, with Voltaire, the
Earl, who remembered Swift in his prime, was fond
of gossiping with Hume and of bantering d'Alembert.
Kind and charitable to all men, he was especially

considerate and indulgent to the young, from the
little exiled Duke of York to the soured Elcho, and
the still unsuspected Glengarry. One exception alone
did the Earl make (unless we believe Rousseau) : he
could not endure, and would not be reconciled to,
Prince Charles. If in this he may seem severe, no
other offence is laid to his charge, though modern
opinion may condemn his cool acquiescence in desperate plots which he probably never expected to
be carried into action. Otherwise the Earl presents
the ideal of a good and wise man of the world,
saved from all excess, and all disappointment, by
the gifts of humour and good-humour. When we
add that ' the violet of a legend,' of unfortunate but
life-long love, blows on the grave of the good Earl,
it will be plain that, though not a hero, like his
brother, Marshal Keith, he was a character of no
common distinction and charm. His life, too, is
almost an epitome of the Jacobite struggle from 1715
to 1757. The Earl was ever behind the scenes.

Though tenth Earl (the first of the hereditary
Marischals to be 'belted earl' was William, in 1458),
George Keith was apt to mock at hereditary *noblesse.*
Stemmata quid faciunt? He had a story of a laird
who grumbled, during a pestilence, ' In such times a
gentleman is not sure of his life.' The date of his
birth was never known. In old age he cast an
agreeable mystery about this point. He was once
heard to say that he was twenty-seven in 1712 ; if
so, he died at ninety-three (1778). Others date his

birth in 1693, others in 1689; d'Alembert says (on the authority of one who had the fact from Ormonde) that he was *premier brigadier* of that general's army in 1712. An engraving from a portrait of the Earl as a young man represents him as then twenty-three years of age. If the engraving was done in Paris, as seems probable, in 1716, he would be born in 1693. Oddly enough the pseudo-Memoirs of Madame de Créquy (who is made to speak of him as her true love) throw a similar cloud over the year of her birth. Concerning the Earl's father, Lockhart of Carnwath writes that he had great vivacity of wit, an undaunted courage, and a soul capable of great things, 'but no seriousness.' His mother, of the house of Perth, was necessarily by birth a Jacobite. The song makes her say:

> I'll be Lady Keith again
> The day the King comes o'er the water.

The Earl's tutor was probably Meston, the Jacobite wit and poet.

The Earl succeeded his father in 1712. His own first youth had been passed in Marlborough's wars; from 1712 to the death of Queen Anne, and the overthrow of hopes of a Restoration by the Tories, he lived about town, a brilliant colonel of Horse Guards, short in stature and slight in build, but with a beautiful face, and dark, large eyes. So we see him in the portrait of about 1716.

The following letter, the earliest known letter of the Earl, displays him as a disciplinarian. Conceiv-

ably the mutinous Wingfeild was a Jacobite, but, by
September 12, 1714, the chance for a rising of the
Guards for King James had passed. Queen Anne
was dead, and the Earl was still colonel in the army
of George 1.

To Lord Chief Justice Parker

Stowe MSS. 750, f. 58.   'September 12, 1714.

'My Lord.—As soon as I heard that your Lordship
had granted a Habeas Corpus for Thom^{as} Wingfeild
one of the private men of His Majesties Second
Troop of Horse Grenadier Guards under my Command, I sent a Gentleman to wait upon your Lordship and to acquaint you with the reasons for my
ordering Wingfeild to be confin'd to the Marshall of
the Horse Guards according to the practice of the
Army, but your Lordship was not then at your
Chambers; I now take the liberty to inform you
that the Prisoner has not only been guilty of uttering
menacing words & insolently refusing to comply
with the establisht Regulations of the Troop, (to
which Regulations he has subscribd) but has also
been endeavouring to raise a mutiny therein, which
crimes among Soldiers being of dangerous Consequences I did intend to have him try'd by a General
Court Martial, that he might have been exemplarily
punisht as far as the Law allows to deter others
from the like practices: but as there is no warrant for holding a Court Martial for the Horse
Guards extant, & I being unwilling to trouble their

Excell^cies the Lords Justices on this occasion, I had ordered my officers to hold a Regimental Court Martial upon him yesterday in order to break him at the head of the Troop, which is the only punishment they can inflict, but they did not proceed then on acco^t of the Habeas Corpus; this I thought fit to acquaint your Lordship with and to assure you that I am &c.

'MARISCHALL.'

From Lockier, Spence got the familiar anecdote of the Earl's conduct at Queen's Anne's death, before the projects for a Restoration of the Chevalier were completed. Ormonde, Atterbury, and the Earl met, when Atterbury bade Marischal go out (with the Horse Guards) and proclaim King James. Ormonde wished to consult the Council. 'Damn it,' says Atterbury in a great heat (for he did not value swearing), 'you very well know that things have not been concerted enough for that yet, and that we have not a moment to lose.' That moment they lost, and a vague anecdote represents the Earl as weeping, after the battle of Sheriffmuir, over the many dead men who might have been alive had he taken Atterbury's advice. D'Alembert, who does not mention Atterbury, attributes the idea of an instant stroke for the King to the Earl himself.[1]

When the rising of 1715 was in preparation,

---

[1] There is a brief sketch of the Earl in his brother's Memoirs (Spalding Club), which cites d'Alembert, and puts the Earl's birth in 1687.

the Earl, according to d'Alembert, wrote to James, telling him that 'a sovereign deprived of his own must share the dangers of those who risked their lives for his sake,' and so made him 'leave his retreat' at Bar-le-Duc. But James's natural brother, the Duke of Berwick, on July 16, 1715, had already given the same advice. 'Your honour is at stake, your friends will give over the game if they think you backward.' James replied that he hoped to be at Dieppe by the 30th of the month. Within five days Berwick was crying off from the task of accompanying his brother, who replied with a repressed emotion, ' You know what you owe to me, what you owe to your own reputation and honour, what you have promised to the Scotch and to me. . . . I shall not, therefore, bid you adieu, for I expect that we shall soon meet.'

It was now not the King who turned laggard, but Berwick who advised delay. '*I find Rancourt*' (the King), he says, ' very much set on his *journey.*' In brief, it was Berwick and Bolingbroke who kept James back, though with great difficulty. He needed no urging (as d'Alembert suggests) by our Earl. · I fear I shall scarce be able to hinder him from passing the sea,' says Berwick (August 6).

Then Louis XIV. died, all was confusion, and the Regent Orléans detained Berwick in France, exactly at the time when Mar went to raise the Highlands. What with Bolingbroke, Berwick, the death of Louis XIV., and the intrigues of Orléans in the Hanoverian interest, James, travelling disguised through an Odyssey of perils, did not leave France for Scotland till mid-December. A month before (November 13) Mar had been practically defeated at Sheriffmuir, and Forster, Mackintosh, Derwentwater and Kenmure had surrendered at Preston. The King thus came far too late, but certainly by no lack of readiness on his part.

D'Alembert makes the Earl utter a fine constitutional speech on the duties of a king, when he proclaimed James at Edinburgh. Unluckily, on this occasion James was never proclaimed at Edinburgh by anybody. The *Éloge* of d'Alembert is eloquent, but it is not history. It has been the chief source for the Earl's biography.

The Earl had doubtless been won over by Mar to resign his English commission, and desert King George for King James. The story is told that, as he rode North from London in 1715 to join Mar in the Highlands, he met his young brother James riding South to take service with King George. He easily induced his brother to share his own fortunes, and Prussia ultimately gained the great soldier thus lost to England. The Covenanting historian, Wodrow, avers that 'Marischal was bankrupt,' and therefore eager for *res novæ*. But he would have been a Jacobite in any case. As to the Earl's conduct when Mar's ill-organised and ill-supplied rising drew fatally to a head at Sheriffmuir, his brother, the Field-Marshal of Prussia, in his fragmentary Memoir,

tells all that we know. The Earl, with 'his own
squadron of horse' and some Macdonalds, was sent
to occupy a rising ground, the enemy being, as was
thought, in Dunblane. From the height, however,
the whole hostile army was seen advancing, and the
Earl sent to bid Mar bring up his forces. There
was much confusion, and the Earl's squadron of
horse was left in the centre of the line. Mar's right
with the Earl routed Argyll's left, while Argyll's
left routed Mar's right. 'In the affair neither side
gained much honour,' says Keith, 'but it was the
entire ruin of our party.' Half of Mar's force,
having thrown down their plaids,[1] were now un-
clothed; many had deserted; the evil news of the
Preston surrender came, the leaders were at odds
among themselves, 6,000 Dutch troops were advancing from England. Seaforth and Huntly took their
followers back to the North, and when King James
arrived at Perth, late in December, he found a
wintry welcome, soldiers few and dispirited, and
dissensions among the officers. The army wasted
away while Cadogan, Argyll, and the Dutch troops,
greatly outnumbering the Jacobites, advanced on
Perth through the snow.

James's army now beat a retreat, with no point to
make for, as Inverness was in the hands of the enemy.
Mar, therefore, advised James, who had not ammunition enough for one day's fight (thanks to Bolingbroke,

---

[1] Plaids worn by the Earl and his brother are preserved in a
house in Fifeshire.

said the Jacobites), to take ship at Montrose. If he
stayed, the enemy would make their utmost efforts
to come up with and capture him. If he departed,
the retreating Highlanders would be less hotly pursued. James consulted Marischal, who wished to
offer no opinion, alleging ' his age and want of experience,' says Keith.[1] Finally, he privately admitted to
Mar that ' he did not think it for the King's honour,
nor for that of the nation, to give up the game without
putting it to a tryall.' Powder enough for one day's
fight could be got at Aberdeen; he hoped to gain
recruits as they went North, and, at worst, James,
if beaten, could escape from the West coast. ' Mar
seemed to be convinced of the truth of this ' (very
like Bobbing John); ' however, a ship was already
provided,' and James, with Mar, Melfort, and others,
eloped; the King characteristically leaving all his
money to recompense the peasants who had suffered
by the war. James was no coward, he had charged
the English lines repeatedly, at the head of the Royal
Household, in the battle of Malplaquet, where he
was wounded. In his journey from Lorraine to the
coast he had run the gauntlet of Stair's cut-throats.
But a Scottish winter, a starveling force, no powder,
and Mar's advice, had taken the heart out of the
adventurer.

---

[1] This remark makes it probable that the Earl was really a young
man. If born in 1693, as some thought, he would be twenty-three
in 1716. (As, indeed, one of d'Alembert's authorities says that he
was.) If a year or two older, he could scarcely have pleaded youth as
a reason for silence.

According to Mar, the Earl had orders to sail with the King, 'who waited on the ship above an hour and a half, but, by what accident we yet know not, they did not come, and there was no waiting longer.'[1] 'The King and we are in no small pain to know what is become of our friends wee left behind.' D'Alembert says that the Earl refused to sail. 'Your Majesty is to protect yourself for your friends. I shall share the sorrows of those who remain true to you in Scotland, I shall gather them, and shall not leave without them.' If Mar tells truth, the Earl can have made no such speech. A modest man, he remained at his duty without rhetoric.

The dispirited and deserted Highland army moved North, and the Earl was sent to ask Huntly whether he would join them—in which case they would fight at Inverness—or not. 'He easily perceived by Huntly's answer that nothing was to be expected from him.' They, therefore, marched to Ruthven, whence they scattered, Keith and the Earl fared westwards with Clanranald's men, and made for the Islands. Hence they sailed in a French ship on May 1, and reached St. Pol de Léon on May 12. There were a hundred officers of them together, and all this destroys d'Alembert's romance, modelled on the adventures of Prince Charles, about the Earl's dangers and the noble behaviour of the crofters among whom he was wandering. An English force was, indeed, at one time within thirty miles of

[1] Mar to 'H. S.' From France, February 10, 1716.

the fugitives, but there was nobody to whom Clanranald's men could have been betrayed, not that
any one was likely to betray them, and the Earl
Marischal and James Keith with them. In truth,
d'Alembert confused this occasion with another, after
Glenshiel fight, in 1719.

Many of the fugitives went to James at Avignon,
but Keith stayed in Paris, where Mary of Modena
received him well. 'Had I conquered a kingdom
for her she could not have said more ' She gave him
1,000 livres, while James granted what he could,
200 crowns yearly. Keith does not say that the
Earl was in Paris, where his portrait was probably
painted at this date. There, however (as is known
from an unpublished MS.), he certainly was, and he
might even, by Stair's mediation, have obtained his
pardon. But he supposed that the cause would presently triumph, and declined to make any advances
to George I. He was now in correspondence with
General Dillon, James's military representative in
Paris. In August, 1717, Dillon writes to him about
one ' Prescot,' who is suspected of intending to murder
James in Italy; he refers to Lord Peterborough, who
was arrested on this impossible charge at Bologna in
September 1717.[1] In 1719 the Earl and his brother
went to Spain. There was then war between Spain
and England, Ormonde was with Alberoni, and was
to be employed. Keith would have gone thither

---

[1] Mr. Eliot Hodgkin's MSS., *Hist. MSS. Com.* xv. ii. Appendix,
p. 230.

earlier, but 'I was then too much in love to think of
quitting Paris.'

Here, in Paris, 1717-18, if ever, would have to be
fixed the Earl's legendary romance with Mademoiselle
de Froullay (Madame de Créquy). The story, a very
pretty one, is given in this lady's Mémoires, an ingenious but fraudulent compilation.

An author best known for his plagiarisms seized
on Madame de Créquy as a likely old person to have
left memoirs behind her. By aid of gossip and books
he patched up the amusing but mythical records
which he attributed to the lady. Why he selected
the Earl as the lover of her girlhood we can only
guess; but dates and facts make the pretty tale
incredible, though it has found its way into Chambers's
account of the Earl's career. Thus, for example, it is
averred by Sainte-Beuve, on the authority of her man
of business, M. Percheron, that Madame de Créquy
was born in 1711. The love story of 1717, told in
her Memoirs, beginning in the Earl's attempt to teach
her Spanish and English, and interrupted by the fact
that he was a 'Calvinist,' is therefore improbable.
The lady was but three years old when her affections,
according to her apocryphal Memoirs, were blighted.
The lovers met again, when the Earl was Prussian
Ambassador at Versailles in 1753. 'We had not
had the time to discover each other's faults, we had
not suffered each by the other's imperfections, both
remained under that illusion which experience destroyed not: we were happy in the sweet thought of

ineffable excellence, and when we met in the wane of
life, and either saw the other's white hair, we felt
an emotion so pure, so tender, and so solemn, that
no other sentiment, no other impression known to
mortals, can be compared to it.' All this is charming, but it cannot conceivably be true! The Earl
composed his one madrigal under the influence of
this elderly emotion (say the pseudo-Memoirs), a
tear stole down his withered cheek, and he assured
Madame de Créquy that they would meet in Heaven.
' I loved you too much not to embrace your religion.'
So runs the romance of the pseudo-Madame Créquy.

In fact, the Earl remained a member of the persecuted Episcopal Church in Scotland. In Rome a
priest tried to convert him, beginning with the
Trinity. ' Your Lordship believes in the Trinity ?'
' I do,' said the Earl; ' but that just fills up my
measure. A drop more and I spill all.'

Madame de Créquy's Mémoires are obviously a
daring forgery, but the ' violet of a legend ' has a
fragrance of its own. The Earl was in 1716, as his
portrait shows, a singularly handsome young man,
with large hazel eyes and an eager face, with a
complexion like a girl's beneath his brown curls.
Madame de Créquy is made to say, by way of giving
local colour, that he greatly resembled a portrait of *le
beau Caylus*, a favourite of Henri III. The portrait
was in her family.

In 1719, to return to facts, the two Keiths were
received in Spain by the Duc de Liria, son of the

Duke of Berwick, who had heard of an intended
expedition to England. In Barcelona the splendour
of their welcome, they travelling incognito, amazed
them. They had been, in fact, mistaken for their
rightful King and one of his officers, who were
expected. From Barcelona they went to Madrid,
whence Alberoni sent the Earl posting all about the
country after Ormonde, who was to command the
invading forces. Ormonde was a kind of figure-head
of Jacobite respectability. He was presumed to be the
idol of the British army at the time of Queen Anne's
death; he had added his mess to the general chaos
of Tory imbecility in 1714, and, in place of playing
Monk's part in a new Restoration, had fled abroad.
A few of his letters of 1719 to the Earl survive : he
hopes for ' the justice which the Cause deserves,' and
when his fleet is scattered in the usual way, reports
the uneasiness of James about the Earl.[1]

The Earl in Spain arranged what he could
with the Cardinal, while Keith passed through
France, then hostile to Spain, and met the exiled
Tullibardine in Paris. Here all was confusion,
the Jacobites—Seaforth, Glendarule, and Tullibardine—being deep in the accustomed jealousies.
They sailed, however, and reached the Lewes,
where Keith met his brother, the Earl ; but here
divided counsels and squabbles about rank and commissions arose. The Earl succeeded in bringing the
Spanish auxiliary forces to the mainland, and was

[1] Add. MSS. 33,950. 1718 1719. British Museum.

C

for marching at once against Inverness. The other
faction, that of Seaforth and Tullibardine, dallied;
the ammunition, stored in a ruinous old castle on an
island, was mostly seized by English vessels. News
arrived that Ormonde's fleet, sailing from Spain, had
been dispersed on the seas, and the Highlanders
came in very reluctantly. The Jacobites landed at
the head of Loch Duich, and were posted on a hill-
side in Glenshiel, commanding the road to Inverness.
Hence the English forces drove them to the summit
of the mountain, and night fell. They had neither
food, powder, nor any confidence in their men, so the
Spaniards surrendered, the Highlanders dispersed,
and Keith thus began his glorious military career in
a style somewhat discouraging.

Lord George Murray, later the general in the
Rising of 1745, was also in this rather squalid
engagement. Keith was suffering from a fever, and
he with his brother 'lurcked in the mountains.' On
this occasion, no doubt, the Earl profited by the
loyalty of his countrymen, among whom (says an
anonymous informant of d'Alembert's) he moved
without disguise. He is even said to have been
present when a proclamation was read aloud offering
a reward for his apprehension. His adventures
increased his love for his own people; indeed, he
certainly espoused the Jacobite cause as a national
Scottish patriot, not for dynastic reasons.

Keith and his brother, after 'lurcking' for months
in the Northern wilds, escaped from Aberdeen to

Holland, in September 1719. Thence they made for
Spain, intending to enter France by Sedan. But as
they had no passports they were stopped in France
and imprisoned. Keith hit on an ingenious way of
getting rid of their Spanish commissions, which
would have been compromising, and a letter to the
Earl from the Princesse de Conti served as a voucher
for their respectability, and procured their release.
They reached Paris when the fever of the Mississippi
Scheme was at its height. Jacobites as needy as
they, the Oglethorpe girls and George Kelly, probably got hints from Law, the great financial adventurer, and founder of the Mississippi Scheme. The
young Jacobite ladies bought in at par and sold at a
huge premium. They thus won their own *dots*, and
married great French nobles. Even poor George
Kelly had a success in speculation. He was, at this
time, Atterbury's secretary, and being involved in
his fall, passed fourteen years in the Tower. In
1745 he was one of the famed Seven Men of Moidart,
but none the dearer on that account to the Earl,
who never trusted him, and, in 1750, caused him
to be banished from the service of the Prince. All
these adventurers, Law, the Oglethorpes, Olive
Trant, Kelly, and the Keiths, may have met in Paris,
after Glenshiel. But the Earl and his brother did
not make their fortunes in the Mississippi Scheme.
They had no money, and Keith frankly expresses his
contempt for the speculations after which all the
world was running mad. The brothers passed to

c 2

Montpellier, Keith attempted to enter Spain by Tou-
louse, the Earl by the Pyrenees. Months later Keith
tried the Pyrenees passes, and there, at an inn, met
his brother, who had been arrested and imprisoned
for six weeks. The King of France had just set him
free, with orders to leave the kingdom, and the
wandering pair of exiles went to Genoa, then a focus
of Jacobite intrigue, whence they sailed to Rome, to
see ' the King, our Master.'

Jacobites lived in an eternal hurry-scurry.
James had been driven from France to Lorraine;
then to Avignon, where Stair planned his assassination;[1] then to Urbino, Bologna, and Rome. Sailing
for Spain, in 1719, he had been obliged to put in
near Hyères, and there to dance all night—the
melancholy monarch—at a ball in a rural inn.
Spain could do nothing for him, and he returned to
Rome, whither Charles Wogan brought him a bride,
fair, unhappy Clementina Sobieska, just rescued from
an Austrian prison. Keith says nothing of her, but
tells how, at Cestri de Levanti, his brother called on
Cardinal Alberoni, now fallen from power and in
exile. The Earl, with some lack of humour, wanted
to tell the Cardinal all about the Glenshiel fiasco, but
was informed that the statesman had no longer the
faintest concern with the affairs of Spain or interest
in the gloomy theme.

From Leghorn the brothers went by land

---

[1] There are copies of his correspondence with the would-be
murderer in the Gualterio MSS., British Museum.

through Pisa, Florence, and Siena to Rome. The
King, 'who knew we were in want of money,' sent
Hay to borrow 1,000 crowns from the Pope, 'which
was refused on pretence of poverty; this I mention
only to shew the genious of Clement XI., and how
little regard Churchmen has for those who has
abandoned all for religion.' His Majesty, therefore,
raised the money from a banker. The exiled King's
chief occupation was providing for his destitute
subjects : most of his letters were begging letters.

The point for which the Keiths had been making
ever since their escape from Scotland was Spain.
Baffled in attempting to cross the Pyrenees, and
penniless, they reached Spain by taking Rome on
their way, James providing the funds with the difficulty which has been described. From Civita
Vecchia they sailed back to Genoa. Now, Jacobite
privateers, under Morgan, Nick Wogan, and other
wandering knights, were rendering Genoa unluckily
conspicuous by making the harbour their head-
quarters. The tiny squadron for years hung about
all coasts to aid in a new rising.

The English Minister, D'Avenant, threatened to
bombard the town if the Keiths were not expelled,
while, if they *were*, the Spanish Minister said that he
would insist on the banishment of all the Catalan
refugees in Genoa. To oblige the Senate of Genoa
in their awkward position, Keith and the Earl
departed, and coasted from the town to Valentia in
a felucca, sleeping on shore every night.

It is probable that the brothers were suspected of a part in that form of the Jacobite plot which chanced to exist at the moment. From 1688 to 1760, or later, there had been really but one plot, handed on from scheming sire to son, and adapting itself to new conditions as they happened to arise. The study of the plot is, indeed, a pretty exercise in evolution. The object being a Restoration, the most obvious plan is a landing of foreign troops in England, with a simultaneous rising of the faithful. First France is to send the foreign troops; and she did actually despatch them, or try to despatch them, at various times—witness La Hogue, Dunkirk, and Quiberon Bay. When France will not stir, other Powers are approached. Sweden would have played this part, in 1718, but for the death of Charles XII. Then Spain made her effort, in 1719, with the usual results. There were hopes, again, from Russia, as from Sweden, and from Prussia in 1753.

After each failure in this kind, the Jacobites tried 'to do the thing themselves,' as Prince Charles said, either by assassination schemes (which Charles Edward invariably set his foot on), or by a simultaneous rising in London and the Highlands, or by such a rising aided by Scots or Irish troops in foreign service landed on the coast. From the failure at Glenshiel to 1722 this was the aspect of the plot. Atterbury, Oxford, Orrery, and North and Grey were managers in England, Mar and Dillon in Paris, while Morgan and Nick Wogan commanded

the poor little fleet.[1] Ormonde, in Spain, was to
carry over Irish regiments in Spanish service. The
Jacobites had the ship prepared years before for the
expedition of Charles XII., with two or three other
vessels. The gallant Nick Wogan, who, as a mere
boy, had been pardoned, after Preston, for rescuing
a wounded Hanoverian officer under fire, was hover-
ing on the seas from Genoa to the Groin. George
Kelly was going to and fro between Paris and
London, 'a man of far more temper, discretion, and
real art' than Atterbury, says Speaker Onslow.

When the scheme for Ormonde's amateur invasion failed, a mob-plot of Layer's followed it; but all
was revealed. Kelly and Atterbury were seized;
Atterbury was exiled, Kelly lay in the Tower, and
Layer was hanged.

Keith says nothing of any part borne by his
brother or himself in these feeble conspiracies. One
Neynho, arrested in London, averred that the Earl
Marischal had been in town on this business, in
disguise, and had shared his room. Neynho merely
guessed that his companion was the Earl, who certainly was on friendly terms with Atterbury. Long
afterwards he wrote (1737): 'I was told in Italy
that Pope had thought of publishing a collection
of familliair letters, particularly of ye Bishop; as
I was honoured with Many, I sent copys of a
part and parts (sic) to Pope.' These, however,

---

[1] The author hopes to tell the story of Mr. Wogan, a charming
character, on another occasion.

could not have been political epistles. The originals must have perished when the Earl burned all his papers, as d'Alembert's authorities report, in 1745.[1]

On the whole, it seems certain that Keith, at least, was not in the plots of 1720–22; Keith, indeed, lay ill in Paris in 1723–24, suffering from a tumour. The Earl now held a commission from Spain, which secured for him a pension, irregularly paid; but, being a Protestant, he never received an active command, except once, in an affair with the Moors. There was no harm, it seemed, in sending a heretic to fight against infidels. His great friend in Spain was the Duchess of Medina Sidonia, who was anxious to convert him.

'She spoke to him of a certain miracle, of daily occurrence in her country. There is a family, or caste, which, from father to son, have the power of going into the flames without being burned, and who by dint of charms permitted by the Inquisition can extinguish fires. The Earl promised to surrender to a proof so evident, if he might be present and light the fire himself. The lady agreed, but the *questadore*, as these people are called, would never try the experiment, though he had done so on a former occasion; he said that fire had been made by a heretic, who mingled charms with it, and that he felt them from afar.'

This was unlucky, as these families whom fire

---

[1] Hist. MSS. Commission, x. i. Appendix, p. 475.

does not take hold on exist to-day in Fiji, as of old
among the Hirpi of Mount Soracte.

The Earl had no trouble with the Inquisition, being
allowed to have what books he pleased, as long as he
did not lend them to Spanish subjects. 'His religious
ideas were far from strict . . . but he could not
endure to hear these questions touched on when
women were present, or the poor in spirit ; it was a
kind of talk which in general he carefully avoided,'
—except among *philosophes*.[1] Hume tells us that
the Earl Marischal and Helvetius thought they were
ascribing an excellent quality to Prince Charles
when they said that he 'had learned from the philo-
sophers at Paris to affect a contempt of all religion.'
It seems improbable that the Earl was more ' emancipated ' than Hume, but his wandering life had made
him acquainted with the extremes of Scottish Presby-
terianism, with the Inquisition in Spain, the devotions
of his King in Rome, the levities of Voltaire and
Frederick, and all the contemptuous certainties of the
Encyclopédistes. The Earl rather loved a bold jest
or two, in philosophic company, and his *mots* were
not always in good taste. As a Norseman's religion
was mainly that of his sword, the Earl's appears to
have been that of his character, which was instinc-
tively affectionate, indulgent, and charitable. If he
had neither Faith nor Hope, which we cannot assume,
he was rich in Charity.

It is, perhaps, no longer possible to trace all the

[1] Letter from Musell Stosch to d'Alembert, *Œuvres*, v. 457.

wanderings of the Earl after his brother entered the
Russian service in 1728. In those years the exiles
were mainly concerned about the quarrels between
James and his wife, which had an ill effect on their
Royal reputation in Europe. The Courts chiefly
solicited for aid at this period were those of Moscow
and Vienna. Spain did not pay her pension to James
with regularity, and the Earl Marischal, then as later,
may have suffered from the same inconvenience. This
may account for his return to Rome, where he resided
in James's palace, about 1730-34. 'He has the
esteem of all that has the honour to be known to
him, and may be justly styled the honour of our
Cause,' writes William Hay to Admiral Gordon, who
represented Jacobite interests in Russia (Feb. 2, 1732).
The little Court at Rome was as full of jealousies as
if it had been at St. James's. Murray, brother of
Lord Mansfield, was Minister, under the title of Lord
Dunbar, while James's other 'favourite' Hay (Lord
Inverness) was at Avignon out of favour, and had
turned Catholic. The pair were generally detested
by the other mock-courtiers. These gentlemen had
formed themselves into an Order of Chivalry, 'The
Order of Toboso,' alluding to their Quixotry. Prince
Charles (aged twelve) and the Duke of York (a hero
of seven) were the patrons. 'They are the most lively
and engaging two boys this day on earth,' writes
William Hay. The Knights of the Order sent to
Gordon in Russia their cheerful salutations, signed
by 'Don Ezekiel del Toboso' (Zeky Hamilton),

'Don George Keith' (the Earl), and so on. They declined to elect Murray, because he had ' the insolence to fail in his respect to a right honourable lady who is the ever honoured protectress of the most illustrious Order of Toboso,' Lady Elizabeth Caryl. A number of insults to Murray follow in the epistle.[1]

All this was rather dull, distasteful work for the Earl. He received from James the Order of the Thistle (' the green ribbon '); but, except perhaps at Rome, he would not wear a decoration not more imposing than that of the Toboso Order. Writing to his brother, he drew a pretty picture of the little Duke of York, who was fond of the Earl, and used to bring his weekly Report on Conduct to be criticised and sent on to Keith, far away in Russia. Keith was asked to comment on it, or, if he did not, the Earl was diplomatist enough to do so in his name. Prince Charles the Earl seems to have disliked from the first. He had already, at the age of thirteen, 'got out of the hands of his governors,' the Earl writes, and indeed the Prince's spelling alone proves the success with which he evaded instruction. But, to please the little Duke, the Earl sent for a sword from Russia. The Duke was a pretty child, and wept from disappointment when his elder brother, in 1734, went off to the siege of Gaeta, while he, a warrior of nine, remained in Rome.

The Earl disliked the tiny jealous Court; the

---

[1] Hist. MSS. Commission, x. i. Appendix, p. 184.

impotent cabals, the priests who tried to convert him. Writing to David Hume long afterwards, in 1762, he said, ' I wish I could see you, to answer honestly all your [historical] questions; for, though I had my share of folly with others, yet, as my intentions were at bottom honest, I should open to you my whole budget.' When he wrote thus he had made his peace with England. Why he did so we shall try to point out later.

Always scrupulously honest (except when diplomatic duties forbade, and even then he hated lying), the Earl told his brother that he found the Jacobite Court at Rome no place for an honest man. He does not give details, but he seems to hint at some enterprise which, in his opinion, was not honourable. James, moreover, was sunk in devotion, weeping and praying at the tomb of Clementina. From this uncongenial society the Earl departed, and took up his abode at the Papal city of Avignon, where Ormonde now resided. He liked the charming old place, and thought it especially rich in original characters. By 1736, however, he had returned to Spain, where, as he said, he was always sure to find ' his old friend, the Sun.' News of the Earl comes through some very harmless correspondence, intercepted at Leyden, in 1736, by an unidentified spy.[1] Don Ezekiel del Toboso (Hamilton) was now out of favour with James, which, judging by his very foolish letters, is no marvel. He resided

[1] Hist. MSS. Commission, x. i. Appendix, p. 452.

at Leyden, corresponding with Ormonde and George
Kelly. George, after fourteen years of the Tower,
since Atterbury's Plot. had escaped in a manner at
once ingenious, romantic, and strictly honourable.
Carte, the historian. was another correspondent ; but
gossip was the staple of their budgets—gossip and
abuse of James's favourites, Dunbar and Inverness.
In Spain the Earl officially represented James, but
his chief employments were shooting and reading.
His Spanish pension was unpaid (he had a small
allowance from the Duke of Hamilton), and he was
minded ' to live contentedly upon a small matter,' he
says, rather than to ' pay court in anti-chambers to
under Ministers whom I despise.' ' I wo na gie an inch
o' my will for an ell o' my wealth,' he remarks, in
the Scots proverbial phrase. A Protestant canton
in Switzerland would suit him best, where a little
money will furnish all that he requires. ' I am
naturally sober enough, as to my eating, more as to
my drinking, I do not game, and am a Knight
Errant *sin amor*, so that I need not great sums for
my maintenance.' A Knight *sin amor* the Earl seems
usually to have been. He must have been over
forty at this time, and he had not yet acquired his
celebrated fair Turkish captive. The Earl, however,
had not given up all hope of active Jacobite service.
' I propose to try if I can still do anything, or have
even the hopes of doing something.' He had a
' project,' and, as far as the hints in his letters can
now be deciphered, it was to remove James, or, at

all events, Prince Charles, from Rome (a place distrusted by Protestant England), and to settle one or
both of them—in Corsica !

The Earl was interested, as a patriotic Scot, in
the hanging of Porteous by the Edinburgh mob.
' It's certain that Porteous was a most brutal fellow ;
his last works at the head of his Guard was not the
first time he had ordered his men to fire on the
people.   I will not call them Mobb, who made so
orderly an Execution.'

To this extent may Radical principles carry a
good Jacobite ! The Earl should have written the
work contemplated by Swift, ' A Modest Defence of
the Proceedings of the Rabble, in All Ages.'

A quarrel with the Spanish Treasurer, who was
short of treasure, ended in somebody assuring the
official that the Earl was a man of honour, ' who
would go afoot eating bread and water from this to
Tartary *con un doblon.*' To Tartary, or near it, the
Earl was to go, though he had been invited by
Ormonde to Avignon.   Till the end of the year
1737, Kelly and others hoped to settle Prince
Charles in Corsica, with the Earl for his Minister.
Marischal was expected by Ormonde at Avignon, in
the last week of December, and thither he went for
a month or two, leaving for St. Petersburg in March,
to visit his brother.   Keith had been severely
wounded at the assault on Oczakow, and the Earl
found him insisting that he would not have his leg
amputated.   The Earl took his part, and brought

Keith to Paris, where the surgeons saved his leg, but where he had to suffer another serious operation. Thence the devoted brothers went to Barège, where Keith recovered health. He returned to Russia, leaving in the Earl's care Mademoiselle Emetté, a pretty Turkish captive child, rescued by him at the sack of Oczakow, and Ibrahim, another True Believer. These slaves, says a friend who gave information to d'Alembert, were treated by the Earl as his children. He educated them, he invested money in their names (probably when he was in the service of Frederick the Great), and he cherished a menagerie of young heathens, whom his brother had rescued in sieges and storms of towns. One, Stepan, was a Tartar; another is declared to have been a Thibetan, and related to the Grand Lama. The Earl was no proselytiser, and did not convert his Pagans and Turks. It is said that he was not insensible to the charms of pretty Emetté.

'Can I never inspire you with what I feel?' he asked.

'Non!' replied the girl, and there it ended.

The Earl made a will in her favour, in 1741, and she later—much later—married M. de Fromont. The love story is not very plausible, before 1741, as Emetté was still a girl when she accompanied the Earl to Paris, during his Embassy, in 1751.

The movements of the Earl are obscure at this period, but in 1742-43 he was certainly engaged for the Jacobite interest in France, residing now at Paris, now at Boulogne. The unhappy 'Association' of Scottish Jacobites had been founded in 1741. Its promoters were the inveterate traitor, Lovat, and William Macgregor, of Balhaldie, who, since 1715, had lived chiefly in France, and was a trusted agent of James. Balhaldie's character has been much assailed by Murray of Broughton, who was himself connected with the Association. As far as can be discovered Balhaldie was sanguine, and even of a visionary enthusiasm, when enterprises concocted by himself were in question. The adventures of other leaders, especially adventures not supported by France, he distrusted and thwarted. The loyal Lochiel and the timid Traquair were also of the Association, which Balhaldie amused in 1742 with hopes of a French descent under the Earl Marischal. Balhaldie had promised to the French Court 'mountains and marvels' in the way of Scottish assistance, and the Earl 'treated his assertion with the contempt and ridicule it deserved,' says Murray of Broughton. The Earl's own letters show impatience with Balhaldie and Lord Sempil, James's other agent in Paris. Thus, on February 12, 1743, the Earl writes from Boulogne to Lord John Drummond, whose chief business was to get Highland clothes wherein the Duke of York might dance at the Carnival. The Earl protests, in answer to a remark of Sempil's, that he 'has more than bare curiosity in a subject where the interest of my King and native country is so nearly concerned (not to speak of my own), where I see a noble spirit, and where I am sensible a great deal of honour is done me, and I add, that I still hope these gentlemen will do me the honour and justice to believe that I shall never fail either in my duty to my King and country, my gratitude to them for their good opinion, or in my best endeavours to serve.' All this was in reply to Sempil's insinuation that the Scottish Jacobites thought the Earl lukewarm. Murray confirms the Earl by telling how Balhaldie tried to stir strife between the Earl and the Scots, who revered him, though Balhaldie styled him 'an honourable fool.' [1]

Lord John Drummond suggested to James's secretary, Edgar, that the Earl should supersede Balhaldie, 'who had been obliged to fly the country in danger of being taken up for a Fifty pound note.' Lord John's advice was excellent. The Earl, and he alone, was the right man to deal with the party in Scotland, who could trust his sense, zeal, and honour. But James, far away in Rome, could never settle these distant and embroiled affairs. He went on trusting Balhaldie, who was also accepted by the party in England. Had James cashiered Balhaldie and instated the Earl, matters would have been managed with discretion and confidence. The Earl was determined not to beguile France into an endeavour based on the phantom hosts of Balhaldie's imagination. Had he been minister, it is highly probable that nothing would have been done at all,

[1] The Earl's letter is in Browne, ii. 448, from the Stuart Papers.

and that Prince Charles would never have left Italy. For Balhaldie continued to represent James in France, and Balhaldie it was. with Sempil, who induced Louis XV. to adopt the Jacobite cause. and brought the Prince to France in 1744. While his father lived, Charles never returned to Rome.

On December 23, 1743, James sent to the Duke of Ormonde. an elderly amorist at Avignon,[1] his commissions as General of an expedition to England and as Regent till the Prince should join. The Earl received a similar commission as General of a diversion, 'with some small assistance,' to be made in Scotland. The Earl was at Dunkirk, eager to sail for Scotland, by March 7, 1744. and Charles was somewhere, *incognito*, in the neighbourhood. But the Earl, as he wrote to d'Argenson, had neither definite orders nor money enough ; in short, as usual. everything was rendered futile by French shilly-shallying and by the accustomed tempest. D'Alembert and others assert that Charles asked the Earl to set forth with him alone in a sailing-boat, to which the Earl replied that, if he went. it would be to dissuade the Scottish from joining a Prince so brave but so ill-supported. It is certain that d'Argenson told Marshal Saxe that the Prince ought to retire to a villa of the Bishop of Soissons, with the Earl for his *chaperon*. The Earl was still anxious for an expedition in force, but d'Argenson distrusted his information on all points.

---

[1] The Rev. George Kelly was a constraint on the old Duke's amours with Madame de Vaucluse !

Charles declined to go and skulk at the Bishop's, and
wrote that ' if he knew his presence unaided would
be useful in England he would cross in an open boat.' [1]

On this authentic evidence the Earl was anxious
to make an effort, and Charles's remark about going
alone in an open boat was conditional—*s'il savait que
sa présence seule fût utile en Angleterre*. But no energy,
no hopes, no courage, could conquer the irresolution
of France. By April Prince Charles was living, *très
caché*, in Paris. Thus his long habit of hiding arose
in the *incognito* forced on him by the Ministers of
Louis XV. The Prince, as he writes to his father
(April 3, 1744), was ' goin about with a single servant bying fish and other things, and squabling for
a pency more or less.' He was anxious to make
the campaign in Flanders with the French army,
' and it will certainly be so if Lord Marschal dose
not hinder it. . . . He tels them that serving in
the Army in flanders, it would disgust entirely the
English,' in which opinion the Earl may have been
wrong. Charles accuses the Earl of stopping the
Dunkirk expedition (and here d'Alembert confirms),
' by saying things that discouraged them to the last
degree: I was plagued with his letters, which were
rather Books, and had the patience to answer them,
article by article, striving to make him act reasonably, but all to no purpose.' [2]

[1] Papers from French Foreign Office. In Murray of Broughton's
Memorials, pp. 499 501.

[2] Charles to James, May 11, 1744. Stuart Papers in Murray
of Broughton's *Memorials*, p. 368.

It was not easy to 'act reasonably,' where all
was a chaos of futile counsels and half-hearted
French schemes. They would and they would not,
in the affair of the expedition of March 1744. We
find the Earl now urging despatch, now discouraging
the French, and, on September 5, 1744, he writes to
James, from Avignon, · there was not only no design
to employ me, but there was none to any assistance
in Scotland.' [1]   The Earl believed that the Prince's
incognito was really imposed on him by the devices
of Balhaldie and Sempil, 'to keep him from seeing
such as from honour and duty would tell him truth.'

Through such tortuous misunderstandings and
suspicions on every side, matters dragged on till
Charles forced the game by embarking for Scotland
secretly in June 1745. The Earl Marischal was the
man whom he sent to report this step to Louis XV.
' I hope.' Charles writes to d'Argenson, 'you will
receive the Earl as a person of the first quality, in
whom I have full confidence.' The Earl undertook
the commission.[2]   On August 20, 1745, he sent in a
Mémoire to the French Court. Lord Clancarty had
arrived, authorised (says the Earl) to speak for the
English Jacobite leaders, the Duke of Beaufort, the
Earl of Lichfield, Lord Orrery, Lord Barrymore,
Sir Watkin Williams Wynne, and Sir John Hinde
Cotton. They offered to raise the standard as soon
as French troops landed in England. When they

<hr/>

[1] Stuart Papers. Browne, ii. 476.
[2] Compare Villettes' letter, *postea*, p. 48.

made the offer, the English Jacobites (who asked
for 10.000 infantry, arms for 30.000, guns, and pay)
did not know that Charles had landed in Scotland.
D'Argenson naturally asked for the seals and signatures of the English leaders, as warrants of their
sincerity. He could not send a *corps d'armée* across
the Channel on the word of one individual, and such
an individual as the profane, drunken, slovenly, one-
eyed Clancarty. The Earl, on October 23, 1745,
tried to overcome the scruples of d'Argenson, but in
vain.[1] Clancarty, it is pretty clear, came over as a
result of the persuasions of Carte, the historian, in
whom the leading English Jacobites had no confidence. 'The wise men among them would neither
trust Lord Clancarty's nor Mr. Carte's discretion in
any scheme of business,' says Sempil to James (September 13. 1745).

Sempil was ever at odds with the Earl, who, says
Sempil. 'insists on great matters.' French policy
was to keep sending small supplies of money and
men to support agitation in Scotland. The Earl did
not want mere agitation and a feeble futile rising;
he wanted strong measures, which might have a
chance of success. 'He can trust nobody,' says
Sempil, 'and is persuaded that the French Court
will sacrifice our country, if his firmness does not
prevent it.' The Earl was right; what he foresaw
occurred. Sempil, however, was not far wrong,
when he observed that the Prince was already

---

[1] Stuart Papers, in Murray of Broughton's *Memorials*, pp. 513–514.

engaged, and a little help was better than none. 'I
am sorry to see my old friend so very unfit for great
affairs,' writes Sempil.   The Earl had ever been
adverse to a wild attempt by the Prince, as a mere
cause of misery and useless bloodshed. He probably
thought that no French support and a speedy collapse of the rising were better than trivial aid, which
kept up the hearts of the Highlanders, and urged
them to extremes.

By October 19 the Duke of York was flattered
with hopes of sailing at the head of a large French
force.   The force hung about Dunkirk for six
months, doing nothing, and then came Culloden.
The Duke was prejudiced against Sempil and his
friend Balhaldie, and already there was a split in the
party, Sempil on one side, the Earl Marischal on
the other.   George Kelly returned from Scotland,
as an envoy to France, but Sempil would not trust
him even with the names of the leading English Jacobites. The secrecy insisted on by Sir Watkin Williams
Wynne, Lord Barrymore, the Duke of Beaufort, and
the others was kept up by Sempil even against Prince
Charles himself. This naturally irritated the Earl,
and, what with Jacobite divisions in France, and
French irresolution, Marischal had to play a tedious
and ungrateful part.   James expected him to join the
Prince, but he, for his part, gave James very little
hope of the success of the adventure.[1]   James him-

---

[1] James to the Duke of York. November 8, 1745. Browne, iii.
452, where all the correspondence is printed.

self, with surprising mental detachment, admitted
that the best plan for the English Jacobites was ' to
lie still,' and make no attempt without the assistance
from France which never came.

The Earl disappears from the diplomatic scene,
on which he had done no good, in the end of 1745.
He obviously attempted to settle quietly in Russia
with his brother. But the Empress ' would not so
much as allow Lord Marischal to stay in her country,'
wrote James to Charles, in April 1747. Ejected
from the North, he sought · his old friend, the
sun,' in the South, at Treviso, and at Venice. The
Prince, in August 1747, wrote from Paris imploring
the Earl to join him, for the need of a trustworthy
adviser was bitterly felt. The Earl replied with
respect, but with Republican brevity, pleading his
· broken health,' and adding, 'I did not retire from
all affairs without a certainty how useless I was, and
always must be.'

At Venice the Earl entertained a moody young
exile, who tells a story illustrating at once his host's
knowledge of life, the strictness of his morality,
and his freedom from a tendency to censure the
young and enterprising.[1]

From Venice the much-wandering Earl retired
to his most sure and hospitable retreat. He joined
his brother, who had now entered the service of

---

[1] The Memoirs of the exile in question, unhappily, have never
been printed, and I do not feel at liberty to anticipate any points
of interest in these curious papers.

Frederick the Great. He reached Berlin in January 1748. Frederick, asking first whether his estates had been confiscated, made him a pension of 2,000 crowns. Frederick loved, esteemed, sheltered, and employed the veteran, 'unfit for affairs' as he thought himself. No doubt Frederick's first aim was to attach to himself so valuable an officer as Keith, by showing kindness to his brother. But the Earl presently became personally dear to him, as a friend without subservience, and a philosopher without vanity or pretence. In his new retreat the Earl was not likely to listen to the prayers of Prince Charles, who, being now a homeless exile, implored the old Jacobite to meet him at Venice. Henry Goring carried the letters, in April 1749, and probably took counsel with the veteran. Nothing came of it, except the expulsion from the Prince's household at Avignon of poor George Kelly, a staunch and astute friend, who was obnoxious to the English Jacobites. Since 1717 Kelly had served the Cause, first under Atterbury, then—after fourteen years' imprisonment—in France, Scotland, and as the Prince's secretary. He had been Lord Marischal's ally in 1745, but Rousseau says that the Earl's failing was to be easily prejudiced against a man, and never to return from his prejudice. Kelly's letter to Charles might have disarmed him. 'Nobody ever had less reason or worse authority than Lord Marischal for such an accusation ; for your Royal Highness knows well I always acted the contrary part, and never failed representing the advantage and even necessity of having him at the head of your affairs. . . . His Lordship may think of me what he pleases, but my opinion of him is still the same.' There seems to be no doubt that the Earl had written to Floyd (whom he commends to Hume as an honest witness) to say that ' from a good hand' he learned that Kelly ' opposed his coming near the Prince.' and had spoken of him as ' a Republican, a man incapable of cultivating princes.' The Earl *was* ' incapable of cultivating princes,' and Rousseau esteemed him for the same. But it was under Kelly's influence that Charles, in 1747. tried to secure the society and services of the Earl. He had been prejudiced (as Rousseau says he was capable of being), probably by Carte the historian. Years afterwards. when the Earl had disowned Charles, Kelly returned to the Prince's household. He never had a stauncher adherent than this Irish clergyman of exactly the same age as his father. History, like the Earl Marischal, has been unduly prejudiced against honest George Kelly.[1]

[1] Letters in Browne, iv. 64 66. Conceivably it was Goring who prejudiced the Earl against Kelly ; he may have conveyed the ideas of Carte and the English party.

II

THE EARL IN PRUSSIAN SERVICE

ABOUT the Earl's first years in the company of the great Frederick little is known or likely to be known. *Deus nobis hæc otia fecit*, he may have murmured to himself while he refused the Prince's insistent prayers for his service, and put his Royal Highness off in a truly Royal way, with his miniature in a snuff-box of mother-of-pearl. The old humourist may have reflected that men had given lands and gear for the cause, and now, like the representative of Lochgarry, have nothing material to show for their loyalty, save an inexpensive snuff-box of agate and gold. No, the Earl would not travel from Venice in 1749 to meet the Prince.

His name occurs in brief notes of Voltaire, then residing with Frederick, and quarrelling with his Royal host. Voltaire kept borrowing books from the Scottish exile, books chiefly on historical subjects. If we may believe Sir Charles Hanbury Williams, then at Berlin, the celebrated Livonian mistress of Keith caused quarrels between him and his brother, and even obliged them to live separately.[1] The

---

[1] See Sir Charles's letter of February 6, 1751, in *Pickle the Spy*, p. 117.

Earl gave much good advice to Henry Goring, the
Prince's envoy at that time, and if he was indeed on
bad terms with his brother (these bad terms cannot
have lasted long), he may have been all the better
pleased to go as Frederick's ambassador to Versailles
in August 1751. Thither he took his pretty Turkish
captive, and all his household of Pagans, Mussulmans,
Buddhists, and so forth. I have elsewhere described
the Earl's relations with Prince Charles, then lurking
in or near Paris; his furtive meetings with Goring at
lace shops and in gardens, his familiarity with Young
Glengarry, who easily outwitted the Earl, and his
unprejudiced tolerance of a perfectly Fenian plot -
the Elibank Plot—for kidnapping George II., Prince
Fecky, and the rest of the Royal Family. The Earl
merely looked on. He gave no advice. His ancient
memories could not enlighten him as to how the
Guards were now posted. 'What opinion, Mr.
Pickle,' he said to Glengarry, 'can I entertain of
people that proposed I should abandon my Embassy
and embark headlong with them?' The Earl had
found a haven at last in Frederick's favour. He was
willing to help the cause diplomatically, to send
Jemmy Dawkins to Berlin, to sound Frederick,
and suggest that, in a quarrel with England, the
Jacobites might be useful. He was ready enough
to dine with the exiles on St. Andrew's Day, but not
to go further. When Charles broke with the faithful
Goring in the spring of 1754, the Earl broke with
him, rebuked him severely, and never forgave him.

He had never loved Charles; he now regarded him as impossible, even treacherous, and ceased to be a Jacobite.

The nature of his charges against the Prince will appear later. Meanwhile, as the Prince had behaved ill to Goring, who fell under his new mania of suspicion, as he declined to cashier his mistress, Miss Walkinshaw, in deference to English and Scottish requests, as he was a battered, broken wanderer, *sans feu ni lieu*, the Earl abandoned him to his fate, and even, it seems, officially ' warned the party against being concerned with him.' After forty years of faithful though perfectly fruitless service, the Earl apparently made up his mind to be reconciled, if possible, to the English Government. Though his appointment as ambassador had been a direct insult to Frederick's uncle, George II., the great diplomatic revolution which brought Prussia and England into alliance was favourable to the Earl's prospects of pardon.

He probably accepted the Embassy not without hopes of being able to do something for the Cause. James certainly took this view of the appointment. But the end had come. The retreat of Charles in Flanders had been detected at last by the English. The English dread of Miss Walkinshaw, and the quarrel over that poor lady, made themselves heard of in the end of 1753. By January 17, 1754, we find Frederick writing to the Earl that he ' will secretly be delighted to see him again.' Frederick

Der Carl Harnemar
engis

bade Marshal Keith send an itinerary of the route
which the Earl ' will do well to follow' on his return
to Prussia. On the same day Keith wrote to his
brother the following letter, which shows that their
affection, if really it had been impaired, was now
revived :—[1]

'17 January, 1754.

'I'm glad my dearest brother says nothing of his
health in the letter . . . 27th Dec., for Count
Podewils had alarmed me a good deal by telling
me that you had been obliged more than once to
send Mr. Knyphausen in your place to Versailles, on
occasion of incommoditys; and tho' I hope you
would not disguise to me the state of your health
. . . yet a conversation I had some days ago with
the King gives me still reason to suspect that it is
not so good as I ought to wish it. He told me that
for some time past you had solicitated him to allow
you to retire . . . and at your earnest desire he had
granted your request, but at the same time had
acquainted you how absolutely necessary it was for
his interest that you should continue in the same
post till the end of harvest, by which time he must
think of some other to replace you ; he asked me at
the same time if your intention was to return here :
to which I answer'd . . . it was, tho' I said this
without any authority from you . . . he told me
that in that case he thought you should keep the
time of your journey and route as private as possible,

[1] These letters are from the printed Correspondence of Frederick.

and that after taking leave of the Court of France
you should give it out that your health required
your going for some time to the S. of France, that
it was easy on the way to take a cross road to Stras-
bourg and Francfort, and after passing the Hessian
dominions to turn into Saxony, by which you would
evite all the Hanoverian Territories and arrive
safely here. Everything he said was more like a
friend than a sovereign, and showed a real tenderness for your preservation . . .'

Frederick did not wish his friend to run any
risk of being kidnapped in Hanoverian territory, by
the minions of the Elector. The Earl could not be
allowed to return at once, for the clouds over Anglo-
Prussian relations were clearing, while England was
at odds with France, both about the secret fortifying
of Dunkirk, contrary to treaty, about the East Indies,
and about North America. So Frederick philoso-
phised, in letters to the Earl, concerning the disagreeable yoke he had still to bear, and about the inevitable
hardships of mortal life in general. He also asked
the Earl to find him a truly excellent French cook.
On March 31, Frederick offered the Earl the choice
of any place of residence he liked, and expressed a
wish that he could retire from politics. He foresaw
the crucial struggle of his life, the Seven Years' War.
' But every machine is made for its special end : the
clock to mark time, the spit to roast meat, the
mill to grind. Let us grind then, since such is my

fate, but believe that while I turn and turn by no
will of my own, nobody is more interested in your
philosophical repose than your friend to all time and
in all situations where you may find yourself.'

Frederick is never so amiable as in his correspondence with the old Jacobite exile.

At this period, Frederick gave the Earl information of Austrian war preparations, for the service of
the French Ministry. Saxony and Vienna excited
his suspicions. He did not yet know that he was to
be opposed also to France. He was occupied with
dramatists and actors, 'more amusing than all the
clergy in Europe, with the Pope and the Cardinals at
their head.' He has to diplomatise between Signor
Crica and Signora Paganini, but hopes to succeed
before King George has had time to corrupt his new
Parliament. Happier letters were these to receive
than the heart-broken appeals which rained in from
Prince Charles, letters which the Earl had hoped to
escape by retiring from his Embassy. Here his negotiations 'had embroiled him with the cooks of Paris,'
but he had acquired the friendship of d'Alembert,
whom he introduced to Frederick. The King thought
d'Alembert 'an honest man,' and agreed with the
Earl's preference for heart above wit. 'They who
play with monkeys will get bitten,' which refers to
Frederick's quarrel with Voltaire. The Earl warned
the wit that some big Prussian officer would probably
box his ears if he persisted in satirising his late host.
'Rare it is,' says Frederick, 'to find, as in you, the

combination of wit, character, and knowledge, and
it is natural that I should value you all the more
highly.'

In May 1754, the Earl, while still pressing to be
relieved from duty, was eager to undertake any
negotiations as to an *entente* between Prussia and
Spain. a country which he loved. There was an
opportunity—General Wall, of an Irish Jacobite
house, being now minister in the Peninsula.

The Earl left Paris in the end of June (carrying
with him to Berlin poor Henry Goring. who was near
death), and accepted the Government of Neufchâtel.
While (February 8, 1756) Frederick's throne was
'threatened by Voltaire, an earthquake, a comet,
and Madame Denis,' the Earl was trying to soothe
Protestant fanaticism, then raging in his little realm.

' They will tell you, my dear Lord,' writes
Frederick, ' that I am rather less Jacobite than of
old. Don't detest me on that account.' It is known,
from a letter of Arthur Villettes, at Berne (May 28,
1756), to the English Government, that the Earl was
making no secret of his desire to be pardoned.[1] The
Earl spoke of the Prince, now, with ' the utmost
horror and detestation,' declaring that since 1744
' his life had been one continued scene of falsehood,
ingratitude and villainy, and his father's was little
better.'

Such, alas ! are the possibilities of prejudice.
The Earl accused Charles of telling the Scots, previous

[1] Ewald, *Charles Edward*, ii. 223.

to his expedition in 1745, that the Earl approved of it. There is no evidence in Murray of Brough-ton that Charles ever hinted at anything of the kind Charles's life, from 1744 till he returned to France, is minutely known. He had not been false and villainous. He had been deceived on many hands, by Balhaldie (as the Earl strenuously asserted), by France, by Macleod, Traquair, Nithsdale, Kenmure, by Murray of Broughton, and he inevitably acquired a habit of suspicion. Lonely exile, bitter solitude, then corrupted and depraved him; but the Earl's remarks are much too sweeping to be accurate, where we can test them. In the case of James we can test them by his copious correspondence. His letters are not, indeed, those of a hero, but of a kind and loving father, who continually impresses on Charles the absolute necessity of the strictest justice and honour, especially in matters of money, ' for in these matters both justice and honour is concerned ' (' Memorials,' p. 372, Aug. 14, 1744). As to politics, James was absolutely opposed to any desperate adventure, any hazarding, on a slender chance, of the lives and fortunes of his subjects. His temper, schooled by long adversity, made him even applaud the reserve of his English adherents, and excuse, wherever it could be excused, the conduct of France, and attempt, by a mild tolerance, to soothe the fatal jealousies of his agents. No Prince has been more ruthlessly and ignorantly calumniated than he whose ' ails ' and sorrows had converted him into a philosopher no

E

longer eager for a crown too weighty for him. into
a devout Christian devoid of intolerance, and disinclined to preach.

The Earl was justified in forsaking a Cause
which Charles had made morally impossible. But he
believed, in spite of Charles's contradiction, that he
had threatened to betray his adherents. This prejudice is the single blot on a character which, once
animated against a man, never forgave.

The correspondence of Frederick with his Governor of Neufchâtel is scanty ; he had other business
in hand—the struggle for existence. On July 8, 1757,
he writes from Leitmentz. thanking the Earl for a
present of peas and chocolate. On October 19, 1758,
he sends the bitter news of the glorious death of
Marshal Keith, and on November 23 offers his con-
dolences, and speaks of his unfortunate campaign.

Probus rixit, fortis obiit, was the Earl's brief epitaph
on his brother. His one close tie to life was broken.
That younger brother, who had fished and shot with
him, had fought at his side at Sheriffmuir, had shared
the dangers of Glenshiel and the outlaw life. who had
voyaged with him in so many desperate wanderings,
to save whom he had crossed Europe—the brother who
had secured for him his 'philosophic repose'—was
gone, leaving how many dear memories of boyhood
in Scotland, of common perils, and common labours
for a fallen Cause !

And there followed—oh philosophy !—a squabble
with Keith's mistress about the frugal inheritance of

one who scorned to enrich himself! 'My brother had just held Bohemia to ransom, and he leaves me sixty ducats,' wrote the Earl to Madame Geoffrin. In December 1758, Frederick determined to send the Earl to Spain, where 'nobody is so capable as you of making himself beloved.' He wanted peace, but peace with honour. The Earl was merely to watch over Frederick's interests, and to sound Spain as to her mediation. The King feared a separate Anglo-French peace, with Prussia left out.

By January 6, 1759, Frederick was trying to secure the Earl's pardon in England, and wrote to Knyphausen and Michell in London. The death of Lord Kintore, the Earl's cousin, devolved an estate upon him. This Marischal wished to obtain, but he had not changed sides in hope of gaining these lands. Andrew Mitchell wrote to Lord Holderness, on January 8, 1759, from Breslau, saying that Frederick had remarked, 'I know Lord Marischal to be so thorough an honest man that I am willing to be surety for his future conduct.' He enclosed a letter to be discreetly submitted to George II., submitting Frederick's desire for the Earl's pardon. By February 5, news reached Prussia that George had graciously consented.

There must have been a delay caused by formalities, for the Earl did not send his letter of thanks from Madrid to Sir Andrew Mitchell 'gratefully acknowledging the goodness of the King' till August 24, 1759.

So there was ' the end of an auld sang.' Charles

was hanging about the French coast, for the expedition under Conflans was preparing to carry him, as he hoped, to England: James, in Rome, was receiving his sanguine letters. It was 1744 over again: but the Earl was now of the other party, and James must have felt the loss severely. The bell which was regularly rung at home for the Earl's birthday, cracked when the news came to Aberdeenshire. 'I'll never say "cheep" for *you* again, Earl Marischal!'—so some local Jacobite translated the broken voice of the old bell. But the Earl manifestly did not win his pardon by discovering and betraying the secret of the family compact between France and Spain, as historians have conjectured. Dates render this, happily, impossible.[1]

The Earl took a humorous view of Jacobite French adventures. 'The conquest of Ireland by M. Thurot has miscarried,' he writes to Mitchell (April 2, 1760). Thurot had but two small ships.

The Earl now desired to visit England on his private affairs, and Frederick granted permission. He went in peace, where he had gone in war, but Scotland no longer pleased him. True, his Bill was carried through Parliament, admitting him to the Kintore estates, and, from the Edinburgh newspapers, he heard of a new honour—he was elected Provost of Kintore !

[1] The story was believed, however, by a contemporary who knew the Earl well.
[2] Mr. Bisset has printed these letters from the originals in the Add. MSS. British Museum.

'I had for me all the blew bonnets to a man, and a Lady whose good heart I respect still more than her birth, tho it be the very highest, she made press me (*sic*) to ask a pension, assuring me it would cost but one word. I excused myself as having no pretention to merit it. She bid me not name her, in leaving you to guess I do not injure her. She said the same also to Baron Kniphausen.'

Years later, from Neufchâtel, he wrote to Andrew Mitchell, 'The Provost of Kintore presents his compliments,' adding some congratulations on Mitchell's pension.

Not even the Provostship of Kintore reconciled the Earl, a changed man, to a changed Scotland. Conceivably he was not welcomed by the Jacobite remnant around the cracked bell. Bigotry, hypocrisy, and intolerable sabbatarianism were what the Earl disliked in his own country. He was also resolute against marrying, declined *faire l'étalon*, as Frederick delicately put it. Early in 1761, he made up his mind to return to Neufchâtel, and to compose the quarrels of Protestants and heretics. At Neufchâtel the Earl made an acquaintance rather disagreeable to most English tastes, the moral and sensible Jean-Jacques Rousseau. The philosopher's account of the Earl is in his 'Confessions.' According to him, Marischal, beginning life as a Jacobite, 'se dégoûta bientôt,' which is not historically accurate. 'La grande âme de ce digne homme toute républicaine' could not endure 'l'esprit injuste et tyrannique' of King James! The wicked people of Neufchâtel, whom the Earl 'tried to make happy,' 'kicked against his benevolent cares.' A preacher 'was expelled for not wanting many persons to be eternally damned.'

Rousseau went to Neufchâtel to escape the persecution which never ceased to attack this virtuous man. Frederick allowed him to hide his virtues in this hermitage, and made some rather slender offers of provision (twelve *louis*, says Rousseau), which exasperated the sage. On seeing the Earl his first idea was to weep (Jean-Jacques perhaps followed Richardson in his tearfulness), so extremely emaciated was the worthy peer. Conquering his 'great inclinations to cry,' with an effort, Rousseau admired the Earl's 'open, animated, and noble physiognomy.' Without ceremony, and acting as a Child of Nature, Jean-Jacques went and sat down beside the Earl on his sofa. In his noble eye Rousseau detected 'something fine, piercing, yet in a way caressing.' He became quite fond of the Earl. Wordsworth has justly remarked that you seldom see a grown-up male weeping freely on the public highway. But, had you been on the road between Rousseau's house and the Earl's you might have seen the author of the 'Nouvelle Héloïse' blubbering as he walked, shedding *larmes d'attendrissement*, as he contemplated the 'paternal kindnesses, amiable virtues, and mild philosophy of the respectable old man.'

I know not whether I express a common British sentiment, but the tears of Jean-Jacques over our Scottish stoic awaken in me a considerable impatience. The Earl was incapable, for his part, of lamentations. Jean-Jacques was too ' independent ' to be the Earl's guest. Later, he conceived in that bosom tingling with sensibility that the Earl had been ' set against him ' by Hume—' Ils vous ont trompé, ces barbares ; mais ils ne vous ont pas changé.' It was true, the Earl could break Prince Charles's heart, but he always made allowances for Jean-Jacques. Rousseau, not knowing that the Earl's heart was true to him, writes : ' Il se laisse abuser, quelquefois, et n'en revient jamais. . . . Il a l'humeur singulière, quelque chose de bizarre et étrange dans son tour d'esprit. Ses cadeaux sont de fantaisie, et non de convenance. Il donne ou envoie à l'instant ce qui lui passe par tête, de grand prix, ou de nulle valeur indifféremment.' Nevertheless the Earl was the cause of Rousseau's ' last happy memories.'

The Earl left Neufchâtel ; he arranged for Rousseau's refuge in England. David Hume, who was dear to the Earl, arranged the reception of Rousseau in England, and every one has heard of Rousseau's insane behaviour, and of the quarrel with Hume. Rousseau wanted to write the History of the Keiths, and asked the Earl for documents. Jean-Jacques was hardly the man to write Scottish family history, and the documents were never entrusted to him.

Here follows the letter on the topic of Rousseau, which the Earl wrote to Hume :—

'Jean Jaques Rousseau persecuted for having writ what he thinks good, or rather, as some folks think, for having displeased persons in great power who attributed to him what he never meant, came here to seek retreat, which I readily granted, and the King of Prussia not only approved of my so doing, but gave me orders to furnish him his small necessarys, if he would accept them ; and tho that King's philosophy be very different from that of Jean Jaques, yet he does not think that a man of an irreprochable life is to be persecuted because his sentiments are singular, he designs to build him a hermitage with a little garden, which I find he will not accept, nor perhaps the rest which I have not yet offered to him. He is gay in company, polite. and what the French call *aimable*, and gains ground dayly in the opinion of even the clergy here ; his enemys else where continue to persecute him, he is pelted with anonimous letters, this is not a country for him, his attachment and love to his native Toune is a strong tye to its neigbourhood, the liberty of England, and the character of my good and honored friend D. Hume F——i D——r¹ (perhaps more singular than that of Jean Jaques, for I take him to be the only historian impartial) draws his inclinations to be near to the F——i D——r, for my part, tho it be to me a very great pleasure to converse

---

¹ Fidei Defensor.

with the honest savage, yet I advise him to go to
England, where he will enjoy *Placidam sub libertate
quietem.* He wishes to know, if he can print all his
works, and make some profit, merely to live, from
such an edition. I entreat you will let me know
your thoughts on this, and if you can be of use to
him in finding him a bookseller to undertake the
work, you know he is not interested, and little will
content him. If he goes to Brittain, he will be a
treasure to you, and you to him, and perhaps both
to me (if I were not so old).

‘ I have offered him lodging in Keith Hall. I am
ever with the greatest regard your most obedient
servant

M.[1]

‘ Oct. 2, 1762.’

Rousseau never went so far north, never took
Keith Hall for a hermitage, nor scandalised the Kirk
Session. After his quarrel with Hume, the Earl
did not write freely to him, saying that he wrote
little to anyone. He thought, he tells another
correspondent, of ‘ turning bankrupt in letters.’
‘ My heart is not the dupe of these pretences,’
sighs Rousseau. He took money from the Earl,
he took money at many hands. He sent a long
deplorable lamentation to Marischal : the Earl has
been deceived, a phantom has been exhibited to him
as his fond J.-J. R. Probably there was no answer, but

[1] From the correspondence of Hume. MSS. in the collection of
the Royal Society of Edinburgh.

the Earl bequeathed to him his watch as a *souvenir*. ' Jean Jacques est trop honête home pour ce monde, qui tâche a tourner en ridicule sa delicatesse.' so the Earl had written from London to Hume in Paris.

He appears, when in England, to have met Hume at Mitcham, and he was devoted to the stout, smiling sceptic, whom he called ' *Defensor Fidei.*'

In 1764 the Earl left Neufchâtel for Potsdam, where Frederick built him a house. This he describes in a letter to Hume. The following note (1765) clearly refers to Hume's report of Helvetius's absurd anecdote, that Prince Charles showed the white feather on starting for Scotland, and had to be carried on board, tied hands and feet, by Sheridan, George Kelly, and others of the Seven Men of Moidart. Hume repeated this incredible nonsense in a letter to Sir John Pringle, who clearly distrusted the evidence.[1] This appears to be the ' certain history' which the Earl asks Hume to get from Helvetius, who had been ' assured of the fact.' By whom ?

To disseminate this fourth-hand scandal of his former master—scandal which, if true, he himself was in a better position to have heard than Helvetius—was perhaps the least worthy act of the Earl.

The David Floyd of whom he writes occurs often in the Stuart Correspondence. He was of the old St. Germains set, being the son of that Captain Floyd, so much disliked by Lord Ailesbury, who

---

[1] Hill Burton's *Hume*, ii. 464-6.

came and went from England to James II., after
1688.

In another letter the Earl advises Hume to
consult Floyd on events ' of which you took a confused note from me at Mitcham.' Among these
facts may be the story, given by Hume on the Earl's
authority, of Charles's presence at the coronation
of George III. No other evidence of this adventure
exists.

Here follows the letter :—

'29 Aprile.

' In answer to your question, the Don quixotisme
you mention never entered into my head. I wish I
could see you to answer honestly all your questions,
for tho I had my share of follys with others, yet as
my intentions were at bottom honest, I should open
to you my whole budget, and lett you know many
things which are perhaps not all represented, I mean
not truly. I remember to have recommended to
your acquaintance Mr. Floyd, son to old David
Floyd, at St. Germains, as a man of good sense,
honor, and honesty : I fear he is dead, he would
have been of great service to you in a part of your
history since 1688. *A propos of history when you
see Helvetius, tell I desired you to enquire of him
concerning a certain history.* I fancy he will answer
you with his usuall Frankness.'

This, then, must refer to Helvetius's lie about the
Prince's cowardice.

The following letters to Hume illustrate the

rather blasphemous *bonhomie* of the Earl, who,
because of Hume's genius and fatness, was wont
to speak of him as ' *verbum caro factum.*' He writes
of his new hermitage at Potsdam, of his garden, his
favourite books (just what we might expect them
to be—Montaigne, Swift, Ariosto), of Voltaire,
d'Argens, and d'Alembert. He incidentally shows,
à propos of a fabled discovery, that Mr. Darwin's
theory would not have astonished him much :—

'Potsdam, ce 11 Sep. 1764.

'Le plaisir de votre lettre, et l'assurance d'amitié
de Madame Geauffrin et de Monsieur d'Alembert, a
été bien rabattu par ce que vous me dites de l'etat
de la santé de M. d'Alembert ; sobre comme il est a
table, comment peut il avoir des meaux d'estomac :
il faut qu'il travaille trop de la tête à des calculs,
ou qu'il allume sa chandelle par les deux bouts, c'est
cela sans doute. Renvoyez-le ici a mon hermitage,
je le rendray à sa, ou ses, belles frais, reposé, se
portant a merveille.

'A propos de mon hermitage dont Mr de Malsan
vous a fait la description, il a voyagé avec Panurge.
et a été chez *Oui-dire tenant école de temoignerie*,
primo, ma petite maison ne subsiste pas, par consequence mon grand hôte ne pouvoit m'y honorer de
sa presence.

'2°. Elle ne sera pas si petite, ayant 89. pieds de
façade, avec deux ailes de 45. pieds de long ; le
jardin est petit, assez grand cependant pour moy, et

j'ay une clef pour entrer aux jardins de Sans-Soucy.
Il y aura une belle salle avec une vestibule, et un
cabinet assez grand pour y mettre un lit, tout a part
des autres appartements, si d'Alembert venoit il
pouvoit y loger et prendre les eaux, mais il est plus
que probable que le Grand Hôte me disputeroit et
emporteroit cet avantage. En attendant son arrivee,
j'y logerais mon ancien ami Michel de Montagne,
Arioste, Voltaire, Swift, et quelques autres.

'Saul et David y seront aussi, quoyque j'aimerais
mieux David F—i D—r—m, surtout en persone, car
le Verbum j'ay, la Caro me manque. Je regrette
bien de n'avoir pas sçu que Me de Boufllers étoit en
hollande quand j'y ay passé, j'aurois été heureux de
la connoitre, par tout le bien que tout le monde dit
d'elle. Son ami et le mien Jean Jaques à été en
chemin pour les eaux en Savoye.

'Voltaire est un antichretien entousiaste, j'en ay
connu plus d'un et qui plus est sans être poëte ; je
ne sais rien de son dictionaire que j'ay cherché ici
inutilement, il viendra, toutes les choses nous vienent,
un peu plus tard a la verité par ou vous étes ; mais
la Société dont vous avez le bonheur de jouir ne
nous viendra pas ; comme je suis tres vieux, lourd,
pesant, bon a rien, il ne faut que Placidam sub
libertate Quietem ; mon hôte, pour me la donner
plus entierement, me batit ma maison ; elle sera
achevée en trois mois ; meublée au printems ; et j'y
pourray loger Octobre 1765.

'Faites moy envisager comme pas impossible que

vous pourriez y venir, que je serois bien content. bon soir.

' Mes respects a Madame Geauffrin.

' Dites a d'Alembert que j'ay une vache pour lui donner de bon lait, cela le tentera plus que le cent mil roubles qu'on lui á offert. N'a pas bon lait qui veut, et vir sapiens non abhorrebit eam. come disoit Maitre Janotus de ses chausses. . . .

' d'Argens est parti hier chercher le soleil de Provence. avant que de se mettre en voyage, il se fit tâter le poux par son medecin a plusieures reprises. le priant toujours bien fort de le dire de bon foye s'il etoit en etat de faire le voyage, les chevaux étoient deja au carosse. il dit qu'il reviendra, et n'en sait rien; le soleil ne le guerira pas de sa hipocondrie, il reviendra chercher le froid, s'il ne creve pas, ce qui est a craindre, son corps est trop delabré. Son frere, grand Jesuite, sa vieille mere, et les Jansenistes Provençeaux tout cela le genera. il soupirera aprés la liberté de philosopher a Sans-Soucy, quoiqu'il se plaint quand il y est; si on lui dit qu'il se porte bien surtout il se fache. Il seroit fort a souhaiter que votre plume fusse employée a nous instruire de la verité, au lieu des disputes sur l'I(l)e de la Tortuga, que je crois l'occupe un peu a present, mais si vous ne vous mettez pas a écrire de votre proprement mouvement, et non pas par com-plesance pour un autre, ne faites rien; il faut y être tout entier.

'Le Chevalier Stuart m'a parlé des decouvertes par le Microscope, par un certain Needham, prêtre, j'ay cherché inutilement cette brochure. Voici le fait come le chevalier Stuart me l'a dit. Il prit un gigot de mouton, le fit rotir presqu'a bruler, pour detruire les animalcules ou leur œufs qui pouvoient y être : il en pris le jus, le mit dans une bouteille bien bouchée, le fit cuire des heures dans l'eau bouillante, pour detruire toute animalcule ou œuf que pouvoit si être introduite par l'air en mettant le jus dans la bouteille ; au bout de quelque tems le jus fermenta, et produisit des animalcules.

'Needham pretend que toute generation ne vient qu de fermentation. Je vous dis mon autheur, vous le connoissez ; il ne parle legerment.

'Cette decouverte me paroit valoir la peine a examiner : ce pourroit être du gibier, come dit Montagne, de M. Diderot. Si la fermentation dans une petite bouteille produit un tres petit animal : celle de tous les elements de notre globe, ne pourroit elle produire, un chêne, un elephant. Je proteste que je parle avec toute soumission à David Hume F—i D——i, et à la sainte Inquisition, s'il trouve que quelque chose cloche dans ce sistême, que je ne fais que raporter, bon soir.'

Other letters to Hume occur in 1765, and are preserved in the Library of the Royal Society of Edinburgh. 'I am going down hill very fast, but easily, as one that descends the Mont Cenis *ramassé*, without

pain or trouble.' He mentions the frost and snow at
Berlin as severe to *un pobre viejo Cristiano Español*.
He sends turnip seed, a bucolic gift, to Helvetius,
and to Madame de Vassé, the lady who concealed
Prince Charles in the Convent of St. Joseph.[1]

He mentions that he sups every night with the
King, and wishes Hume to share these festivals.

The Earl was infinitely happier with Frederick
and the gay freethinkers at Potsdam than in Scotland, where so many friendly heads had fallen, where
every sight recalled unhappy things ; where the lairds
drank too much, and the ministers preached too long,
and wits were scarce, and people wanted him to
marry and beget heirs (here he had Frederick's sympathy), and still the cracked old bell kept up its
peevish lament, *Disloyal, Loyal, Loyal, Disloyal* !

Such was the Earl's correspondence with Hume;
they are the letters of a kind, good, humorous old
pagan. To d'Alembert also he wrote freely. 'I
have read with much pleasure four volumes of your
works, and was really pleased with myself when I
found that I could understand them. I want to use
my rights as an old fellow, and tell anecdotes.' Then
he gives a Scotch story, which would be more amusing in Scots than in his French. Of Frederick, he
says that (unlike Carlyle) he is ' gey easy to live wi', '
l'homme du monde le plus aisé à vivre. He announces
' David Hume is elevated to the sublime dignity of
a Saint, by public acclamation : the street where he

---

[1] *See* ' Mlle. Luci,' later.

dwells is entitled La rue de *St. David.* Vox populi.
vox Dei. Amen.' Again,—the old sinner!—

'I have received an inestimable treasure, plenary
indulgences *in articulo mortis*, with power to bestow
some of them on twelve elect souls. One I send to
good David Hume : as I wish you all good things in
both worlds, I offer you a place among my chosen.'

The philosopher took a simple pleasure in drol-
leries which no longer tempt us—we have now been so
long emancipated.

The Earl said that in Spain he would have felt
obliged to denounce Frederick to the Inquisition.
Frederick has given the old exile medicines to make
him love him, as Prince Hal did to Falstaff. 'If he
had not bewitched me, would I stay here, where I
only see a spectre of the sun, when I might live and
die in the happy climate of Valencia ?'

So he slipped down the hill in a happy, kind old
age. In summer he rose at five, read for an hour,
wrote his letters, and burned most of those which he
received. Then he had his head shaved, and washed
in cold water, dressed, took a drive, or pottered in
his garden. Heaven made gardens, surely, for the
pottering peace of virtuous eld. At twelve he dined,
chiefly on vegetables, taking but one glass of sherry.
He had always four or five guests, and, after dinner,
left them 'to make the coffee'—that is, to enjoy a
siesta. He never remembered to have remained
awake a moment when once his head touched the
pillow. Then he took coffee, played piquet, pottered

F

again in the garden, supped on chocolate, and so to bed early. He read much, and thanked a slight loss of memory for the pleasure of being able to read all his favourite authors over again. Rabelais, Montaigne, and Molière were his favourites in French, in English, Shakspeare and the old dramatists. Terence and Plautus he studied in Latin, the Greek writers 'in cribs.' Tragedy he could not abide ; mirth he loved, and d'Alembert's informant had come on him laughing aloud when alone. He was full of anecdote, and, having known everybody of note for some seventy years, his talk was delightful. For music, he preferred the pibroch in a strange land, as did Charles, alone and old in Italy. One touch of nature !

He was kindness itself, and loved giving ; from Rousseau he met, we are told, the usual amount of gratitude after the quarrel with Hume. But, judging from what Rousseau himself says, on this occasion he was not ungrateful. If he heard, in conversation, a tale of misery, he made no remark, but sought out and succoured the person in distress. To every one who visited him he insisted on making some little present. He maintained a poor woman in comfort ; nay, ' down to spiders and frogs, he was the friend of all created things ' Being a piquet player of the first force, he would only stake halfpence, and, when his winnings accumulated, laid them out in a feast of fat things for Snell, his big dog. Like Lionardo da Vinci, he could not bear to see a caged bird.

In his last years he was drawn about in a garden chair, his legs failing him. His mortal agony was long and patiently borne : never before had he been ill. 'Can your physic take fifty years off my life?' he asked the doctor. He died merely of long life, on May 25, 1778. In 1770 he had described himself to his kinsman, Sir Robert Murray Keith, as ' nearly eighty.' In 1778, then, he cannot have been ninety-two. as Mr. Carlyle supposed—probably he was about eighty-five. Years of trouble and sorrow these years would have been to another, but ' a merry heart goes all the way.' Physically. and mentally, and morally. the Earl had ever been an example of soundness. In his latest illness he was never peevish. Once ' he wished he were among the Eskimo, for they knock old men on the head.'

The Earl was not a great man. In conspiracy, in war, in government. in diplomacy, he was a rather oddly ineffectual man. He had. in short. a genius for goodness. and an independence of spirit, a perfect disinterestedness, an inability to blind himself to disagreeable facts, and to the merits of the opposite side—a balance, in fact, of temperament and of humour—which are inconsistent with political success. We may wish that his taste in jokes had been less that of the *philosophes.* We may wish that, if the Cause was indeed hopeless, he had deserted it without reproaching his old master. He might have abstained from disseminating the tattle of Helvetius. There is very little else which mortal judgment can find to

reprehend in brave. honest, generous, humorous, kind
George Keith. who was, without Christian faith, the
pattern of all the Christian virtues. He was of two
worlds—the old Royalist world, and the Age of Revolution—yet undisturbed in heart he lived and
died.

Vetustæ vitæ imago,
Et specimen venientis ævi.[1]

[1] In the papers of Ramsay of Ochtertyre occurs perhaps the only
unkind reference to the Earl. Ramsay reports that, being told about
the destitution of the child of his nurse (who had sold her cow and
sent him the money in 1719), he made no remark. A reference to
p. 66, *supra*, will show that silence followed by kind deeds was the
Earl's way when he heard a story of distress. Ramsay mentions that
he sold his lands cheap when he finally left Scotland.

III

MURRAY OF BROUGHTON

IN black contrast to the name, the character, the happy life and peaceful, kindly end of the good Earl Marischal stand the infamy, the ruined soul, the wretched existence and miserable death of John Murray of Broughton. 'No lip of me or mine comes after Broughton's!' said the Whig father of Sir Walter Scott, as he threw out of window the tea-cup from which the traitor had drunk. Murray was poisonous; was shunned like a sick, venomed beast. His name was blotted out of the books of the Masons' lodge to which he belonged; even the records of baptisms in his Episcopal chapel attest the horror in which he was held for thirty years, for half his life. Yet this informer remained, through that moiety of his degraded existence, true in heart to the Cause which the Earl Marischal forsook and disdained, true to his affection for his Prince; and it is even extremely probable that, after he became titular King, Charles, on a secret expedition to England, visited Murray in his London house.

The vacant, contemned years, when his beautiful wife had ceased to share his infamy, were partly

beguiled in the composition of the 'Memorials,'
which Mr. Fitzroy Bell has edited, with reinforce-
ments from the Stuart MSS., the papers in the
Record Office, and the archives of the Quai d'Or-
say. In these we find a spectacle which is rare: a
traitor convicted, exposed, detested, yet still cling-
ing to the Cause which he wrought for and sold,
still striving to batter himself into his own self-
respect, and to extenuate or bluster out his own
dishonour. The Earl Marischal has left us no
memoirs; a manuscript which he gave to Sir Robert
Murray Keith has been lost. But Murray's papers
are still in the possession of his great-grandson by a
second marriage, Mr. George Siddons Murray, who
has generously sanctioned their publication.

John Murray, of Broughton, in Peeblesshire, was
born in 1715, being descended from a cadet of the
house of Murray of Philiphaugh. His father, Sir
David Murray, was out in the Fifteen, but afterwards lived peacefully, developed the lead mines of
Strontian, and died before the Forty-five. His son,
educated at Edinburgh and Leyden Universities,
visited Rome in 1737-8, carried thither his ancestral
politics, and inflamed them at the light of Prince
Charles's eyes, 'the finest I ever saw.'[1] He found
Charles 'the most surprizingly handsome person of
the age,' a description not borne out by the miniature in enamel which he gave to his admirer in a

---

[1] Murray to a lady. Quoted in *Genuine Memoirs of John Murray,
Esq.* (London: 1747), p. 9.

diamond snuff-box.[1] Here we see 'the complection
that has in it somewhat of an uncommon delicacy;'
we see large brown eyes, an oval face, and the bright
hair hanging down below the perruque, that hair
which is treasured in a hundred rings, sleeve-links,
and lockets. But genuine portraits of the Prince do
not account for his epithet of 'bonnie,' and for his
almost involuntary successes with women. He had
'an air,' and was, indeed, a good-looking boy enough;
but he was no Adonis, the lower part of his face
tending early to overfulness. However, he won
Murray's heart, and he never lost it.

Returning, in 1738, to Broughton, on the Tweed,
Murray found himself a near neighbour of Lord
Traquair, then residing in his ancient château, which
lent its bears to Tully Veolan. The house has a
legend of an avenue gate never to be opened till the
King comes again; but Lord Traquair, a Jacobite
from vanity, did nothing to promote a Restoration.
He feebly caballed, and at Traquair Murray may
have drunk loyal healths enough to float a ship.
Inclined for more active measures, he succeeded old
Colonel Urquhart as Scottish correspondent of Edgar,
the King's secretary in Rome. The appointment was
approved of by the Duke of Hamilton, who, dying in
1743, left the Garter, the gift of King George, and
the Thistle, the gift of King James! The new Duke
was Jacobite enough to subscribe 1,500*l.* to the

---

[1] The diamond box has gone; the miniature, published by Mr.
Fitzroy Bell, is in my possession.

Cause and to accept James's commission just before
the Prince landed, but he held aloof from the Rising.
Murray went into his business as Jacobite
organiser with a cool and clear head. He knew the
value of documentary evidence, and when he could
he secured the signatures of adherents. In 1741 the
'Association' was formed, by Traquair, Lovat, Macgregor or Drummond of Balhaldie (described in the
essay on the Earl Marischal), the bankrupt Campbell
of Auchenbreck, father-in-law of Lochiel, and Lochiel
himself, the only honest man of the cabal. In
March 1741, Murray was introduced to Balhaldie.
That chief promised mountains and marvels, including 20,000 stand of arms already stocked. Visionary
weapons were these, as the swords which fell from
heaven into Clydesdale in 1684. Murray was invited
to trust Lovat, which he was disinclined to do. having
heard from Lochiel and from general rumour of that
rogue's unfathomable and capricious treachery.
Murray yielded, however, and the Association was
launched. First came the question of supplies.
The Scots were loyal, but, as a rule, would not part
with a bawbee. Hay of Drumelzier kept a good
grip of the gear; Lockhart of Carnwath had no
money by him; the Duke of Hamilton evaded the
question; and Lovat and Balhaldie opposed the
recruiting of new associates, who. if brought in,
would have rebelled against such incompetent or
treacherous managers.

Nothing occurred till, in December 1742, Balhaldie

sent some of his Ossianic prophecies of a French
invasion to Traquair. Murray did not believe in the
predictions, and only the feeblest attempts at organising
the country into districts were made. Auchenbreck
was to manage Argyllshire, Traquair was responsible
for Scotland south of Forth. Neither brought in
an adherent. Weapons were lacking, and Balhaldie
gave no information about a plan of campaign. It
was absolutely necessary to know what France really
intended. and, at the end of 1742. Murray himself set
out for Paris. In London he heard of the death of
Cardinal Fleury—a great blow to the cause. He
found in Paris that Balhaldie was beguiling France
with exaggerated accounts of what the stingy and
disorganised Scots were prepared to do. Murray
was merely mocked by Cardinal Tencin, and from
Amelot got only vague expressions of goodwill, and
the warning that 'such enterprizes were dangerous
and precarious.' Yet Balhaldie seemed much elated,
and returned to England with Murray to put heart
into the English adherents. In England Murray
found Colonel Cecil as little satisfied with Balhaldie
as himself, but the Celt hurried about with a great
air of business, and sent for Traquair to come to town.

Traquair did go to town, carrying a letter of
Murray's, to be forwarded to the Earl Marischal. By
the advice of Balhaldie (who was the last man that
ought to have seen the letter) Traquair burned it.
This was a new offence, and, in brief, the feud between Murray and Balhaldie became inveterate.

In London Traquair did nothing. He never wrote to the party in Scotland, and he brought back nothing but the names of the English leaders, the Duke of Beaufort, Lord Orrery, Lord Barrymore, Sir John Hinde Cotton, and Sir Watkin Williams Wynne. When Murray, in turning informer, divulged these names, except that of Beaufort, he told Government nothing which every man who cared did not know. But the English were thrown 'into a mortal fright,' as Balhaldie found so late as 1749. They were always in a mortal fright, always insisted that their Scottish allies should not even know who they were. Thus concerted movements were made impossible. Murray was dashed by the discovery that the English party was a mere set of five or six *nominum umbræ*. Doubtless there were plenty of Squire Westerns, who were ready to drink healths.

> Were our glasses turned into swords,
> Or our actions half as great as our words,
> Were our enemies turned to quarts,
> How nobly we should play our parts.
> The least that we would do, each man should kill his two,
> Without the help of France or Spain,
> The Whigs should run a tilt, and their dearest blood be spilt,
> And the King should enjoy his own again ! [1]

There may have been more serious intentions. In a Devonshire house I saw, once, a fine portrait of James III., and learned that the great-grandfather of the owner had burned compromising papers. Such

---

[1] *A Collection of Loyal Songs.* Printed in the year 1750.

papers of English Jacobites, if any existed, seem always to have been destroyed.

Traquair had done nothing; from Barrymore he got a promise of 10,000*l.*, from the rich Welsh baronet he got only excuses. Lovat, according to Murray, said, in the Tower, that Beaufort had promised to raise 12,000 men, · whereby he exposed before the warders a nobleman to the resentment of Government whom I had been at great pains to represent . . . . as no ñays privy to or concerned in our scheme.'

The year 1743 ended, and at its close (December 23) James announced to Ormonde and to the Earl Marischal the French King's resolution to help him. Balhaldie brought the Prince to France, early in 1744. Nothing was done, nothing was concerted. An attempt to engage the Cameronians, through Kenmure and Sir Thomas Gordon of Earlstoun, was a predestined failure. After Midsummer, 1744, Murray determined to visit France, watch Balhaldie, and see the Prince. He casually discovered that a Mr. Cockburn left the Jacobite cypher lying loose on his window seat, or under a dictionary! These were pretty characters to manage a conspiracy; but we have seen equal stupidity in 'Jameson's Raid.' In London Murray saw Dr. Barry, whom he later betrayed, as far as in him lay. He crossed to Flanders, and met Balhaldie gambling in the Sun tavern at Rotterdam. Balhaldie vapoured about buying arms, though · he had not credit for a *louis d'or*,' and bragged about the travelling chaise

(the Prince's famous *chese*) which he had designed for
his Royal Highness. Not to pursue these chican-
eries, Murray exposed Balhaldie and Sempil to
Charles, whom he met secretly behind the stables of
the Tuileries. The Prince took it very coolly, without loss of temper or excitement, but announced
his intention to visit Scotland next summer (1745) if
he came with a single servant. Murray replied that
his arrival would ever be welcome, 'but I hoped it
would not be without a body of troops.' Murray
then pointed out that, in such an adventure, 'he
could not positively depend on more than 4,000
Highlanders, *if so many*,' and that even these would
infinitely regret the measure.

Murray has been accused, by Maxwell of Kirkconnell, of putting Charles upon this enterprise. In
fact, his error lay in not formally and explicitly
warning the Prince from the first. Later he did send
warning letters, but Traquair did not try to deliver
them, and Young Glengarry failed in the attempt.

The result of Murray's disclosures, and of a
written Memorial which he sent in, was to undeceive
Charles as to Sempil and Balhaldie. His letters to
James are proofs of this, and now the split in the
party was incurable. Murray went to and fro,
undermining Balhaldie. Balhaldie, at the end of
1744, sent Young Glengarry from France, to work
against Murray on the mind of Lochiel. That chief
brought the two future traitors, Glengarry and
Murray, together, and the Celt came into the Low-

lander's bad opinion of Balhaldie. This was early in
1745. Murray now made the mistake of trying to
pin men to a declaration, in writing, that they would
join Charles, even if he came alone. His duty was
to discourage any such enterprise, which, unaided by
France, could only mean ruin. On the other hand,
he actually engaged Macleod, the chief of the Skye
men. With Stewart of Appin, Macleod chanced to
be in Edinburgh. Murray gave him a letter from
Charles, and described the character of that Prince.
' Macleod declared, in a kind of rapture, that he
would make it his business to advance his interest as
much as was in his power, and would join him, let
him come when he would.' This occurred at a
meeting in a tavern attended by the persons already
mentioned, with Traquair, Glengarry, and Lochiel. Of
these men, Appin did not come out, Traquair skulked,
Macleod turned his coat, Glengarry became a spy,
Murray was Murray, and only Lochiel saved his
honour. Next day, by Murray's desire, Lochiel
extracted from Macleod a written promise to raise
his clan, even if Charles came unaided and alone.

How Macleod kept his promise we know. He
sent his forces to join Loudon's detachment in
Hanoverian service; the whole array was frightened
back in an attempt to surprise and capture Charles.
They all ran like hares from the blacksmith of Moy,
with one or two gardeners and other retainers of
Lady Mackintosh, and the only man slain was
Macrimmon, Macleod's piper, the composer of the

prophetic lament, 'Macleod shall return, but Macrimmon shall never!' Murray comments with great
severity on Macleod's treason, and, in his promise,
and that of others, finds justification for Charles's
adventure, and an answer to the question, 'Why he
made an attempt of such consequence with so small
a force?' All this leaves Murray in a quandary. To
send such promises (as he did) was to encourage
Charles in a desperate project. To be sure Murray,
later, did attempt to stop Charles; but he should
never have sent him these signed encouragements,
both from Macleod and Stewart of Appin. But
Murray, he says, now changed his mind; he made out a
journal of all his proceedings, showing Charles (most
inconsistently) that all the party, except the Duke of
Perth, 'were unanimous against his coming without
a force.' These papers Murray entrusted, for Charles,
to Traquair, who was going to England, and meant
to proceed to France, using this very singular expression, 'that he would see the Prince, *though in
a bawdy house*. The present Earl of Weymss and
Laird of Glengarry [Pickle] can vouch this. The
latter has since repeated it to me in my house in
London.'

Traquair now went to London, but he never
went to France, nor did he transmit the warning to
Charles. Meanwhile Murray extracted 1,500*l.* from
the new Duke of Hamilton (a new fact), and the
Duke of Perth paid an equal sum, and even offered
to mortgage his estate. Hamilton also gave a verbal

promise to join Charles ' with all the forces he could
raise.' Murray again wrote to Charles, saying that
he must bring at least 6,000 men. Perth, Elcho, and
Lochiel signed this letter. This letter was sent by
one John Macnaughten. Did it ever arrive? In the
Stuart Papers is a letter signed 'J. Barclay,' and
undated. It is clearly from Murray to Charles, and
announces the journal entrusted to Traquair, but
contains no warning.[1]

In a letter of March 14, 1745, to James, Charles
refers to this letter announcing the journal and other
despatches, which had not arrived—as Traquair
never sent them. On April 9, Charles appears to
refer to Macnaughten's budget of letters as not yet
deciphered.[2]

From London Traquair sent only a note of doubt-
ful and, at best, of insignificant meaning. Nothing
whatever was settled or arranged. Then came Sir
Hector, chief of the Macleans, to Scotland, where he
was arrested. Now, Murray reflected that the epistle
sent by Macnaughten ' contained rather a wish than
an advice, and might not be sufficient to prevent the
Prince's coming.' Murray therefore sent, as a final
warning, that set of papers which Traquair had not
forwarded, entrusting it to Young Glengarry, at the
end of May 1745. But Glengarry did not succeed
in seeing Charles, who was thus left without warning
not to come. Perhaps no warning would have stopped

[1] Browne, ii. p. 476.
[2] Stuart Papers, in Murray of Broughton's *Memorials*, pp. 392 395.

him ; at all events he received none, and the die was cast. The Prince embarked on June 22.

Murray's whole book is one of self-justification. He may clear himself of having suggested the unaided enterprise to Charles. But, partly through the frivolity of Traquair, partly through the zeal of Murray, Charles was left without decisive admonition. He saw his party distracted : for a year and a half France had treated him 'scandalously' (as even the patient James averred), and he determined to force the hands both of France and the Jacobites. He pawned the Sobieski rubies—'the Prince would wear them with a very sore heart on this side of the water'—he put his life to the hazard. If ever an attempt was to be made at all, Charles did well. England was empty of troops. A success or two, the Prince reckoned, must unite the distracted party on the one hand, and tempt or compel France to action on the other. His motto was de l'audace ! If all men had been Lochiels, if the Duke of Hamilton, Macleod, Traquair, Lovat, Beaufort, Barrymore, Orrery, and the rest, had honour and truth, if France had such a thing as a policy, and could seize an opportunity, Charles would have won the Crown. But many men are not Lochiels, and, if France had a policy, it was not to restore the Stuarts, but to use them as a mere diversion.

By the end of May Macnaughten returned, with news that Charles would be in Scotland by July. This caused Murray much chagrin, but he at once warned Perth, Lochiel, and Macleod. To the Duke

of Hamilton he gave the Prince's commission, · which
he accepted with great cheerfulness.' Murray then
went to Lochiel, who remarked that every man of
honour was bound to rise, and who quite trusted
Lovat and Macleod. He leaned on broken reeds.
Lovat temporised, Macleod turned his coat. Here
Murray's MS. breaks off, and he continues the history
of the Rising 'from Moidart to Derby.'

The military part of Murray's 'Memorials' is full
of reflections on Charles's 'unparalleled good nature
and humanity,' and his strategic skill. Murray had
desired to be an aide-de-camp: he clearly thinks himself a good judge of warfare. He was obliged to be
Secretary, but did not covet that office. He, alone,
had any previous personal knowledge of Charles, with
whom he was such a favourite as to excite the
jealousy of Lord George Murray and of Maxwell of
Kirkconnell. These jealousies were of perilous consequence. Maxwell, writing after Murray was the
most detested man on earth, charges heavily against
him: ' He began by representing Lord George as a
traitor to the Prince ; he assured him that he had
joined on purpose to have an opportunity of delivering
him up to Government.' Lord George heard of this,
and was deeply affected. Prestonpans nearly opened
Charles's eyes, but Lord George's 'haughty and over-
bearing manner prevented a thorough reconciliation,
and seconded the malicious insinuations of his rival.
. . . He now and then broke into such violent
sallies as the Prince could not digest. . . .'

G

Now the loyalty of Lord George is beyond all
shadow of suspicion. Till his death, in 1760, he was
the faithful and devoted subject of King James. Even
Murray, in his MSS., does not breathe a word
against him. But, if Murray did, at first, conceive
suspicions, and suggest precautions, it is impossible
to blame him. What was Lord George's position?
He had been out, at Glenshiel, in 1719, with his
brother, Tullibardine. He was pardoned, and was residing in Scotland. He never appears as a Jacobite in
the negotiations of 1740–45. His brother William,
who, but for his steady Jacobitism, would have been
Duke of Atholl, came over with Charles. The
actual Duke, de facto, Lord George's brother James,
deserted Blair Atholl on the approach of the Highlanders, and went to London. Tullibardine (William)
assumed the title of Duke, and occupied Blair.
Lord George also joined the Prince. But Murray
had to ask himself, was Lord George in earnest?
Murray knew the treachery of the times, and had
employed James Mohr Macgregor, known to be a
Hanoverian spy, to beguile Cope and the Lord Chief
Justice. Was Lord George, Murray would think,
playing James Mohr's part on the other side?

Murray had reason for suspicion. As late as
August 20, 1745, after the standard was raised at
Glenfinnan, Lord George wrote to the Lord Advo-
cate from Dunkeld. He announced that, on the
following day, he and Old Glengarry would wait on
Cope at Crieff. Cope was marching North to fight

the Prince. Lord George talked of 'the Pretender,' and sent information. He *did* wait on Cope. As late as September 1, he was corresponding with his Hanoverian brother, Duke James, but, on September 3, he announced to his brother that he was about to join the Prince. 'Duty to King and Country overweighs everything.' [1]

As a matter of fact, Lord George simply, if rather suddenly, changed his mind, engaging, like Lord Pitsligo, 'without enthusiasm,' and it seems without hope. He thought that honour called him. But to Murray Lord George's conduct in first colloguing with Cope, and then rallying to Charles, must have seemed suspicious. It *was* suspicious: to Cope it must have appeared the blackest treason. 'Lord George,' Murray would say, 'is betraying somebody; now, whom is he betraying?'

A curious piece of gossip has lately come to light. It was said that one of the Highland army, in England, had a squabble with a wayfaring man, and broke his staff, in which was found a letter from the Whig brother Duke James, to Lord George, suggesting that, in a battle, he should desert, carrying over the Atholl men. Probably the story is false, and based on the sending *to* Duke James of letters, by one of his servants, concealed in the shank of a whip. In any case, Lord George was never really reconciled to Murray, and Charles (after Lord George counselled

---

[1] *Chronicles of the Atholl and Tullibardine Families*, iii. pp 8, 17. (Privately printed: edited by the Duke of Atholl.)

retreat at Derby, retreat at Stirling, and the abandonment of the surprise at Nairn) never trusted,
never forgave him. wished to imprison him in France,
and shut his door against him.   James in vain remonstrated, Charles was implacable.

At Carlisle. on the march southwards. there was
a great quarrel.   Lord George resigned his commission, offering to serve as a volunteer.   Charles
accepted the resignation.   The Duke of Perth was
acting as commander-in-chief.   He was a Catholic.
and Lord George deemed that this would have an
ill effect, besides he himself was a much senior and
infinitely more experienced officer.   Lord George
also urged that Murray 'took everything upon him.
both as to civil and military.'   The Duke of Perth
then resigned his command, apparently on the advice
of Maxwell of Kirkconnell, who praises his magna-
nimity.   Murray also. he himself tells us, withdrew
from the councils of war. 'which seemed to quiet
Lord George a good deal.'   Lord George became
general in chief, and distinguished himself by skill
and personal bravery.   But the quarrel was
never reconciled.   Unluckily Murray gives no
account of the decision to retreat from Derby.
Then no more councils were held. and 'little
people' (that is. Murray) were allowed to advise: till Lord George and the chiefs sent in a
remonstrance.

Murray breaks off in his narrative at Derby, and
does not resume it till after Culloden.   He had fallen

ill at Elgin, in March 1746, where Charles also had a severe attack of pneumonia.[1]

Murray was carried across country to Mrs. Grant's house in Glenmoriston. Everything fell into worse confusion after his departure, his successor, John Hay of Restalrig, being incompetent. At Glenmoriston Murray heard from Archibald Cameron of the defeat at Culloden. In the shape of a letter from a friend of Mr. Murray of Broughton, he describes and justifies his own conduct after 'the wicked day of destiny.'

It is, perhaps, less easy to justify the conduct of his master. The irredeemable point in Charles's behaviour in Scotland was his withdrawal from the remnant of his army, which met at Ruthven. There is much obscurity as to the details, as to whether a place of rendezvous had been fixed upon or not. But Charles knew where the army and officers were; he received a scolding letter from Lord George, and he declined to return to the forces. His distrust of Lord George had revived; he knew that there were men who would not scruple to win their pardon by betraying him, and, with Sheridan, O'Sullivan, O'Niel, and others, he made for the islands.

Murray, after news came of the defeat, was carried to Fort Augustus, and thence to Lochgarry's house.

[1] Charles was nursed at Thunderton House, by Mrs. Anderson (née Dunbar) of Arradoul. In some mysterious way Charles was able to secure for Mrs. Anderson's son an appointment under the English Government. So says a tradition preserved by Miss Janet Lang, a great-great-granddaughter of Mrs. Anderson.

Hoping even yet to rally a force, he met the wounded and outworn Duke of Perth at Invergarry, to no result. He then was carried to Lochiel's country, and Lochiel determined to wage a guerilla war in the hills, expecting French assistance. Murray sent Archy Cameron to Arisaig to get news of Charles, but Archy learned from Hay of Restalrig that the Prince had already taken boat for the Isles. Archy disbelieved Hay, but Charles had really gone, or was on the very point of going (April 26). Certain news reached Murray and Lochiel; the chief determined to remain with his clan, on a point of honour, and Murray stood by Lochiel, as also did Major Kennedy. They could have fled in the French vessels which landed the gold of the fatal treasure, but they were resolute to stand by each other.[1] Those who departed were the dying Duke of Perth, a sacrifice to his own chivalrous devotion; Lord Elcho, who presently tried to gain his pardon; old Sir Thomas Sheridan, who soon afterwards died, heart-broken, at Rome; Lord John Drummond, Lockhart of Carnwath, and Hay of Restalrig.

Murray now arranged for the burial of the French gold, and then Glenbucket, with the poet-soldier John Roy Stewart, Clanranald, Lochgarry, Barisdale, Young Scotus, and Lovat, held a council. Lovat proposed holding out in the hills, and promised the

[1] See 'Cluny's Treasure,' postea. A writer in the Athenæum (July 9, 1898) appears to think (as was thought at the time) that Murray now intended to turn informer, and keep what he could of the French gold. This is not my impression.

aid of his son, Simon, and 400 Frazers. Murray
suspected the old fox, and proposed that all should
sign a 'band' of mutual fidelity. Lovat would not
sign !

The allies were to rendezvous in ten days at Loch
Arkaig, and, later, the meeting was deferred for
another week. But the Master of Lovat ' was never
so much as heard of' at the tryst ; Lochgarry brought
but 100 men, and Murray accuses him of treacherous
intentions, this on the suggestion of Barisdale. Now
Lochgarry left, and did not return, nor did his
sentinels bring in news of an approaching English
force. Of all this Lochgarry says nothing in his
report to Young Glengarry, published by Mr. Blaikie.
But, as we know with absolute certainty that Barisdale was an infamous coward, liar, and traitor, while
Lochgarry was loyal to his death, we need not accept Barisdale's evidence against a cousin whom he
detested. However it happened, no news came from
Lochgarry, and, if Murray himself had not sent out
scouts, the whole party, with Lochiel, would have
been taken near Loch Arkaig.[1]

The game being now up, Murray made his way
South, in exceedingly bad health, aggravated by ex-
posure and fatigue. His idea was to get a ship on
the East Coast, where Lochiel would join him, and
to escape. But Murray was captured, through information given by a herd-boy, at the house of his
sister, Mrs. Hunter of Polmood. He certainly did

---

[1] See ' A Gentleman of Knoydart,' *postea*.

not intend to be captured, and he says that. even
after he was taken, he tried to arrange about a ship
for Lochiel. He also vindicates the conduct of his
wife, who was about to bear a child, and he justifies
his honesty in money matters. Now in money
matters Murray's hands were clean, and there is
no real ground for the charges against poor
Mrs. Murray. But what Murray does not say, is
that, as soon as he was approached, after his capture, by the Lord Justice Clerk, he promised ' to
discover all he knew.'[1] He did not tell *all* he
knew, but on August 13, being examined in the
Tower, he told a great deal. About Traquair he
spoke out : he named the English Jacobite leaders, he
told his tale about Macleod in the tavern meeting,
he sheltered Macdonald of Sleat, and even screened
Lovat as far as he dared : in fact, he took revenge
on half-hearted Jacobites, and, for some reason. did
his best to hang Sir John Douglas. He sent in an
account of the Clans, in substance much like that in
the MS. of 1750.[2] He betrayed the secret of the
Loch Arkaig treasure, and asked to be allowed to
go to the spot, and point it out to the agents of
Government. In reply to Murray, Traquair and Dr.
Barry lied firmly, under examination, and Sir John
Douglas refused to answer any questions. They
suffered imprisonment, but escaped with life for lack

---

[1] Lord Justice Clerk to Newcastle, July 10, 1746. Murray's
Memorials, p. 418.
[2] *The Highlands in 1750.* Blackwood, 1898.

of corroboration. Some legal jugglery was needed
before Murray could be accepted as King's Evidence,
but the trick was played, and the Laird of Broughton
publicly ' peached ' at Lovat's trial. He declares
that he peached with economy. 'The utmost care
was taken to conceal everything that was not known
by his own letters, of which he was so sensible that
he sent me thanks by Mr. Fowler (Gentleman
Gaoler of the Tower), for my forbearance, and said
he was not the least hurt or offended by anything I
had said.'

Such are Murray's excuses. He could have told
more, and Lovat might have died without his testimony, on the evidence of various Frazers. Murray
was pardoned in June 1748. He tried to provoke
Traquair to a duel and vapoured with cloak and
sword behind Montague House. He associated with
Young Glengarry, whom he very probably thought
an honest man, and his visits a privilege. Glengarry
doubtless got from Murray information about the
Loch Arkaig treasure, and, perhaps, picked up a few
crumbs of intelligence for his employers. His wife
had not left Murray, in 1749, when he reconciled his
lady to the loss of her repeater, pawned by a priest
named Leslie for the relief of Young Glengarry, who
was starving.[1] When Mrs. Murray left her intolerable lord is not exactly known, nor is anything
certain about her later fortunes. In May 1749,
Stonor tells Edgar that Murray's ' late actions have

---

[1] Leslie. Paris, May 27, 1752. Browne. iv. 101.

not only the appearance of a knave but a madman,
and it is the opinion of most people he is really also
the latter, several of his family having been disordered in their senses. and his present situation
sufficient to cause it in him. as he can't but feel the
sting of such a conscience. finds himself the outcast
of mankind, and *is in circumstances extremely indi-
gent.*' It follows that he did not keep the money
buried in the garden of Menzies of Culdares, some
4,000l.[1] Traquair had Murray arrested by a warrant
of the Lord Chief Justice. for provoking a breach of
the peace.[2]

In 1764, Murray sold Broughton. His agent was
Sir Walter Scott's father, and, as we all know, Mr.
Scott threw the cup from which Murray had drunk
out of the window. The younger Dumas, probably
by a chance coincidence. uses this in his play.
'L'Étrangère.' After selling Broughton, Murray is
said to have lived in London, and family tradition
avers that he was visited by Charles, whom he introduced to his little boy as · your *King.*' This ought.
then, to be dated 1766, or later. Murray is said to
have justified Stonor's letter, already cited, by dying
in a madhouse, on December 6, 1777. He was sane
enough, certainly. when he wrote his ' Memorials.'
Such was Murray of Broughton, in spite of his
treachery a devoted believer in the Cause ; till his

---

[1] See 'Account of Charge ' in Chambers's *Rebellion*, p. 522 ;
and, later, ' Cluny's Treasure.'
[2] Stuart Papers. Browne, iv. 59. Mr. Fitzroy Bell does not
remark on all this evidence.

capture, a brave. loyal. and constant supporter of the
Cause ; a man by nature honourable. and a lover of
honour in others. as in Lochiel and the Duke of
Perth. He sinned, when he did sin, in violation of
every tradition of education, and. in turning Informer,
wrenched every fibre of his moral nature. His servant, a poet of the time remarks, set his master an
example.

> Behold, the menial hand that broke your bread.
> That wiped your shoes, and with your crumbs was fed.
> When life and riches, proffered to his view,
> Before his eyes the strong temptation threw.
> Rather than quit integrity of heart.
> Or act, like you, th'unmanly traytor's part,
> Disdains the purchase of a worthless life.
> And bares his bosom to the butcher's knife.

But Murray renounced honour and lingered on
the scene.

> And whither, whither, can the guilty fly
> From the devouring worms that never die ?

' Lead us not into temptation.' The view of death
brought Murray face to face with a self in his breast,
which, it is probable, he had never known to exist :
that awful contradictory self to which each of us has
yielded, though few in such extremity of surrender.

IV

MADEMOISELLE LUCI

In 'Pickle the Spy' mention was frequently made
of 'Mademoiselle Luci,' the mysterious young lady
who, from 1749 to her death in 1752, was the
French Egeria of Prince Charles. An exile, without
a roof to cover his head in any land but the States
of the Pope, to which he declined to go, the Prince
was sheltered in the Parisian convent of St. Joseph
by Mlle. Luci and the lady styled *La Grande Main*
in the cypher of the Prince's correspondence. By
dint of some research, I discovered that Mlle. Luci
was Mlle. Ferrand, while La Grande Main was her
devoted friend, Madame de Vassé. Both were very
intimate with a person always alluded to in the
Prince's correspondence as *le philosophe*. As Montesquieu lived in the same street (the Rue Dominique)
as these ladies (who directed the Prince's philosophical studies), as he was on friendly terms with
Charles, Lord Elibank, Bulkeley, and other Jacobites,
I concluded that the *philosophe* of the correspondence
was probably the author of 'L'Esprit des Lois.'
This was a blunder which criticism should have

detected. The *philosophe* was not Montesquieu, but the Abbé Condillac. The proof is in the preliminary chapter of his 'Traité des Sensations;' he there dedicates that important psychological work to Madame de Vassé, and deplores the death of their beloved Mlle. Ferrand. Condillac, clearly, was their friend, *le philosophe*. Mlle. Ferrand, it seems, was the instructor of Condillac, as well as the protector and literary adviser of Prince Charles.

'You know, Madame,' says Condillac to Madame de Vassé, ' to whom I owe the light which at length scattered my prejudices. You know what part she had in this book, that lady so justly dear to you, so worthy of your friendship and esteem. I consecrate my work to her memory, and I address you that I may share the pleasure of speaking about her and the pain of our common sorrow. May this book be the monument of your friendship, and preserve it unforgotten.'

A volume on the relations of sense and thought, like Condillac's, is not the place to which one naturally turns in search of information about a girl who loyally served a proscribed Prince and a forsaken Cause. Yet it is Condillac who attests for us ' the keenness, the just balance, of Mlle. Ferrand's intellect, and the vivacity of her imagination, qualities apparently incompatible, when carried to the pitch at which she displayed them.'

The scheme of Condillac's psychology cannot be discussed in this place, but he says that he owed every-

thing to Prince Charles's friend. 'She enlightened me
as to the principles, the plan, and the most minute
details, and I ought to be the more grateful, as she
had no idea of instructing me, or of making a book.
She did not remark that she was becoming an author,
having no design beyond that of conversing with me
on the topics in which I was interested. . . . Had
she taken up the pen, this work would be a better
proof of her genius. But there was in her a delicacy
which forbade her even to contemplate authorship.
. . . This treatise is, unhappily, but the result of
conversations with her, and I fear that I may have
sometimes failed to place her ideas in their true
light.'

Had Mlle. Ferrand survived, Condillac thinks that
she would not have allowed him to acknowledge her
influence on his work. 'But how can I, to-day, deny
myself the pleasure of this act of justice? Nothing
but this remains to me, in our loss of a wise adviser,
an enlightened critic, and a true friend. You, Madame,
will share the pleasure with me, you who will not
cease to regret her while you live.' The philosopher
speaks of 'the intellect, the loyalty, the courage,
which formed these ladies for each other.' Loyalty,
courage, wit, these women laid them at the feet of
a Prince not their own, and solely recommended to
their tenderness by his misfortunes.

'Your friend, in dying, had this one consolation,
Madame, that she was not to survive you. I have

seen her happy in this reflection. "Speak sometimes
of me with Madame de Vassé," she said to me, " and
let it be with a kind of pleasure."' Such was the girl,
so brilliantly endowed, so brave, so affectionate, who
did Prince Charles's marketing, bought him novels and
razors, directed his choice of books, was the channel
through which his secret correspondence passed, was
jealously regarded by his mistress, Madame de Talmond, and died before the end of all hope had come,
before the Prince was renounced even by his own.
To the angry Madame de Talmond she wrote, 'I am
strongly attached to your friend [the Prince] and for
him would do and suffer anything short of stooping
to an act of baseness.'

There must have been something in Charles,
beyond his misfortunes, to win so much devotion
from a woman of the highest intellect.

Mlle. Ferrand died, after a long illness, in October
1752. Her memory is preserved only by a note in
Grimm's correspondence, by the touching tribute of
Condillac, and by the discovery of her kindness to a
proscribed Prince. While she protected and advised
him, she was inspiring a renowned philosopher, and
keeping a secret which every diplomatist in Europe
was eager to learn. We naturally desire to know
whether Mlle. Ferrand was beautiful as well as talented
and kind. But researches in France have not brought
to light any portrait either of Mlle. Ferrand, or of
Madame de Vassé, who long survived her friend, and

was in correspondence, about 1760, with the Earl Marischal.[1]

[1] Unable, at first, to learn even the real name of Mlle. Luci, I appealed, in despair, to a lady who occasionally sees 'visions' in crystals. 'What can you see of Mlle. Luci ?' I asked, by letter, giving no hint of any kind as to the lady's date or connections. The seeress replied that, in an ink-bottle on her writing-desk, she saw a girl of about twenty-eight, dark, handsome, rather like Madame Patti in youth. Her dress was that of the middle of the eighteenth century. On her shoulder was laid another lady's hand, a long, delicate, white hand, with a 'marquise' diamond ring. '*La Grande Main*,' I exclaimed, ' the hand of La Grande Main ! '—whom we later discovered to be Madame de Vassé.

The coincidence was certainly pretty, but, unless a portrait of Mlle. Ferrand can be discovered, we must remain ignorant as to whether she was correctly represented in the ink-picture ; whether a true refraction shone up from the dead past, the afterglow of a romance.

V

THE ROMANCE OF BARISDALE

WHILE the Lowlanders, for nearly fifteen hundred years, had cast on Highland robbers the eyes of hatred and contempt, Sir Walter Scott suddenly taught men to think a cateran a very fine fellow. The unanimity of a non-Highland testimony had previously been wonderful. ·'The Highlanders are great thieves,' says Dio Cassius, speaking for civilisation as early as A.D. 200–230. Gildas, in the sixth century, calls the Highlanders (Picti) ·a set of bloody free booters, with more hair on their thieves' faces than clothes to cover their nakedness.' Early mediaeval writers talk of the *bestiales Picts* ('the beastly Picts '), and later Lowland opinions to a similar effect are too familiar for quotation. To Scott was left the discovery of the virtues of the honest cateran, who looked on cattle-stealing as an ennobling occupation in the intervals of war.

Sir Walter's opinion ran through Europe like the Fiery Cross. His grandson, Hugh Littlejohn, stirred up by the ·Tales of a Grandfather,' dirked his small brother slightly with a pair of scissors in a childish enthusiasm! Even the moral Wordsworth, moved by

Scott, had a good word for Rob Roy. Yet about that
hero Sir Walter cherished no illusions. He knew
Rob's Letter of Submission to General Wade, after
1715. Rob, of course, had been out for King James,
but he coolly says to Wade: 'I not only avoided
acting offensively against his Majesty's' (King
George's) 'forces, but, on the contrary, sent His
Grace the Duke of Argyle all the intelligence I could
from time to time of the strength and situation of
the Rebels; which I hope his Grace will do me the
justice to acknowledge.'

'All the *demerits* ascribed to him by his enemies
are less to his discredit than this one *merit* which he
assumes to himself,' says Jamieson.[1] The double-
faced traitor, Rob's son, James Mohr, one of the
bravest of men, *chassa de race*. The truth is that a
life of plunder, however romantic and however little
regarded as immoral or degrading by Highland
opinion, really did foster, in educated men, the most
astonishing perfidy. This is the last vice we look
for in the generous cateran; and, indeed, the outlaws
of Glen Moriston were as loyal to their Prince as
Lochiel. But the prevalent opinion that robbery,
sanctioned by tradition, does not degrade the general
character, can be proved to be an error. We read
about Cluny that, in 1742-5, he held the usual
belief. 'He was certain it' (the habit of robbery)
'proceeded only from the remains of barbarism, for
he had many convincing proofs that in other respects

[1] *Burt's Letters*, ii. p. 334.

the dispositions of the people in these parts were
generally as benevolent, humane, and even generous,
as those of any country whatever.'[1]

Cluny was right about the untutored mass of the
people, but he was wrong about a few educated chiefs,
who encouraged and lived on an unfortunate tradition. Thus Sir Walter Scott writes about the thief
whose history we are to narrate, Macdonnell of
Barisdale : 'He was a scholar and well-bred gentleman. He engraved on his broadswords the well-
known lines :

> Hae tibi erunt artes, pacisque imponere morem,
> Parcere subjectis, et debellare superbos.'[2]

Barisdale knew what was right ; his following knew
only his will. He was the blackest of traitors ; they
were true as steel.

The specially robber tribes in 1715–45 were
those of the dispossessed Macgregors, whose hand
was, necessarily, against every man's hand ; of the
Macdonnells in Knoydart ; and of some of the
Camerons in Lochaber and Rannoch. Old Lovat,
too, discouraging schools, kept up sedulously the
ancient clan ideas. No other sections of the Highlanders are accused, even by Whigs, of robbery.
Mackays, Mackenzies, Grants, Mackintoshes, Macphersons, Macleans are not blamed, and such gentlemen of the Camerons and Macdonnells as Lochiel,
Scothouse, and Keppoch are specially exculpated.

---

[1] MSS. in the Cluny Charter Chest. Privately printed, 1879, p. 16.
[2] *Waverley*, i. p. 161 (1829).

Lochiel was a reformer within his clan. The gallant
Keppoch had forsworn the predatory habits which,
in 1689, made his people threaten Inverness. Of
Scothouse we shall hear the most excellent report.
Now, it cannot be by a mere fortuitous coincidence
that all the Highland traitors, James Mohr, Old
Lovat, Glengarry, Barisdale, and some others, come
precisely from the homes of cattle thieves, and from
a factitious hothouse of old clan ideas; from the
Macgregor country, Knoydart, the worst part of
Lochaber, and Rannoch. Yet, so strange was the
condition of the North, that we find Barisdale, the
meanest wretch of all, recognised as an acquaintance
by so high a Lowland dame as the ' Great Lady of
the Cat,' the Countess of Sutherland.

We now proceed to the story of the chief who
loved a Virgilian quotation.

In the army of Charles Edward there was no man
more detested and feared than Col Macdonell of
Barisdale. According to a curious tract, ' The Life
of Archibald Macdonell of Barisdale, who is to Suffer
for High Treason on the Twenty Second of May, at
Edinburgh, By an Impartial Hand,' [1] Col of Barisdale was son (? grandson) of the second brother of
Alastair Dubh Macdonnell of Glengarry, the hero of
Sheriffmuir, being thus a cousin of Glengarry. He
was a man of prodigious muscular force, six feet
four inches in height. He is said to have caught
and held a roedeer; and, on one occasion, to have

---

[1] London: 1754.

heaved a recalcitrant cow, probably stolen property, into a boat. There lay, in the present century, on the gravel-drive before Invergarry House, a large boulder, and beside it a short pin of iron was fixed into the ground. Only a very powerful man could lift the boulder on to the pin, a few inches in height, but Barisdale could heave it up to his knees. So write, from tradition, the two 'Stuarts d'Albanie,' in 'Tales of the Century' (1847). They add that Barisdale's courage did not match his strength, and that he yielded in single combat to Cluny.

Returning to our 'Impartial Hand' (by his minute local knowledge a native of Ross or Moray), we find him nowise partial to Barisdale. 'Colonel Ban,' as he calls him, married a Miss Mackenzie of Fairburn, and, having a small estate in Ross-shire, could raise two hundred of the clan. He thus, says Murray of Broughton, declared himself independent of Glengarry, his chief, an indolent drunkard. Being acquainted with the Mackenzie estates, he used his knowledge in the surreptitious acquisition of cattle. He would then throw the blame on the Camerons; and that, says our author, is precisely the cause of the bad name for cattle-stealing which the Camerons have unhappily acquired. One day Barisdale, with his Tail, met Cameron of Taask, with *his* Tail, and was charged by Cameron with his misdeeds. Words grew high, claymores were drawn, and a finger of Cameron's left hand was nearly lopped off. The intrepid chieftain, acting on the Scotch proverb,

'Better a finger off than aye wagging,' tore the injured limb from his hand, bound the wound with a handkerchief, 'and so fell to work on Barisdale,' whom he sliced on the pate. 'The skin and a lock of his hair hung down,' and their devoted tenants, anxious observers of the fray, separated the infuriated chieftains. Barisdale was presently arrested on a charge of theft, but his Tail perjured themselves manfully, and he got off on an alibi.

The neighbours, finding the hero so stubborn, paid him 'black meal' (*sic*), in return for which he promised to protect their herds. But his genius pointed out to him a more excellent way, and Barisdale became the Jonathan Wild (as Waverley says) of Lochaber and Knoydart. He was a thief-catcher, and also an accomplice of thieves, as interest directed or passion prompted.[1] He kept his tenantry, or gang, in rare order, and 'had machines for putting them to different sorts of punishment.' One machine was merely the stocks, where, outside of the chieftain's drawing-room windows (which commanded a fine view of the sea), many a poor thief sat for twenty-four hours, with food temptingly placed just out of his reach. Thus Barisdale struck terror, inspired respect, and accumulated wealth.

A more cruel engine than the stocks had Barisdale, a triumph of his own invention. In 'The Lyon

---

[1] This is confirmed by the Gartmore MS. in Burt; by MS. 104, in the King's Collection; and by Murray of Broughton, in his paper on the Clans.

in Mourning.' Mackinnon, who helped Prince Charles
to escape from Skye, says that Captain Fergusson
(noted for his ferocity) threatened him with torture.
'The cat or *Barisdale* shall make you speak,' said
the Captain. The engine is described as one in
which no man could live for an hour. The 'Impartial Hand' gives this account of it : 'The
supposed criminal' (that is, any man who would not
give Barisdale a share of his booty) 'was tied to an
iron machine, where a ring grasped his feet, and
another closed upon his neck, and his hands were
received into eyes of iron contrived for that purpose.
He had a great weight upon the back of his neck, to
which, if he yielded in the least, by shrinking down-
wards, a sharp spike would infallibly run into his
chin, which was kept bare for that very purpose.'
Barisdale was also apt to waylay herring-fishers, and
make them pay, as toll, a fifth of what they had
captured, alleging certain seignorial rights.

'It is well known,' says the author of 1754, ' that,
from the month of March to the middle of August,
some poor upon the coast have nothing but shell-
fish, such as mussels, cockles, and the like, to support
them. Poverty reigns so much among the lower
class that scarce a smile is to be seen upon their
faces.' Barisdale also reigned upon the coast.

Such was life in the Highlands in the golden
days of the Clans, before sheep, Lowlanders, evictions, emigration, and deer forests brought, as we
are told, discontent and destitution. The poor lived

on mussels and cockles, some tenants eked out a scanty livelihood by stealing their neighbours' cows, and the genial Barisdale kept all in good order. For Barisdale's prowess we are not obliged to rely on the ' Impartial Hand ' and the Gartmore MS. alone. In ' The Highlands of Scotland : a Letter from a Gentleman at Edinburgh to a Friend in London,' we meet our Col again. This manuscript [1] is in the King's Collection, 104, in the British Museum. The author is an *enragé* Whig and Protestant, but a close observer. From him we learn how cattle-stealing paid ; for at first blush it looks like the practice of those fabled islanders ' who eke out a livelihood by taking in each other's washing.' The business was extended over a wide area ; the Macdonells did not merely harry the Mackenzies and Rosses.

Speaking of Knoydart, our author says : ' Coll. Macdonell of Barisdale, cousin-german of Glengarry, took up his residence here, as a place of undoubted security from all legal prosecution. He entered into a confederacy with Lochgarry and the Camerons of Loch Arkaig, with some others as great villains in Rannoch. This famous Company had the honour to introduce theft into a regular trade ; they kept a number of savages dependent on them for the purpose, whom they out-hounded ' on predatory expeditions.

They robbed from Sutherlandshire to Perthshire, Stirlingshire, and Argyle. When the thieves were

---

[1] Published (1898) as *The Highlands in* 1750 (Blackwood).

successful these gentlemen had a dividend of the
spoil. When unsuccessful, the thieves lived on the
country which they traversed. To denounce them
was ill work. A gentleman, known to our author,
was nearly ruined by Barisdale & Co. He caught
two of the Macdonalds, who were hanged. Fifteen
years later his son, going to Fort William, vanished.
The tribe, says our author, demanded 'blood for
blood.'

By these devices Barisdale compelled his neighbours to pay, in blackmail, 'above double their
proportion of the land-tax in Seaforth's, Lovat's,
and Chisholme's country.' He captained a kind of
'Watch.' But Barisdale's 'Watch' was expensive
and unsatisfactory to his subscribers. As early as
1742 we have found Cluny setting up an opposition
in business. Cluny's Watch is described at great
length by the author of a kind of memoir of the
chief, written in France in 1755–1760. The writer's
object is to show how much Cluny lost by his loyalty
to the Stuarts, and how much he deserves the en-
couragement of Louis XV. He established, for the
discouragement of theft, 'a watch or safeguard of
his own trusted followers.' The nobility and gentry
'were surpris'd at Cluny's success, and enveyed so
much his happiness, that they applyed to him with
one accord. to take them under his protection, and
cheerfully offered to join in a voluntary subscrip-
tion. . . .' Among the subscribers are the Duke of
Gordon, the Earl of Airlie, the Earl of Aberdeen.

Forbes of Culloden, the Mackintosh, Grant of Grant,
and even the Duke of Argyll.   These facts attest
the extent of Barisdale's raids.

Cluny was highly successful, rescuing 'even those
who had never applyed to him.'   The subscriptions
amounted to 20,000 livres, and the Dukes of Atholl
and Perth, with Seaforth, were about to join.   It
was now that a preacher, thundering against theft,
was interrupted by a listener who ' desired him to
save his labour upon that point, for Mons. de Cluny
alone would gain more souls to heaven in one year,
than all the priests in the highlands could ever do
in fifty.'

The English Ministry, hearing of Cluny's fame,
now sent him, unasked, a captain's commission in
Loudon's regiment, worth 6,000 livres yearly.   But
he threw up his new commission when he joined
Prince Charles.   Cluny's spirited behaviour, says MS.
104, 'took the bread out of their mouths.' the mouths
of Barisdale & Co.   But ' Barisdale, by the former
trade (theft) and the latter expedient (blackmail),
lived at a very high rate, and mortgaged a large sum
of money on Glengarry's estate.' where he was a
wadsetter.

Cluny's opposition may have led to his duel with
Barisdale, as reported by the Stuarts d'Albanie.
Barisdale was, as we have seen, like Lochgarry, a
wadsetter of Glengarry's ; that is, he received from
Glengarry certain lands, redeemable after a specified
interval of time, in exchange for money paid, or bills,

or perhaps for cattle, which he was skilled in pro-
curing. We do not find that the chief, Glengarry,
could or did exercise any authority in controlling
the excesses and depredations of his independent
cousin Col. For this he is blamed by the author of
the Gartmore MS., but his Mackenzie following made
Col too strong for his chief.

Ignorant, perhaps, of the character of Barisdale,
unwilling, at least, to dispense with his aid, Prince
Charles visited him in August 1745, made him a
colonel, and gave a major's commission to his son,
young Archibald Macdonnell of Barisdale, a lad of
twenty in 1745. Our 'Impartial Hand'[1] declares that
Coll, though at Prestonpans, was not under fire,
which seems improbable. Barisdale may have been
with the Prince in the second line (fifty yards behind
the first, says the Chevalier Johnstone), or, in the
oblique advance of the first line, Lochiel and James
Mohr may have routed the English before Barisdale
could engage. But, in a letter of Thomas Wedderburn to the Earl of Sutherland, we read (September 26, 1745), 'Three troops that were making
their way for Berwick were pursued by Barisdale,
and 150 men, who all stript to their shirts, on foot,
who overtook the dragoons, I suppose by turning a
hill and gaining ground that way, and made them
prisoners, for which Barisdale was made a knight

---

[1] He is a Lowlander, and avers that Scotland rarely lost a battle
except when the Highlanders were engaged, as at Flodden.

bannarett ' [1]—knighted. that is, like Dalgetty, on the field.

After Prestonpans, according to the Impartial one, confirmed by the 'Culloden Papers,' and by Broughton's 'Memorials,' Barisdale, by Sheridan's advice, was sent north, to work on Old Lovat. Sheridan reckoned that no man was likely to have so much influence with that subtle schemer as the bluff Barisdale, with ' his devouring looks, his bulky strides, his awful voice, his long and tremendous sword, which he generally wore in his hand, with a target and bonnet edged broad upon the forehead.' Barisdale, thus accredited, worked both on Lovat and Lord Cromarty, who raised his peaceful tenants by threats of burning their cottages and cattle.[2] Cromarty might have reported, like a Highland recruiting officer in later days, ' The volunteers are ready; they are all lying bound hand and foot in the barn.' Many of the Highlanders did not want to fight, though they fought so well. Barisdale also sent · the bloody cross,' we are told, through the Frazers, who marched reluctantly under the Master of Lovat, a St. Andrews student, himself as reluctant as he was brave. At Falkirk, Barisdale is said to have been with the second line, and later ' he set out to collect the public money, the greater part of which he kept to himself.'

Just before Culloden, Barisdale was engaged in

---

[1] *Sutherland Book*, ii. 256.
[2] MS. 104 says that they went out most reluctantly.

the not uncongenial duty of reducing the shires of
Ross and Sutherland. In the latter county Lord
Reay. with the Mackays and the Earl of Sutherland,
were for King George; Lord Loudon also was
quartered with his force in Ross-shire. Lord Cromarty. with the Mackenzies. Mackintoshes. Mackinnons. Macgregors. and Barisdale's Macdonnells.
did little. retiring to his own house. Barisdale was
anxious to burn the house of Ross of Balnagoun. but
Lochiel. who had arrived with Lord George Murray.
intervened. At Dornoch. Barisdale went to church.
where the Rev. Mr. Kirk. a gentleman connected
with the Duke of Argyll. had the courage to pray
for King George. Barisdale leaped up. swaggered.
fumed. and. it is rather absurdly said. threatened to
put Mr. Kirk in his famous engine of torture. The
chivalrous Duke of Perth protected Mr. Kirk, saying
that all brave men were his friends. and asked the
clergyman to dinner.[1] Lord George Murray. finding
Cromarty incompetent. and Barisdale mainly occupied in burning granaries. now took the command.
and Loudon crossed the Firth into Sutherland.
Perth then led the Prince's forces across the Firth.
and Loudon hastened to withdraw into central
Sutherland.

Neither side was anxious to come to blows.
Macdonnell of Scotus, a man 'brave. polite, obliging.
of fine spirit and sound judgment,' says the Chevalier
Johnstone, had a son with Lord Loudon. and was

[1] The Impartial Hand.

reluctant to engage. Later, to his intense joy, he took this son a not unwilling prisoner. Meanwhile Barisdale, on March 20, captured the Castle of Dunrobin. The Earl of Sutherland fled, under cover of a fog, and escaped to an English ship. The Countess stayed at home ; she was a daughter of the Earl of Wemyss by his third wife, was a young lady of twenty-eight, and had a young nephew, Lord Elcho, with the Prince. According to the 'Sutherland Book' (i. 420), one of Barisdale's officers threatened her with a dirk, and, some one jogging his elbow, she was actually scratched. To this the Countess, as we shall see, herself bears witness. But it is by no means certain that the lady, coming of a Jacobite family, was an unwilling prisoner of the Prince's men. It was irksome to her, no doubt, to see her rooms littered with hay on which the Highlanders slept, and to observe the robbery of her plate. But the two following intercepted letters, from the Cumberland Papers, display the Countess as an adorer of Prince Charles, and Barisdale as a *preux chevalier*.

Letter from The Countess of Sutherland to the Young Pretender, written with MacDonell of Barisdale's own Hand.

·March 26, 1746.

·The treatment I mett with Friday Last oblidges me to presume to oCoast your Royall Hyness For a protection to prevent the Lyke Usadge in the Future. However my Lord Sutherland Acted, It's known over

the most of this Kingdome my particular attachment
to your Royall Hyness' Family, and were itt ordinaire
in one of my sex to go to the Field to Fight For
my Prince and Country. I would make as aerly ane
appearance as anie, and hade not my Coch horses
and sadle horses being caryed away I woud presume
the Honnaire to waith of your Royall Hyness. Least
my letter be too tediouse I will only give one Instance
of my usadge. a man holding a drawn durk to my
brest gave a scrach of a wound which merk itt
well beare: but this day Barisdale coming here.
being my acquaintance. in his presence I sent a
gentleman to all the men of my Lord Sutherland's
that were in arms desiring them to disperse and
return to their homes in order a proper Draught be
made of them For your royall Hyness service. My
success I can not determine as I can not Depend
upon much assistance. but if matters were further
att my Disposall all the Fensable men in Sutherland
woud be on your Royall Hyness armie as I am quite
affrighted. From the Hylanders I beg to petition
your Royall Hyness protection how Soone pasable
and I always am and ever will,' &c.

On March 27, 1746, from Tarbat House Lord
Cromarty writes in answer to the Countess of Sutherland, acknowledging her letter, and promising protection to all her people who submit.

Then we have Barisdale's *billet* to the lady :

Col McDonell to Lady Sutherlande

'Andmore: March 27, 1746.

'My Faire Prisoner.—I presume these with the offer of my most Respectfull humble Duty to my Lady Sutherland, my Regiment is ordered back againe to Sutherland For which I am verrie sorrie, if anie hardships must be used, itt shoud in the Least Fall to my Shaire. I will have one Certaine pleasure in Itt that it well give the oportunity of being For once more my Lady Sutherland's Saife guard. I Forwarded your Ladyship's letter by one Captt Lewlessnent, and sent itt Inclosed to his Grace, and held Forth my Lady Sutherland's zeall For our Cause, and the Friendship she particullarlie expected From him, and represented the Horses taken away, and pleaded For her Interest to have them, att Least my Ladys Favourites, returned. I go this Day to Inverness myself and shall talk to His Royall Hyness in regard to what my Lady Sutherland woud Exspect off Favours From our side, and what is Actuallie Deue to her. After my return, shall have the pleasure of waitting off your Ladyship att Dunrobine, and allways will be Nott onlie your Lady's prisoner in the strictest Confinement, but your Ladyships most obdtt. and most humble sertt. while

'COL. McDONELL.'[1]

An odious tale is told by the 'Impartial Hand,' about Barisdale's conduct to his wife's young sister.

[1] These letters are in the Cumberland MSS. at Windsor Castle.

We do not trust the Impartial one where we have not corroboration, and, to his fair prisoner, Lady Sutherland, Barisdale certainly displays a tender gallantry. But she may not have regretted that her Barisdale was occasionally absent. Cumberland was approaching, and, on the eve of Culloden, Lord Cromarty was captured in 'The Battle of Golspie,' while dallying over his *adieux* to 'his favourite Amazon,' the Countess of Sutherland, as the Impartial one invidiously declares.

The Countess must have managed her diplomacy adroitly, for the Whig author previously cited says, 'It is a pity the present Earl of Sutherland should be such a weak man, but his lady behaved very honourably, though her brother (nephew) the Lord Elcho, was engaged in the Rebellion.'[1] The lady's letter to Prince Charles was not known to our author.

Barisdale, leaving his fair prisoner, marched south, and halted at Beauly, on the night before Culloden. 'He might easily have reached the field, had he been any way resolute or brave.' But like the Master of Lovat and Cluny, Barisdale came up too late. The fugitives passed through Inverness, under his eyes, and Barisdale also made off.

He was at the Meeting of the Chiefs at Murlagan, on May 8, when it was determined to rally in a week, and a treaty was made, that all should hold together.

---

[1] MS. 104. King's Library.

I

in spite of the Prince's defection.[1] When the week ended, nobody came to the tryst but Lochgarry, who retired at once, Lochiel. and Barisdale, with three or four hundred of their clans. But the Rev. John Cameron, in ' The Lyon in Mourning ' (i. 88) accuses Barisdale of promising to return next day, as a blind, and of sending instead two companies of infantry in English service, to capture Lochiel. They were recognised by their red crosses, and Lochiel escaped, ' which was owing to its not being in Barisdale's power '—to catch him, ' rather than to want of inclination,' says Mr. Cameron. Murray of Broughton represents Barisdale as accusing his cousin and enemy, Lochgarry, of treachery, and believes that both were equally guilty, but Lochiel was as incapable of suspecting as of being guilty of treason. In his Letter to the Chiefs, of May 26, he says that Clanranald's men refuse to leave their own country, that Glengarry's men have yielded up their arms (induced thereto, we shall see, by Old Glengarry), that Lochgarry promised to return, but did not, and that, ' trusting to Lochgarry's information, we had almost been surprized.' But he never hints at a suspicion of Barisdale.[2]

On June 10, says the ' Impartial Hand,' Barisdale and Young Barisdale both surrendered to Ensign Small, in a cave. But Barisdale, it is known, got

[1] See Mr. Mackenzie's *History of the Camerons*, pp. 233–244, where the documents are given.
[2] *History of the Camerons*, p. 236.

a protection, on his promise to deliver up Prince Charles. He laid several schemes to this end, and had two companies to seize the Prince at Strath-fillan. Sheridan, however, 'who had a talent for reading men with as great freedom and judgement as others do books.' warned the Prince, who kept out of Barisdale's clutches.[1] So says the Impartial Hand.

His story of the protection for Barisdale was true, as witness the following letters from the Cumberland Papers, at Windsor Castle.

From G. Howard to Col. Napier, A.D.C. to D. of C.

'July 5th. . . .

'A person passed me here yesterday morning whom I took to be lawful Prey, but, to my great concern, he produced a Pass-port for himself and 4 servants with their arms &c, syned by Sir E. Faulkner : it was dated only the day before yester-day. The person was McDonald of Barisdale, who is so particularly zealous for hanging our officers. 1 asked him if he had seen H.R.H. (Cumberland). He said no, but that a friend got him his Protection.'

Lord Albemarle to Duke of Cumberland

'July 26th.

'The Complaint is universal against Barisdale, therefore 1 shall not renew his protection, but drive

---

[1] Sheridan can scarcely have been Charles's adviser at this time. It may have been O'Sullivan.

and burn his country to punish him for having made
such a bad use of your goodness. Glengarry is much
commended for his behaviour.'

Finally, Barisdale had already induced several
Macdonnells to lay a written information against Old
Glengarry, their chief.

How did Barisdale. who had played a part so
conspicuous, manage to obtain a protection from
Sir Everard Faulkner? That is the point which we
shall later find him explaining with singular candour.   Protected he was, and. in pursuit of information, he had the singular impudence to venture,
with his son, in September 1746, on board the ship
which was to carry the Prince. Lochiel, Lochgarry,
and other gentlemen to France.   They could not
but be aware that Barisdale had made his submission, and was come on no good errand.   Lochgarry
was his bitter enemy.   They therefore put Barisdale
and his son in irons, shut them down under hatches.
carried them to France. and there imprisoned these
gentlemen of Knoydart on a charge of treason.   Mr.
Fraser Mackintosh, a very innocent writer, thus
describes the high-handed outrage : ' Barisdale was
so unpopular with the Camerons. that, without the
slightest warrant, they took it on themselves to deport
Coll Macdonnell, and his son Alexander [Archibald?]
to France.'   Mr. Fraser Mackintosh attributes this
unwarrantable action to ' the Camerons.' with whom
Barisdale was generally ' unpopular.'   But, of course,

the seizure was warranted by Charles, Prince Regent,
who is said to have knighted Barisdale on a stricken
field. The seizure was more than justified, and was
not due to poor Col's 'unpopularity.'

Col languished in a French prison till 1749. In
March he ventured back to Scotland, finding himself,
after his release, very 'unpopular' in Flanders. He
was promptly culled like a flower by his old captor,
Ensign Small, and was brought before Erskine for
examination. Erskine writes that he found the tall
bully 'under visible terror.' France had imprisoned
him. England was likely to give him what 'he wad
be nane the waur o' '—a hanging. His house was left
unto him desolate; he would flirt no more with fair
captive Countesses: no one trembled at his frowning
brows: it was Barisdale's turn to tremble, as he did.
He was locked up in Edinburgh Castle, where, at
least, he was safe from avenging dirks. He there
penned the following explicit confession, in hopes of
a pardon, and pay as a spy. Perhaps Cumberland
refers to Barisdale's earlier services in this capacity,
in a letter of August 2, 1749. Cumberland speaks
of 'the goodness of the intelligence' now offered to
Government. 'On my part I bear it witness, for I
never knew it fail me in the least trifle, and have
had very material and early notices from it.' [1]

Here, then, follows Barisdale's confession to the

---

[1] *Pickle*, p. 160. I at first conjectured that this letter might refer
to Pickle himself, but Barisdale, who was in touch with Cumberland
in 1746, just after Culloden, is more probably the person hinted at.

Justice Clerk in Edinburgh. It entirely disposes of
Mr. Fraser Mackintosh's suggestion that the Camerons
seized Barisdale because he was ' unpopular.'

Narrative given in by Barrisdale to the Justice Clerk

(*H. O. Scotland.   Bundle* **41.**   *No.* 13.   *State Papers.   Domestic*)

April 10th, 1749.

' His Royal Highness, the Duke of Cumberland,
sent a protection by Sir Alexr. Macdonald to
Barisdale, upon delivering to him of which, he told
him, in Consequence of the Favours the Duke
intended for him, he should cause all such as he
would have any Influence with, surrender their arms
directly, which Barisdale did at the Barracks of
Glenelg immediately thereafter; by which the Concert of those that imagined to make any further
resistance was broke, and he gave all the Assurances
Sir Alexr. desired of him, to be a good faithful subject, yt would give all obedience to the Government,
which Since he has perform'd. *But from that time the
Jacobite party design'd to ruine Barisdale,* and endeavoured, with all Calumny's, to make him odious to all
partys and all Persons.   The Pretender's Son having
returned from the Isles to the Continent (mainland),
Sir Alexr. Macdonald wrote to Barisdale, desiring to
inform him of some particulars, which he did very
distinctly, and soon after his R. Highness [Cumber-
land] left Fort Augustus, my Lord Albemarle, then
Commander in Chief, desired Sir Aler. McDonald to

send for Barisdale to Fort Augustus. Sir Alexr. Macdonald wrote to him, and accordingly Barisdale
waited of my Lord Albemarle at Fort Augustus,
at Sir Alex. McDonald's Lodgings, where before Sir
Alex: McDonald, his Lordship told Barisdale, as the
Pretender's Son was now returned from the Isles to
the Continent (mainland), if he hop'd for the Continuance of his R. Highness's Favours, he must lay
himself out in giving Assistance to have the Person
of ye Pretender's Son sez'd.

'Barisdale answered, in Sir Alexander's Presence,
that Sir Alexr. never made any such Proposal to
him from his R. Highness (Cumberland); and if he
was a Man supposed formerly in the Jacobite
Interest, and *upon getting a better Light*, to forsake them
it would be very inconsistent wth. Honour, for a Man
so supposed, to go such Lengths. But for his share,
were he to do his utmost to comply with his Lordship's desire, he could expect little success in it,
since all the Jacobite Party were upon their Guard,
even the meanest Highlander, to give no Intelligence
to any he had Influence with.

'His Lordship and he parted that Day: my Lord
Loudoun, Sir Alexr. McDonald, and Barisdale,
being at a Bottle that night, resumed all that past
at that Communing—Loudoun said, "I own what his
Lordship desires of you, may not be easy for you
to perform, but such Information as you can best
receive, you can transmit to his Lordship and you
can make an Observe upon each, according to

the Credite you give yourself to the Information."

' My Lord Albemarle, the next day, at Sir
Alexander's Lodgings, insisted as the Day before;
and Barisdale agreed, such Informations as he could
learn, he would transmit them, wt. Remarks upon
them of the Credite he thought they deserved—
My Lord Albemarle gave a Continuance upon the
Protection for ten Days more, which was a short
time for Barisdale to go to his country, and find
Informations and then transmit them to Fort
Augustus.

' However he sent two different Informations wt.
Remarks upon them : is not certain which of the two,
my Lord Albemarle or my Lord Loudoun's Hands
they came to, as the Bearer of them brought back no
Answer in writing : But at the End of the Ten Days of
my Lord Albemarle's Protection, B. was rather more
distrest than any who were not before protected.

' Some few days thereafter, being at Sir Alexr.
McDonald at Slaite, hearing two French ships coming
to Ariseg, Sir Ar. McDonald desired Barisdale to go
to these Ships, in order to learn some things he
wanted to be inform'd of, and Barisdale coming to
the shore before the Ships, under Pretension of great
Friendship was invited aboard, there being at the
Ships severals he was acquainted with ; But soon
after he was aboard, found his Mistake, would not
be allow'd afterwards to come ashore, was carried to
St. Malos, seated upon the River La Luare where he

was prisoned about 2 years and four months. The
7th. of February last, with a Sentence of Banishment
to leave France in a few Days, was liberated : which
Sentence is now in the hands of the Governor of
Fort Augustus.

· The Accusations laid against him by the Pretender's son and likewise laid before the Court of
France were sent to Barisdale enclosed in a Letter,
wrote and signed by George Kelly, the Pretender's
Son's Secretary. of which there is a Copy herewith.'

He now offers services unconditionally [1]—· but is
sorry to be prevented in his Design of going to
London as he entended to throw himself in his R.
Highness the Duke of Cumberland's Hands. hoping,
as he still does. for his Highness' Protection and
Friendship, as promised to him by Sir Alexander
MacDonald in his R.H's. Name at their first Con-
ference. when he delivered to him the protection, in
the obtaining of which Barisdale will be capable. as
he is most willing. of doing essential Services to his
R. Highness and the Government in the North of
Scotland :—and says · it may appear most reasonable,
however, for the Family he is descended from. or the
Clan he is of. have been attach'd to the Pretender's
Family, that his cruel. uncommon. and severe usage
from that Family will not only make him most faithfull
to the Government. but as stiff an Enemy as that Family
have upon Earth. For it is well known the Pre-

---

[1] This does not look as if the Duke alluded to him in the letter
of August 9, where he talks of the price of information.

tender's Son exprest at Paris to some of the Scots,
who were sorry for Barisdale's treatment, that while
it was in his power, Barisdale woud never recover
his Liberty, at least while he was in France, for that
he was well assured, if ever he return'd to Scotland,
being well assured B. being both resolute and
Revengefull, he woud prove a very destructible
Instrument to his Interest.'

Here are the Jacobite charges against Barisdale :—

Copy of George Kelly, the P.'son's Secretary's Letter
'Paris, May 3rd, 1747.

'. . . Did you not own publickly, that upon his
R.H's. Approach to Inverness, you advertised the
Lord President and the Lord Loudoun of the same,
and advised them for their further Safety to retire
from thence? . . . Did you not, without asking their
Advice or Approbation, Surrender yourself to the
Enemy, and enter into certain Articles with them? . . .

'Whether, after receiving a Protection from the
Enemy, you did not engage and promise to appre-
hend the Person of H.R.H. and deliver him up to
them within a limited time? . . . .

'Whether or not you did not impose on several
Gentlemen of Glengary's Family, by asserting that
he had promised to deliver them up to the Enemy,
and that he was to receive 30l. sterling Premium for
Each Gentleman he should put into their Hands?
Did these gentlemen sign an information against
Glengary? And were his letters ordering them to

take up arms delivered up to Lord Albemarle, upon
which your Cousine, Glengary, was apprehended?'

And now the whole truth is out. as concerns
Col, third of Barisdale. His cruelties, his thefts, his
swaggerings, have ended in deliberate treachery,
and this worthy chieftain is found endeavouring to
do what the humblest peasant disdained even to
contemplate, to deliver up the fugitive Prince.

Barisdale took no profit by his iniquity. The
Ross people, whom he had harried, burned his famous
stocks, and his house, with its ' eighteen fire-rooms,
and many others without fires. beautifully covered '
(roofed) ' with blue slates.'

He himself died in 1750, in Edinburgh Castle ;
six soldiers. with no mourners, carried his bulky and
corpulent carcase to a grave ' at the foot of the *talus*
of the Castle.'

So says the Impartial Hand. Of Barisdale's
classical lore, and of his courtesy to a fair captive,
we have seen proof. For the rest, a more worthless
miscreant has seldom stained the page of history.
It was time that such a career as his should be made
impossible.

Young Barisdale skulked for years in the Highlands. a kind of Hereward, pursued by the English
troops. He was usually accompanied by five or six
of his Clan. armed, and in the prohibited Highland
dress. He supported life in his father's fashion,
mainly by robbing the herring fishers of a fifth of

their takes, under some pretence of a legal claim. His tenants, spoiled by the English troops, probably could contribute little to his maintenance. He is often mentioned in the Cumberland Papers, and, after he had been the guest of young Glengarry's uncle, Dr. Macdonnell, that physician talked indiscreetly as follows.

On Sept. 30, 1751, Captain Izard, of the Fusiliers, writes : 'Dr. Macdonald, brother of Glengarry, living at Cailles on Loch Nevis, told that young Barisdale lay at his house the Monday before, and took boat thence to carry his sister home, and he proposed going to the Isle of Skey' (Skye).[1]

He was taken at last on July 18, 1753, in a wood near Lochourn in Morar, and was tried in Edinburgh on a charge of High Treason, on March 11, 1754. With him was Macdonald of Morar, five or six other Macdonalds, and Mackinnons, a MacEachan, and others. He disputed the indictment, which described him as 'of Barisdale,' on the score that his grandfather had only been 'a moveable tenant of Glengarry's, without any right in writing whatsoever.' This plea was disregarded, and he was condemned to be hanged on May 22, bearing his sentence 'with great composure and decency.' Being respited, he lay in the Castle till 1762, when he took the oaths, and was released.

By a curious freak of fortune, young Barisdale's son Col, in 1788, 'held a Commission to regulate the Fisheries. This, in the height of the fishing

---

[1] Cumberland MSS. See 'A Gentleman of Knoydart,' *postea*.

season, was no easy task, and required a firm hand.
Not only were there disputes among the fishermen
themselves, but, apparently, thieves made it a regular
trade to attend, and pick up what they could. . . .
The poor fishermen now suffer from piracy in another
form. If there were officials like Barisdale armed
with sufficient powers, trawling within the limits
would soon be extirpated,' writes Mr. Fraser
Mackintosh.[1] The fishermen have never been fortunate. Before trawling came in they had to do with
the portentous Col of Barisdale. Perhaps, of the
two, they may prefer the trawlers.

Thus, in a generation, the son of Archibald and
grandson of Col, the former a brigand and thief
alike of cattle and herrings, became a peaceful
subject, and protector of the very class of fishermen
whom his grandsire had plundered. We may drop
a tear over old romance, but reality has its alleviating
features. There is absolutely no kind of villainy
of which Col of Barisdale was not eminently guilty.
Oppression, cruelty, cowardice, theft, and treachery
were all among his qualities, were all notorious, yet,
till after Culloden, Col could laugh at the law, and
was not shunned by society.

.   .   .   .   .

We have seen that Col accuses Sir Alexander
Macdonald of Sleat of corrupting his honour, and
advising him to sell himself. This may, or may not,
be true. The sympathies of Sir Alexander had been

[1] *Antiquarian Notes*, pp. 152, 153.

Jacobite, before 1745, but Murray of Broughton
states that in 1741 he was very angry when Balhaldie
put his name on a list of adherents presented to the
French Court. 'He declared he had never given him
any authority to do so.' A statement to the contrary
effect will be found in Mr. Mackenzie's 'History of the
Macdonalds,' page 234. In 1744, Murray represents
him as ready to rise if French troops were landed.
Murray repeats, in justice, that Sir Alexander's promises were purely contingent; they depended on the
existence of a 'well-concerted scheme,' and there was
none. But Sir Alexander not only did not come out,
he was won over by Forbes of Culloden to the
Hanoverian Cause. 'I should be sorry,' says Murray,
'to have so bad an opinion of mankind as to think
any of them cappable of attempting an apologie for
him.' Murray, in his examination, lied in Sir Alexander's interests, saying 'he always absolutely refused to have anything to do with the Pretender.'
But, after Preston Pans, Sir Alexander, moved by
that victory, said, in the hearing of Malcolm Macleod
of Raasay, that he would now raise 900 of his clan
and march south to fight for King James. Next
morning, however, he received a letter from Forbes
of Culloden, and instantly 'was quite upon the grave
and thoughtful, and dropt the declared resolution of
his own mind.'[1] In fact, he turned Hanoverian.

Later, in the crisis of the Prince's wanderings,
Sir Alexander was not at home when his wife, Lady

[1] *Lyon in Mourning*, i. 147.

Margaret, connived with Flora Macdonald to secure
Charles's escape from Skye. Lady Margaret wrote
to Forbes of Culloden that Flora was ' a foolish girl,'
and thanked God that *she* knew nothing of the
Prince's being in hiding near her house. Sir Alexander, on the other hand, confessed to Forbes that
Flora put his wife ' in the utmost distress by telling
her of the cargo she had brought from Uist.' [1] It was
fortunate for everybody, himself included, that Sir
Alexander was away from home. He wrote the
following letter to Cumberland, confessing nothing :—

*From Sir Alexander McDonald to H.R.H. giving
intelligence of Pretender's movements*

'Sconsar, Isle of Sky, 1746.

'Sir,—This morning Capt. Hodgson remitted to
your R. Highness all the intelligence I had then got ;
in rideing a few miles I was informed of the Pretender's whole progress since he landed in this island.
By the letter remitted to your R.H. he was left at
Portree, 14 miles from my house near which he
landed ; at Portree he met one Donald McDonald,
who was in the Rebellion, and who put him into a
boat belonging to the Isle of Rasay, which feryd him
into that island ; after staying there 2 nights he returned in the same small boat to the neighbourhood
of Portree, attended by one Malcolm McLeod. That
night he and his companion lay in a byre ; next day
(the Pretender in shabby man's apparel since he left

[1] *Culloden Papers*, pp. 290-292.

Portree) they found their way into a part of Mac-
Kinnon's estate, and having found McKinnon, though
disguised and lurking himself, he found a boat which
next day convey'd the Pretender, MacKinnon, and
one John MacKinnon, into Moror. They sail'd from
this island on Saturday last. MacKinnon was taken
in Moror by a party from Sky, and John McK. was
this day seized . . . they are both on board the
Furnace and confirm to a trifle the above relation.

'ALEX. MacDONALD.'[1]

The Baronet tells as little as may be ; he does not
implicate Flora, and, of course, shields his wife. His
own position was awkward.

Sir Alexander died in November 1746, when
about to visit Cumberland in England. It is to his
credit that he did his best to protect the loyal Kings-
burgh. But his vacillations were extreme, and if he
really helped to corrupt Barisdale, his behaviour is
without excuse. 'Were I to enumerate the villains
and villainies this country abounds in I should never
have done,' wrote Cumberland to the Duke of Newcastle. 'Some allowance must be made for Sir
Alexander's behaviour in the Forty Five,' says Mr.
Fraser Mackintosh. It was not precisely handsome.
The epigram on his death, which has variants, ran
thus :

If Heaven be glad when sinners cease to sin,
If Hell be glad when traitors enter in,
If Earth be glad when ridded of a knave,
Then all rejoice ! Macdonald's in his grave.

VI

CLUNY'S TREASURE

THE bayonets of Cumberland scarcely dealt a deadlier blow at Jacobitism than the spades which, in gentle and unaccustomed hands, buried the treasure of French gold at Loch Arkaig. About this fatal hoard, which set clan against clan, and, literally, brother against brother, something has been elsewhere said. But the unpublished reports given by spies and informers in the Cumberland Papers and the Record Office throw a great deal of unexpected light on the subject.

Our purpose is, first to offer what may be called official statements as to the original amount and hiding places of the treasure. Next we shall examine the stories as to the disposition and diffusion of the money. These will indicate that the charges of ' embezzlement ' and ' villainy ' brought by Young Glengarry against men so noted for their loyalty as Dr. Cameron and Cluny Macpherson are false. In our evidence will occur the testimony of informers, whose names, as they were persons of no historical importance, it seems needless to reveal. But their revelations were employed by Government in securing the

K

condemnation and banishment of Lochiel's brother, Cameron of Fassifern.

On the whole subject of the hoard we have several statements by Murray of Broughton. The least copious is contained in a tract which professes to be written by a friend of Murray ; really it is from his own pen.[1]

Murray, who had been in very bad health since the Prince was in Elgin before Culloden, found himself skulking with Lochiel in a wood near Loch Arkaig. He heard at the same moment of Charles's flight to the isles, which he condemned, and of the arrival of French ships with money. Most of the party resolved to scatter, but Lochiel declared ' that to desert his Clan was inconsistent with his honour and their interest,' and, by his desire, Murray remained with him, ' unable to refuse the desire of a person for whom he had such a regard, and with whom he had lived so many years in the strictest intimacy.' Major Kennedy, too, though, like other officers in French service, he might have surrendered safely, most generously clave to Lochiel. In later years Kennedy recovered for the Prince a remnant of the French *louis d'or*.

Murray was next carried to the bay opposite Keppoch, where the French ships were lying. They had been attacked by British vessels of war, but had previously landed 35,000 *louis d'or* in six (seven ?)

[1] *Memorials of Murray of Broughton*, p. 270, et seq.

casks. One cask, however, was already missing.
The five casks were conveyed to Murray, and of the
stolen cask all but one bag of gold was recovered.
Next day the Duke of Perth, who was dying, with
his brother, Lord John Drummond, Elcho, old Sir
Thomas Sheridan, the Prince's tutor, the younger
Lockhart of Carnwath, and others sailed for France
in the ships. Murray paid Clanranald, Barisdale,
and others their arrears, with allowances for widows
and wounded men, out of the French gold. He then
sent off the remainder of the hoard under Archy
Cameron's care, and returned to Loch Arkaig.
Fifteen thousand louis were buried ' in three several
parcels in the wood,' and the empty casks were filled
with stones, and carried about with Murray, 'so as
to give no Jelousy to the other Clans of his having
more confidence in the Camerons' than in them.
Near the foot of Loch Arkaig, Murray caused Dr.
Cameron to bury 12,000 louis, reserving about 5,000
for expenses.

Murray travelled south and was captured in
Tweeddale. On August 27, 1746, when in the
Tower, he wrote to an English official, 'last time I
had the honour to see you, I offered to lay my hand
upon the 15,000 *louis d'or*, and am still certain I can
do so, but as the season is now advancing, and
the parties will probably soon be called in, it is not
in that event impossible but the money may be
raised.' (It was ' raised ' by Dr. Cameron.) In his

Examination (August 13. 1746) Murray had already
betrayed the secret of the casks of gold. But the
English could never discover the treasure.

Elsewhere, in a paper of accounts, Murray tells,
in defence of his pecuniary honesty, all about the
disposition of the *louis d'or*.

He accounts for various sums, including 40*l.* to
Lochiel, who, like the gallant gentleman he was, had
given every penny in his possession 'to his own
people about.' Mr. Murray 'chided him for being
too easy to give money to whoever asked it.' A sum
of 3.868*l.* was buried in the garden of Mrs. Menzies
of Culdairs. This, we presume, was the bulk of the
5,000 louis reserved. Murray corroborates (as in his
tract) an anonymous informant's story, presently to
be given, about the stealing of a cask of money, and
restitution made after confession to Father Harrison.
The penitent however, an Irishman, kept 700*l.*, as
stated in the anonymous information. Murray
reckons at 15,000*l.* a sum buried near Loch Arkaig.
by Dr. Archibald Cameron, Young Macleod of Neuck,
Sir Stewart Threipland, and Major Kennedy. There
were fifteen bags containing 1,000*l.* each; one
parcel was put under a rock, in a burn, and two in
holes, near at hand. dug by the four gentlemen.
Another sum of 12.000*l.*, in two parcels, was carried
by Dr. Cameron and Mr. Macleod, from Lochiel's
house of Achnacarry, and buried near the *lower* end
of Loch Arkaig. Lochiel received 1,520*l.* for the
Prince's immediate needs, and the rest is scrupulously

accounted for by the unhappy Secretary. His stories are consistent throughout.[1]

Another description of the arrival and burial of the gold has never been published. It is from the Cumberland Papers, and must have been written about 1749-1750. This is proved by the writer's mention of Barisdale as still alive, and in prison. Now young Barisdale (Archibald) is not meant, for he was not taken till 1753.[2] His father, Coll Macdonnell of Barisdale, on the other hand, was taken in March 1749, and died in Edinburgh Castle on June 1, 1750.[3]

We now offer this anonymous intelligence of 1749-1750, as to the arrival, burial, and later fortunes of the French gold.

Intelligence sent to Col. Napier from Scotland about Seven Casks of Money for the Rebels

Cumberland Papers. Memoir for Col. Napier.

·Soon after the Battle of Culloden a french privateer anchored in Loch Nonha in Arisaig, where Doctor Cameron, Brother to Lochiel, Cameron of Dungallen, prisoner in Edr. Castle, and many other Rebels were then sculking. One of his Majesties' 20 gun Ships and 2 Sloops were cruising on the West Coast, immediately got intelligence of the privateers,

---

[1] Chambers's *Rebellion* of 1745. Appendix. But compare *Memorials*, p. 286, where Murray represents himself as poor, though he had the 5,000 *louis*, unless he had sent them on in front.

[2] *Scots Magazine*, July 1753, p. 362.

[3] *Ibid.*, 1750, p. 254.

and came up and attacked them. but before the
action began they had landed 7 Casks of money
and committed it to the Charge of Doctor Cameron,
who was upon the shore wth. a great many others
of the Camerons and Mc.Donalds. who flocked from
all Corners to see the engadgement. and among
others Mc.Donald of Barrisdale, now prisoner, was
also present and Alexd. Mc.Lachlan in Lidderdale
and Aide-de-Camp to The Pretender.

'When the action was over. The Commander of
the Privateers. having heard of the Battle of Culloden.
insisted to have the money put on board again. *But
the Rebells beg'd to be excused*, and Doctor Cameron
conveyed away six of the Casks to Loch Morrer. 3
miles from Loch Nonha : (The 7th Cask being stole)
and there he got a boat and went wth. it to the head
of ye Loch and from thence got in to Loch arkick :
And having dismissed all the Country people. He
wth. Major Kennedy. a french Officer. and Alexd.
McLeod son to Mr. John McLeod advocate. took the
money out of the Casks. and put it underground in
the head of Locharkick. in the midle of a Wood.

·There was £6 or 7,000 st. in each Cask, All put up
in separate Bags, £1,000 in Each bag. They afterwards
carried away the empty Casks themselves (none being
present but the 3 persons above named) and when
at a considerable distance from the place where the
Money was hid. They caused the Country people
put them under ground in a different place in order
to deceive.

'After this was over. All persons were employed to enquire after the Cask that was stole during the engadgement. And by the Assistance and authority of a priest (Father Harrison) who is great in that country (all Roman Catholics) the money was recovered except £700, and That is still amissing, . . . It is not well known what became of this broken Cask afterwards But Dr. Cameron had the Manadgement of it and all the rest, and it is imagined That The money divided at the meeting with Lovat, at the head of Loch arkick, was part of it, and £3,000 was given to one Donald Cameron at Strontian to Conceal, wch he again delivered to The Doctor, but got not one shilling for himself. [Is this the money hidden at Culdares?] Severals of the Country people got each a Louis d'or and some of their gentlemen got each 2 or 3 and that was all the Distribution made among the Camerons.

'His Majestie's troops afterwards search'd the woods of Locharkick for this money. and were often round the place where it was, and missed very narrowly finding it. for being hid by Gentlemen. not used to work, it was very unskilfully done. and the stamps and impression of their feet visible about the place. But as soon as Dr. Cameron found a proper opportunity. He went and took up the money and hid it in two different places of the wood. In one of them he put 12,000l., wch he shewed to his own son. and another man. That in case he was taken, it might not be lost altogether. and the other part he put in a place which he shewed to nobody. And thus it remained till a Ship arriv'd in Loch Nouha to carry off the Pretender &c. When the above Ship arriv'd He (the Pretender) was sckulking in one of the Glens of Brad Badenoch where he had been for some time conceal'd in a place under ground. with Lochiel, Cluny Mcpherson, and some other person. Upon receiving Intelligence of the arrival of this Ship, It seems it was concerted That Cluny should remain in Scotland and have the Charge of the money. And having come all together from Badenoch to Locharkick, they got Dr. Cameron, who went and shew'd Cluny the 2 different places where the money was: Left him in that Country, and the rest went and embarked with the Pretender in Loch Nouha. Whether there was any of the bags then taken up (as is probable) carried with them, or how many. is what I am not informed of.

'But Certain it is that Cluny immediately after Carried the £12,000 to Badenoch And there were in Company wth. him Angus Cameron (of Downan) a Rannoch Man, brother to Gleneavis, McPherson of Breachy (Breakachy), a brother in Law of his own, and his piper.

'The other part of the money. was shew'd to no Living but himself, and he either did not find an opportunity, or did not think convenient to come for it, untill a month afterwards, when he came and carried it also away, but I am not justly Informed who were wth. him. nor how much was of it, tho' It

is generally believed That he got betwixt £20 and
£30,000 in all.

'It is said by Cluny's Friends that the Pretender,
after embarking, sent a note to Cluny with particular
instructions how he was to manadge the money and
to whom he was to give any part of it,[1] and *they say
that he has conformed in the most exact manner to his
Instructions*, but The other Rebells in the highlands
grumble egregiously That he has not done them
justice. I have only heard That he gave £100 to
Lady Keppoch [2] and have reason to think That if he
made any other distributions it was to some other of
the principall Gentlemen of The Different Clans, to be
given away among their people, and that those have
thought fit to retain all to themselves.

'I know it is strongly suspected that Cameron of
Glenevis, whose Brother (Angus) was wth Cluny at
Carrying away the £12,000, has received a Large
proportion by some means or other, and there is
great reason to think so, as he was almost bankrupt
before the rebellion and is now shewing away in a
very different manner, particularly This year about a
month ago, there were 120 Louis d'ors sent from
him to a man in Locharkeek to buy Cattle for him ;
and some of the Camerons having lately threatened
to be resented of him for his behaviour about yt
money, he met with them, and parted good friends,

---

[1] This is accurate. The note exists to this day.
[2] This was by the Prince's desire.

which is supposed to have been done by giving them considerably.

'Barrisdale tells that Cole or Major Kennedy was to embark much about the same time yt he came from France, was to land on the West Coast in order to meet with Cluny, and carry away the money, but I have not yet learned any thing wth regard to him, And am apt to believe That he has rather landed on the Eastern Coast and my reasons for this Conjecture are: That one Samuel Cameron (Brother to The above men'd Cameron of Gleneavis) Major in the Regt. which was Lochiel's in the French Service, was at Edr. and came in a Chaise with the famous Mrs. Jean Cameron to Stirling, where they parted, and she came to her house in Morvern about the middle of March, and he took some different route: It is supposed That he came over on a message wth. regard to that money, and I the rather believe it as his two brothers seem to have been concerned in it, and I am apt to think that Kennedy and he have come together, but this is only my own conjecture. Another reason which induces me to believe That he would Chuse to land on the E. coast is That Cluny would not probably Like to march with that money or trust himself among the highlanders, who would probably not let it pass without partaking liberally.

' It has been said That the French Officer Cameron came to Mrs. Jean Cameron's. but I am certain he has not come, else I would have got Intelligence of

him, for I have had a sharp look out for him and all
others of that Kind. And I think he would not
probably venture so near the Command and specially
after hearing of Barrisdale's fate' (taken in March
1749).

'It is said That his Two Brothers and Cluny have
differed about the money, and therefore Cluny would
not see this French Officer nor trust him wth anything and some say He is gone back again, but how
far This is true I can't positively determine.

'The above is all that I have been able to learn
wth regard to that money from first to last, and
I am much convinced that the Substance of it is
true.'

[Unsigned.]

Even before the probable date of this intelligence,
Government knew that Cluny's fidelity to his trust
had embittered his relations with the Camerons of
Glenevis and Glengarry's people. There is a curious
anonymous note of January 26, 1748,[1] written by a
man who could spell, and was something of a
scholar. '*Scyphax*,' he says, 'is still in the country
and there are disturbances between him and the
Dorians and *Ætolians* over the goods left by the
Young Mogul.' Scyphax is Cluny, the Dorians are
the Camerons, the Ætolians are the Glengarrys; the
Young Mogul is Prince Charles: 'Nothing but steal-

---

[1] Scots Papers. Record Office.

ing and plundering prevails in all quarters here.'
The writer may have been a Presbyterian minister.

The author of the long letter of intelligence is
unknown, but he can hardly have been an English
officer, like Ensign Small, who did much secret
service in the Highlands. *His* name is always signed
to his Reports, as when he tried to catch Lochgarry
on shipboard, in 1753. The information, however
obtained, is accurate, and, so far, entirely exculpates
Cluny from the various unpleasant accusations
brought by his enemies.[1]   Major Kennedy really
went from France to Newcastle, and received 6,000*l.*
for Charles, a sum conveyed to him, at what peril
we may imagine, by Macpherson of Breakachy.[2]

We now consider the various accounts given
of embezzlement by Dr. Cameron and Cluny. It
is certain that, in November or December, 1749,
Young Glengarry, Lochgarry, and Dr. Cameron were
in Cluny's country, that they handled the treasure,
that they quarrelled, and that they carried their
dispute before the exiled James in Rome. Dr.
Cameron accused Young Glengarry of obtaining the
money by a forged order from James ; while Glengarry charged Cluny and the Doctor with ' embezzlement ' and ' villainy.' Cameron, he said, declared
that the Royal Family had given up all hopes of a
restoration, and told the Highlanders that they must

---

[1] See p. 141, note 2.
[2] Letters between the Major and the Prince are published in
Pickle the Spy.

Prince Charles
circ 1747

now shift for themselves. He also took 6.000 louis
d'or of the Prince's money, 'and I am credibly
informed.' says Glengarry. 'that he designs to lay
this money in the hands of a merchant in Dunkirk,
and enter partners with him.'[1] Again, in an undated letter to Charles, of about March 1751, Glengarry denounces the embezzlement and 'villainy' of
Cluny and Dr. Cameron.[2] He acknowledges having
taken 'a trifle' himself. Another account, clearly
from a Macdonnell source, occurs in old Gask's hand,
among his papers.[3] Dr. Cameron is here, as by Glengarry, credited with absorbing 6,000l., while Cameron of Glenevis is said to have 'intercepted' 3,000l.,
and Cluny, 'for his estate' gets 10,000l. This reads
like a variant of Young Glengarry's tale told to
Bishop Forbes in April 1752. According to that
version, Cluny and Lochiel took security from Charles
for the full value of their estates before they joined
the Royal Standard. This full value is the 10,000l.
which Cluny is said to have 'embezzled.'

Now the only independent evidence against Dr.
Cameron is contained in a letter of his uncle,
Cameron of Torcastle, to Prince Charles.[4] In this
Torcastle denies that he himself touched the money,
and avers that he knew nothing of it, till Dr.
Cameron 'told it himself at Rome, where I happened
to be at the time' (1750). This letter is singularly

[1] Glengarry to Edgar, Jan. 16, 1750. Browne, iv. p. 66.
[2] Browne, iv. p. 79.
[3] *Jacobite Lairds of Gask*, p. 276.
[4] Nov. 21, 1753. Browne, iv. 117.

inconsistent with another unpublished letter from Douay. of August 28, 1751. The epistle was intended for Cameron of Glenevis. but was intercepted by Colonel Crawfurd. Governor of Fort William. The Colonel attributed its authorship to Cameron of Torcastle, and if the attribution be correct, the letter contradicts Torcastle's accusations of his nephew, Dr. Cameron. Whoever the author of the Douay letter may be, he speaks of · the industrious malicious designs and scandalous untruths, publicly handed about against Lochiel's family by Gl——ry.' · Chalmers (Dr. Cameron) knows very well that when truth comes out, these people will fall with scandal into the trap they have contrived for others. . . . All that Chalmers (Dr. Cameron) saw or had access to *was his expenses.*' The writer then speaks of the ' unprecedented method Gl——ry &c. took to get att their sinister ends,' and about Gl——ry's ' misrepresentations of Chalmers to Mr. Young,' the Prince. Singular irritation against Lochgarry is also expressed.[1]

On this showing Dr. Cameron got no 6,000*l.*, but only his expenses. Now, that Dr. Cameron should receive his expenses was perfectly legitimate. But, if he took 6,000*l.*, as Young Glengarry declares, his character is lost. In 1750, 6,000*l.* was a fortune. Dr. Carlyle, writing of that time, speaks about a minister who married a lady with a tocher of 4,000*l.*, which then was equivalent to an estate. When executed

---

[1] Scots Affairs. Record Office.

in June 1753, Dr. Cameron left his family destitute.
Consequently he cannot have helped himself to
6,000*l.*, and put it into commerce, as Glengarry
alleged. That he did nothing of the sort, we have
the very curious evidence of an Informer in 1753.
This man, declaring that he is afraid of being
informed against by Young Glengarry, informs
against him. He says, in his information :

'In Sep. 1749 Dr. Cameron told him (the Informer) he had come over to get some money on
behalf of Lochiel's Family ; That Fassfarn got from
Clunie £6,000, took it to Edinburgh the following
winter, and put it in the hands of John Mc.Farlane,
W.S.¹ Dr. Cameron at the same time got £350: and
Fassfarn £400 more to be employed in making good
certain claims on the estate of Lochiel.

'Says he saw Dr. Cameron a day or two after,
who denied either he or Fassfarn had got any
money, alledging that Cluny would not give it without orders from the Old Pretender : That the Doctor
was off to Rome (1750) to get these, with only £100
for expenses. That the following winter he (the
Informer) met Young Glengarry, who disproved this
by giving him a copy of the Accounts in Clunie's
writing of all the money.'

Here follows Young Glengarry's *alleged* copy of
Cluny's accounts :—

---

¹ The husband of the lady who pistoled the English Captain after
1715.

'*A State of Clunie McPherson's Intromissions*

		£	s.	d.
' By Cash given Dr. Cameron and Fassfern, *secured with Fassfern for use of young Lochiel* .		6,000	0	0
„	sent to Lochiel by Angus Cameron and Donald Drummond, brother to Bohaldie .	1,000	0	0
	given the Dr. when last in Scotland to carry his Charges to and from Rome . . .	350	0	0
	at 2 different times by Angus Cameron to the Clan Cameron and others needy . .	800	0	0
,.	charged by Clunie for his Estate . . .	5,000	0	0
,,	„ ,. for his Commission . .	1,000	0	0
.,	„ „ for 30 Men from September 1746 -Sep. 1749 .	1,627	10	0
,,	charged by Clunie as his pay, at half-a-guinea per diem during said time . .	542	10	0
,.	charged by Clunie as Maintenance of his Family	1,400	0	0
,,	charged by Clunie for Brechachow (Breakachie)	800	0	0
,.	given to young Glengarry Nov. 1749 . .	300	0	0
,,	given by Clunie to his Clan	500	0	0
,,	„ Fassfern to pay Publick Burdens on Lochiel's Estates, viz. Cess and Teinds due by the Tenants .	200	0	0
,,	given Fassfarn to defray the Expences in carrying on the Claims on Lochiel's Estate	100	0	0
,,	Alleged by Clunie to be in Angus Cameron's hands.	500	0	0
,,	in Clunie's hands	4,880	0	0
		£25,000	0	0

' N.B.—Young Glengary got £1,900 at Edinburgh from Mr. Mc.Dougald at the sight of Mr. John Mc.Cleod of Nuck, Advocate, of which Glencarney got £80 and Glencoe £50. But this money had no connection with Clunie's Intromissions, having been carried to the South by Mr. John Murray.'[1] [Part of the 5,000 louis kept by Murray?]

[1] State Papers, Scotland, 1753.

According to this statement, said to be produced as Cluny's, Dr. Cameron did *not* receive 6,000*l.* for himself. The money went to the support of the exiled family of Lochiel, who had died in 1748. The large claims made by Cluny rest, as before, on the word of Young Glengarry.

In May 1753, Fassifern himself, then a prisoner in Edinburgh Castle, was examined. He declined to give any evidence against anybody on any charge. He admitted that in 1749 he received 4,000*l.* from Evan Cameron of Drumsallie, now dead, for Lochiel's family. He asked no questions, but deposited it with Mr. Macfarlane, W.S., who lent it out to Wedderburn of Gosford, in Fassifern's name. Fassifern acted as a near relation for his exiled nephew, Lochiel's son.

Thus the money which Dr. Cameron is said to have seized, was used for the support of Charles's best friends, the family of his most renowned adherent. So vanishes the charge that Dr. Cameron speculated with the money.[1]

As to Cluny's retention of money, the same difficulty occurs as in the case of Dr. Cameron. He arrived in France a destitute exile, when, by Charles's command, he ceased to skulk in the caves of Ben Alder, and crossed to join the Prince in 1754. There is no trace of the value of an estate in his possession, though Charles, in ordinary gratitude, owed him much more than he is said to have

---

[1] S.P.S. Bundle 44, No. 28 29.

claimed. Thus it is certain that Archibald Cameron did not help himself to the Prince's money; while the story about Cluny is inconsistent both with his honourable poverty and with figures, for these accounts make no allowance for 6,000 louis, certainly conveyed to Charles by Major Kennedy. The whole scandal rests merely on the word of Young Glengarry.[1]

---

[1] It is plain that the account given on p. 144, and said by the Informer to be ' in Clunie's writing,' is absolutely wrong, cannot be by Cluny, and is meant to incriminate that chief. Not only are the 6,000 louis carried to Charles by Kennedy omitted, but the ' treasure ' intercepted by Downan and Glenevis does not appear, while 2,000 of the 27,000 louis are left out of the reckoning. ' The State of Clunie McPherson's Intromissions,' in short, is a fraudulent document. It bears traces of confused manipulation in various interests.

VII

THE TROUBLES OF THE CAMERONS

THIS affair of the treasure caused endless calamities, especially involving Cameron of Glenevis, a place within two or three miles of Fort William. The relationship of this family to the head of the clan, Lochiel, stands thus: Archibald Cameron of Dungallon, who died in 1719, was the husband of Isabel Cameron of Lochiel. By her he left two sons and three daughters, of whom Jean married Dr. Archibald Cameron of Lochiel, the last Jacobite martyr; while Mary married Alexander Cameron of Glen Nevis.[1] Glenevis, or Glen Nevis, was not out in the Rising of 1745, but he was imprisoned in 1746, and released in 1747.[2]

The house of the Camerons of Glenevis, according to Mr. Mackenzie's 'History of the Camerons,' was of very ancient standing. It was 'generally at feud with Lochiel, and this feeling of antagonism came down even to modern times. Indeed, it has been maintained that the Glenevis family were

[1] *Lyon in Mourning*, i. 310. *Antiquarian Notes*, by C. Fraser Mackintosh, p. 225.
[2] *Lyon in Mourning*, i. 147.

originally not Camerons at all, but Macdonalds, who
settled there under the Macdonalds of the Isles,
before the Camerons had any hold on the district.'
They are also spoken of as Macsorlies. However
this genealogical point may be settled, there was no
love lost between Glenevis and Young Glengarry.

The Glenevis family, though not overtly engaged
for the Cause, suffered from the brutalities of the
victors. In spite of Glenevis's abstinence from
the Rising, his family was persecuted. Mrs. Archibald Cameron communicated to Bishop Forbes a
lamentable story of how her sister, Glenevis's
wife, was stripped by Cumberland's men, under
Caroline Scott, and only permitted to keep a single
petticoat. Her little son's gold buttons and gold
lace were cut off his coat, and the child was
wounded by the knife.[1] This story, which has contemporary evidence from the lips of Lady Glenevis's sister, Mrs. Archibald Cameron, has received
the usual picturesque embroidery of Highland tradition. Dr. Stewart ('Nether Lochaber') got the tale
from some ladies named Macdonald, in this fashion :
the infuriated soldiery, finding none of the plate and
jewels which Lady Glenevis had buried, observed
a bulky object under her plaid. Slashing with
swords at the plaid, to discover the supposed treasure, they wounded the lady's baby, a child of a few
months old. Mrs. Cameron's less romantic version,
if either, is correct.[2] The brothers of Glenevis were

---

[1] *Lyon,* i. 309-10.   [2] *Nether Lochaber,* pp. 188, 189.

Allan, who fell at Culloden—*felix opportunitate mortis* ; Angus of Dunan or Downan, in Rannoch ; and that unhappy Samuel, called Crookshanks, whom Dr. Cameron, before his execution, denounced as 'the basest of spies.' He was in French service, but was drummed out, after Dr. Cameron's death.

In October 1751, Colonel Crawfurd, commanding at Fort William, received from head-quarters information about Glenevis's and Angus's share in the treasure. Fassifern, Lochiel's brother and representative, was also denounced. The Colonel took to the duties of policeman with a will, and the following letter from him describes his arrest of the accused :—

From Lieut.-Col. Crawfurd to Churchill

Cumberland Papers.   Fort William : Oct. 12, 1751.

. . . . 'When I received the Packet from the Express, I without hesitation affected a surprise and concern at receiving the news of our Cloaths being stranded, and pretended to consult him about the nearest way through the Hills to Aberdeen, near which Place I saw the misfortune had happened ; this answerd extremely well in blinding our good Neighbours in the Town of Maryburgh,[1] who are for the greatest part ready enough to give Intelligence to the Country, of any Movements made by the Garrison. I then employed Captn. Jones to execute the warrant upon Fassifarn, and that he might be at no loss in not knowing the Man or the Country, I

[1] Now Fort William.

sent Mr. Gardiner along with him, whose zeal and readiness to assist you are no strangers to. They pretended to go in the German Boat on a fishing scheme, and turning up Lochiel, they soon got to his house, and secured him and every Thing of Paper Kind, bringing all to the Garrison.

'As soon as they were set out for Fassifarn I pretended to take a walk out of the Garrison, to see if I coud make a purchase of Hay for my Horses, and taking Mr. Douglas, the Sheriff substitute, out with me,[1] by way of shewing me the Road and Country, I allowed only two more officers to accompany me, that we might give no suspicion of our Intentions, which would have been soon discovered had I allowed more or sent a Party.

'However, notwithstanding these precautions, we were told at going to the House, that Glen Nevis was walk'd out with his Brother in Law, Dungallon, and still persisting that we shoud be glad to see Glen Nevis, to talk with him about his Hay, I prevailed on his wife to send a messenger for him into the Fields, which having done I took care, that no other Intelligence should go from the House, and then proceeded to search for his Papers : but I soon perceived that a Consciousness of Guilt, had made him secrete almost every Paper, and the hearing that Dungallon[2] had come to his House in the

---

[1] This Mr. Douglas gets a very bad character from John Macdonnell, of the Scotus family, in his Memoirs.

[2] Dungallon had only been released from Edinburgh Castle in October 1749.

Middle of the preceeding Night, confirmed me in my suspicions that we should see no more of Glen Eves or Dungallon. I then ordered the Parties who were in readiness to go round the Hill, and come down upon the Head of the Glen, making a strict search, but it was to no purpose. You'll please to observe that Dungallon, by way of blinding Douglas, had wrote him on the Wednesday, that it woud be some Days before he coud be in this part of the Country, and yet that very night, near the middle of it, did he come to Glen Eves' house, and for what Intention may be easily guessed.

'It is however some satisfaction that notwithstanding the pains they have been at, to conceal their treasonable practices, yet by their remissness I have found some Old Letters among Cloaths, which will greatly help to put their transactions in a proper light, and part of wch I have now enclosed for your perusal. [The letters enclosed are not in the Cumberland Papers.] The Letter I have marked No. 1. is a Letter from Glen Evis to his brother Angus Cameron, in the beginning of which you'll see that Fassifarn and he are not in concert, and that Fassifarn complains of them both, as I imagine for having got too great a share of the money, and Glen Eves' hint to Angus is, not to look upon Fassifarn as his friend.

'In No. 2. You see Angus in his proper Colours appointing the Congress with Cluny (in December 1749); and it would not be amiss that the Name of the Place, Catlaick, should be well observed on that worthy Gentleman's Account. You see that Loch Gary was in the Country, and on what accounts; likewise the errand of young Glengary. Whether the " Crookshanks " there aludes to Cluny as a Cant word for his having a wry Neck, or to a Brother of Glen Evis [Samuel, the spy] who is an officer in the French Service, and has crooked legs, I am not certain, but I believe it is to the Latter.

'You will likewise observe by this letter that a correction is to be made in the key of your Intercepted Letter, that Angus is Brother to Glen Eves and not to Fassifarn. I daresay you are no stranger to the part that Angus has Acted from the beginning in relation to the great Money Affair, and that no one excepting Cluny knows more of it. I am fully persuaded that Mrs. Chalmers (Mrs. Archibald Cameron) is charged with orders upon his Bank stock, however unwilling he may be to part with it——'

On October 14, Glenevis tired of hiding, and surrendered himself to Crawfurd. No harm was found in Fassifern's papers, which had been seized, and he, with Angus MacIan, a brother (or half-brother) of Lochgarry, was admitted to bail.

On October 22, Colonel Crawfurd wrote an account of Glenevis's examination to Churchill, who forwarded it to the Duke of Newcastle. Now we must ask how Government, which in 1749–50 knew only the anonymous account of the treasure already quoted, was, in 1751, informed that Lochgarry, Young Glengarry, Cameron of Glenevis, and his brother Angus, had meddled with the spoil in December 1749? Readers of 'Pickle the Spy' will remember that Pickle (that is, *ex hypothesi*, Young Glengarry) dates his services as a paid informer from 1750–51. Young Glengarry, then, may have been himself the source of the intelligence about the plunder, and that, as we shall see, was the strong opinion of Glenevis.

In any case this is the earliest hint of suspicion against the honour of Young Glengarry which we have encountered. The eternal feud of Macdonnells and Camerons may have suggested the notion of Glengarry's treachery to the mind of Glenevis; Cluny being out of the question, and he not knowing any one out of prison, except Young Glengarry, who had the necessary information. Glenevis's brother, Angus, and Angus MacIan were in prison with himself, and Lochgarry was with his regiment in France.

Crawfurd says of Glenevis, and his suspicions:

'He seems to think that all the Intelligence procured against him has been by means of Young Glengary : this you may believe I am at no great pains to desuade him from, as the greater Enmity gives the better chance of your coming at truth. He does not deny but that his brother, (Angus) Lochgary, Young Glengary, Angus McIan and he went into Badenoch in the winter 1749, after the Troops were gone from thence, with a view of meeting Clunie, but that while Lochgary, and young Glen-

gary had their Interview at a sheiling opposite to
Dalwhinnie, he was desired by Clunie to keep at the
House of Dalwhinnie till sent for; and that neither
Angus nor he coud be allowd to speak with him,
tho he sent repeated messages by Clunie's Piper,
and a young Brother of Clunie's. That he lay in the
same Room with Young Glengary at Dalwhinnie, and
early in the morning, the young Brother of Clunie
brought Glengary a Bag which might contain two or
three Hundred guineas, and counted them out to
him, and that he understood Glengary got, in the
whole, by that expedition about Two Thousand;[1] he
farther says that the money remitted abroad by Cluny
was carried away by his Brother in Law Mc.Pherson
of Brechachie to Major Kennedy in the North of
England . . .' (So Gask also says.)

On October 31, Crawfurd again writes to Churchill.
He had recommended on October 21, that Angus
Cameron 'should be allowed the quiet enjoyment of
his treasure.' He now remarks that Glenevis has
been admitted to bail. 'He says, in the Scotch
phrase, that *it is hard to have both the skaith and the
scorn*'—that is, to be molested, though he has not got
much of the French gold. 'He blames his brother
Angus for having acted a weak and foolish part in

[1] This includes the money got by Glengarry in Edinburgh, out of
Murray's original 5,000 *louis*, entrusted to his brother-in-law, Mr.
Macdougal. Compare Murray's *Memorials*, p. 304, where he denies
that Mrs. Murray brought any large sum from the Highlands. The
reverse is stated by Ramsay of Ochtertyre, and it is plain that, by
Mrs. Murray's means, or otherwise, a large sum was conveyed by
Murray to Edinburgh.

quitting (parting) with so great a share of the money
that had fallen into his hands, which, he says, did not
exceed £2,500, tho' most people call it £3,000, and
of which he knew his brother had paid £1,000 for the
use of Lochiel soon after his going to France' (1746).
Next we find a repetition of Glenevis's charges
against Young Glengarry, as his betrayer. The
accusation, too, that Young Glengarry forged King
James's name (alluded to by James in a letter to the
Prince, March 17, 1750, as a story reported by Archy
Cameron) is urged by Glenevis.

'He (Glenevis) still continues full of resentment
against Young Glengary, believing that he is the
Author of all the information against him and his
Brother Angus, not being able to account for our
knowledge of the Badenoch meeting in any other
way. He confirms what I wrote of the young Gentleman in my last, only that the £2,000 was not of Clunie's
money, but of what was left by the Secretary Murray
in the hands of Mr. Mc.Douel his brother in Law, and
that his credentials for receiving the money was from
the old Pretender, *but that he was sure they were
forged.*' They certainly *were* forged.

One thing is to be observed about Glenevis's
doubts of Young Glengarry. In this year, 1751, and
onwards, that hero was allowed by Government to
live in London, in Beaufort Buildings, Strand, whence
he communicated with Charles and James, as a
strenuous Jacobite agent. His letters are printed by
Browne from the Stuart MSS. Yet Government, if

only from Glenevis's evidence just given, knew that Glengarry was at least as guilty as Glenevis and his brother of the only crime charged against them on this occasion—namely, dealing with French gold that had been landed for the use of Prince Charles. Where the treason to King George came in, unless they were using the money for Jacobite purposes, or depriving his Majesty of spoils of war, or of treasure trove, does not appear. Yet the Camerons, Glenevis, Dunan, Fassifern, were all kept in durance at Fort William, while Young Glengarry, implicated in their vague offence, was permitted to live, and even to make love, in London. To this point we return later (p. 207). Government had their own reasons for sparing Glengarry, while punishing his accomplices. These accomplices, again, averred that Glengarry had 'peached' upon them, as doubtless he had. The Camerons were released, but before very long, they and Fassifern were all imprisoned again in Edinburgh Castle, on a charge of treasonable dealings with the attainted. This was part of a plan of Government's for 'uprooting' Fassifern, who represented the exiled Young Lochiel in the eyes of the Clan. The action of Government makes another chapter in the history of the sufferings after Culloden. Meanwhile the casks of louis d'or had done their task, and sown among the Clans the dragon's teeth of distrust and of calumny. We cannot tell where the remainder of the gold went, though Cluny probably took what was left over to France, in 1754, as Charles commanded him to do, getting no more for his trouble, perhaps, than did poor Duncan Cameron in Strontian—'not a shilling.' As for Glenevis and his brother, they seem to have finally been fobbed off with the skaith and the scorn, and with very little else but the company of Colonel Crawfurd, so anxious to talk about their hay crop.

Such is an example of Highland life after Culloden. There are midnight meetings at lonely sheilings, there is digging and delving by hands that knew the claymore better than the spade. Letters are opened in the post office, secret murmurs fly about carrying charges of indefinite guilt, reported by unknown spies. No man can put confidence in another : each neighbour *may* have been bullied or bribed into babbling, and, when the laird sees the English colonel saunter along the avenue, Highland hospitality struggles in his heart with a natural inclination to drop out of a back window, and steal up the glen into the hills. A gentleman is apt to be less often on his estates than in Fort William prison or in Edinburgh Castle. No wonder that many joined the new Highland regiments when they were raised, and preferred King George's pay to domiciliary visits from King George's colonels!

VIII

JUSTICE AFTER CULLODEN

The Uprooting of Fassifern

THE years 1752–1754 were full of trouble for Highlanders. The Prince was intriguing desperately with
Scotland, and with Prussia. The Elibank Plot was
matured and betrayed. Dr. Cameron and Lochgarry
were stirring up the Clans. Cluny remained as un-
takable as Abd-el-Kader. The Government were
alarmed at once by Pickle, by their ambassadors
abroad, and by Count Kaunitz. The Forfeited
Estates had been nationalised, 'for the improvement
of the Highlands,' factors had been appointed to
raise and collect rents: evictions were threatened;
agrarian discontent had been aroused; Campbell
of Glenure had been shot in the wood of Letter-
more.[1] The reports of all these things flew from
township to township, from strath to strath, as
fleetly as the fiery cross. The Highlands, in 1752,
were boiling like a caldron. Old tenants were
being turned out that men of a hostile Whiggish
clan might occupy their hereditary holdings.

---

[1] See Mr. Stevenson's *Kidnapped* and *Catriona* and the printed
Trial for the Appin Murder.

Ensign Small, an officer who knew Gaelic, and was
engaged in secret service, found murmurs of a rising
even in the Islands. The Duke of Newcastle was
jotting down alarmed notes, 'to be at any expense
in order to find out where the Young Pretender is.
Lord Anson to have Fregates upon the Scotch and
Irish coast.' [1]

The consequence of this official flutter was a
crowd of arrests and trials. James Stewart, on a
charge of being accessory to Glenure's slaying, was,
to speak plain words, judicially murdered. He was
confined in Fort William, and denied access to his
advisers; the charges and evidence against him were
kept from him till too late, he had a jury of hostile
Campbells at Inveraray, the Duke on the bench, and
he was hanged as accessory to a murder in which
the alleged principal was not before the Court.
Political necessities and clan hatred killed James
Stewart (1752).

In 1753 Dr. Cameron was caught, and hanged in
London, denouncing as informer his kinsman, Samuel
Cameron. The famed Sergeant Mohr Cameron was
taken (by treachery, General Stuart hints and
tradition proclaims; both are right), and he 'died
for the law.' His alleged crime was cattle theft,
but, as a sergeant in French service, he was probably regarded as a Jacobite agent. The Sergeant
was captured in mid-April, 1753 : a few days later
Angus Cameron, brother of Glenevis, was taken at

---

[1] Add. MSS. 32,995, 6, 33.

the same place, his house of Dunan or Downan, in
Rannoch. On May 6 Fassifern, Charles Stewart,
writer in Banavie, Fassifern's agent, and Glenevis,
were lodged, with Angus Cameron, in Edinburgh
Castle. On July 7 Young Barisdale, Young Morar,
and others, were culled like flowers at Lochourn,
while Young John Macdonnell, 'Spanish John,' was
also arrested.

Of all these, the most important prisoner was
Fassifern. He had been taken, as we saw, in
October 1751, and released, as nothing could be
found against him in the affair of the Cluny Treasure.
He was Lochiel's brother and representative, and consequently chief, for the time, of the Camerons. He
had not been out in Forty-five. A man of commerce, a
burgess of Glasgow, he had tried to dissuade Lochiel
from exposing himself to the dangerous charm of
the Prince. But he was naturally anxious to save as
much as possible of Lochiel's estate for the family.
There were several lawful claims on it, which
Government was bound to respect and he to press.
Moreover he, with 'Glenevegh' (Glenevis), had been
denounced by Pickle as agents between the Southern
and Northern Jacobites.[1] In addition to all this,
Fassifern was trying to keep the old Cameron
tenants, Jacobites, in their holdings, and evict tenants
who had the bad taste to be Whigs.

As early as May 1751 he had been denounced
for these offences by Captains Johnston and Mylne,

---

[1] December 1752. *Pickle*, p. 176.

of the Bulls, in garrison at Inversnaid. 'He falls on
ways,' writes an informer whose letter they forward,
'of turning out any from their possessions, who he
knows to be well affected to His Majesty.' He
encourages Jacobites to settle near the forts, for the
purpose of a sudden assault.[1] He has 'plenty of
the Pretender's money' to use for these purposes.
Clan sentiment, not Jacobitism, may have influenced
Fassifern, and Glenevis, at least, was hardly the man
to play the part of Jacobite agent.

The original charge against Fassifern in May
1753 was that of 'correspondence with persons
attainted.' But the game of the Government was to
get rid of him on any pretext. Colonel Crawfurd
had come from Fort William to Edinburgh, and, on
June 4, 1753, wrote a long letter to the Lord Justice
Clerk. 'The uprooting of Fassifern,' he says, with
candour, ' is what we ought chiefly to have in view.'[2]
He has found witnesses, or rather has heard of them
(it seems kinder to omit the names of these gentlemen), who avow that Fassifern tampered with them
to threaten the late Glenure's wife, and to murder
Glenure. That unlucky man was factor for
Lochiel's as well as for Ardsheil's forfeited estate.
and was expected to evict Cameron tenants. 'The
Lord Advocate said that, if this did not hang Fassie-
fairn, it would at least send him to Nova Scotia.'
Perhaps, the Colonel thinks, Breakachie may be

---

[1] State Papers, MS., April 15, 1751.
[2] Cumberland Papers.

induced to inform against Fassifern! That culprit has only sent 100*l.* to Lochiel's family in France, and has made Lochiel's tenants work on his estate, instead of on the county roads.

These last were not hanging matters. And, somehow, Breakachie, a perfectly loyal gentleman, and kinsman of Cluny's, did not give the desired information. The witnesses as to the suborning of Glenure's murder by Fassifern would not kiss the book, or, perhaps, had never promised their evidence at all. Angus Cameron and Glenevis were discharged on bail, on July 3. No proof of treasonable correspondence, or suborned murder, or anything else existed, or could be found against Fassifern. Pickle, of course, could not be produced in Court. The Colonel does not conceal the discomfort of his reflections, and Government is perplexed as to the details of the process of ' uprooting ' the representative of Lochiel. On June 10 Fassifern and Charles Stewart petitioned that they might be put on their trial. But what were they to be tried for? It was an awkward situation.

The resources of civilisation, however, were not exhausted. On August 6 the Duke of Argyll came to Edinburgh and, next day, took his seat in the Court of Session.

That day the Lord Advocate sprang a fresh charge on the accused. They might not have been holding treasonable correspondence, or even suborning murder, but they had been mixed up in—forgery!

The Lord Advocate suspected that certain deeds had been forged, to substantiate claims made by Fassifern on Lochiel's estate. These claims rested on old papers and bonds of various dates, from 1713 to 1748. There was 'credible information' (how obtained we shall learn) that five of these deeds were forged. Fassifern's lawyer, Mr. Macfarlane (husband of pretty Mrs. Macfarlane who shot the Captain), had no longer the vouchers, the original papers from which he drew up the claims. These vouchers had been in a bag at Mr. Macfarlane's house; but 'some time in Summer' (1752) Fassifern (being in Edinburgh) had sent for the bag, and had returned it in a few hours.

The papers were no longer in it. Fassifern, being examined, could remember having abstracted no such deeds as interested the Court. Next day Fassifern asked for a copy of his statement, 'as he was apprehensive he might have inadvertently fallen into some mistakes in the hurry of the examination, which he was extremely desirous to rectify.' The Lords refused his petition : he might have a copy of his examination 'when he is brought upon trial.' Next day he was charged with being guilty, or 'art and part in forging the deeds, or of using them, knowing them to be forged.' He was to be detained in prison till his trial.

He protested that he had already lain in prison for three months, on a charge (Pickle's) of 'being privy to unlawful designs carried on by disaffected

persons'—namely, a rising to follow on the kidnapping
of the Royal Family. He 'has reason to believe that
no such prosecution is seriously intended,' which
is pretty obvious, Pickle not being producible. but
absent, at that very hour, in France, with Prince
Charles! Moreover Fassifern was not told on
whose information he was examined, though he was
'heckled' for several hours.

The charge of forgery was, in fact, based, as usual,
on the evidence of an Informer, whom we need not
name. Here is a report of his accusations:—

'. . . Says he has been certainly informed that
Fassfarn caused Forge several Grounds of Debt, in
Order to be the Foundation of Claims upon the
Estate of Lochiel, some of which were written by
Charles Stewart present prisoner in the Castle, and
Lochiel's name was Forged by one Allan Cameron of
Landavrae. who could write like him, and there were
Forged Discharges by Lochiel to his Tenants for
Crops in 1746 and Proceedings in Order to prevent
the Government from getting payment of the Rent
of 1746 and arrears.'

Says on knowing this he 'instantly told Crawfurd'!

Now even the Government's plea against Fassifern says no word of 'forged discharges of Lochiel to
his tenants!'[1]

The interest of this case is partly the mystery—
had Fassifern really been concerned in tampering

---

[1] *Scots Magazine*, July 1753, p. 362.

with documents?—partly the procedure, which we
know had political motives, and was iniquitous in
method. As to Fassifern's guilt, if any, we are not
likely to learn the truth; as to the kind of justice he
got—there can only be one opinion.

On August 10 Fassifern was 'ordained' to receive a full copy of his examination. He was anxious
that the evidence of an aged solicitor, Alexander
Stewart, in Appin, a man over eighty, and unable to
travel, should be taken by commission. This Stewart
had written, or witnessed, several of the old disputed
deeds, and was the only person alive able to testify,
of his own knowledge, to their authenticity. Fassifern also remonstrated against being described, in
the Lord Advocate's charge, as 'the immediate
younger brother of Donald Cameron, late of Lochiel,
attainted.' He 'ventures to hope that this is not
meant to make a point of dittay.' It was obviously
meant to suggest prejudice. He asked for bail, after
his already long imprisonment. Bail was refused by
the Lords of Session, nor would they examine Alexander Stewart by commission; but they promised to
remove Fassifern from the Castle to the Tolbooth.
The full charges, or 'improbatory articles' against
him, he was not to receive.

On August 24 the prisoner once more protested
against 'the practice of dropping out charges one
after the other,' which unpleasantly resembles the
system of Titus Oates. If the Government, as appears
certain, had this accusation of forgery pigeon-holed

before they locked up the prisoner in May, why did they not bring it forward at first? Fassifern's imprisonment, he justly remarks, 'approaches to a kind of torture.' He is denied the free use of pen and ink, so necessary in his preparation of a defence. An armed sentinel is in his room day and night. This petition was so far successful that pen and ink were given, but what he wrote was inspected, and even his lawyer's chief clerk, Mr. Flockhart, could only visit him by special license. He was allowed to take the air, under a guard, but he seems to have been detained in the Castle, at least the Deputy-Governor is charged to remove the armed sentinel.

In January 1754 articles of accusation were placed before the Lords of Session, and witnesses were examined, including old Alexander Stewart, who was brought from Appin 'in a chaise.' He attested that, as early as 1713, he had written and witnessed some of the deeds, and again in 1728. Appin (whom one of the deeds especially concerned) gave evidence as to the authenticity of others, and quoted Lochiel's remarks to him, in 1746, about 1,000l. borrowed from Fassifern in 1741, and a bond given for the money by himself. He averred that Charles Stewart, writer in Banavie, accused now of forging that instrument, had really written and witnessed it, with Torcastle (in exile) and others (Culchenna and Lundavra), now dead. On these grounds Fassifern petitioned for bail. He had lain in prison for ten months, and his eyes were so impaired that he

could not see to read. He must sink *sub squalore
carceris*, and be 'uprooted' in earnest.

To all this plea it was replied 'that many persons,
even of those who would not do injustice in private
affairs. are too easily induced to countenance an injustice done to the public'—that is. by getting public
money out of the forfeited estates. Fassifern, with his
'connections and influence, might, if at liberty, use
means to prevent discoveries.' There is thus one law
(an unpleasant law) for the rich, and another for the
poor. Finally Fassifern's 'coolness and silence on the
loss of papers of such consequence, notwithstanding
his being confessedly a sensible careful man, were
mentioned as very suspicious circumstances.'

No doubt they *are* suspicious, but that a 'sensible
careful man,' of the best family, should, as charged.
forge a bond of 90*l*. from his own gardener, still in
his service, is also a very improbable kind of accusation. Fassifern and Charles Stewart were, therefore,
left *sub squalore carceris* (March 6, 1754).

In August 1754 they again petitioned for bail.
They had lain in gaol for fifteen months on no capital
charge. 'There is not one of the deeds under challenge that does not seem to be supported by unim-
peachable evidence,' as of Appin, a man of honour,
and old Alexander Stewart. 'They have suffered
punishment beyond bounds already, without example,
and since The Happy Revolution, neither heard of
nor dreamed of in our neighbouring country.' England.

Bail was not granted, and the Lord Advocate told a very extraordinary and, it may be said, inconsistent tale.   His witnesses, he alleged, 'have thought fit to stand a second diligence for compelling them to appear, and, though wrote to, have not given any answer.' Of course there may be two interpretations of this reluctance, or even three.   The witnesses may be coerced by local sentiment, or may not care to take oath to their evidence, or may have reason to suppose that they are not really wanted, as the Crown manifestly merely wishes to keep Fassifern out of his own country.   The evidence of one informer has been given as to forged discharges of Lochiel's.   The Government, however, dropped that slander, while keeping up other charges, not supported by evidence given in Court.

The Advocate then carries back the origin of the trouble to the Loch Arkaig treasure.   In some quarrel about this, a person was 'heard to declare, that, in self defence, he would make known to persons in the King's service what he knew, or had learned, concerning forged deeds prepared by Fassfern and Charles Stewart.'   This information he actually gave to Colonel Crawfurd.   This was certainly one of the witnesses who would not answer to his subpœna, or come to the trial in spite of repeated 'diligences.' Lochaber was not likely to be a happy home for him afterwards ; *Lochaber no more!* would probably be the burden of his song.   Even Glenevis had three shots fired at him, in November 1752, between Fort

William and his own house. So he alleges in a
memorial, or petition, in the State Papers. The
Colonel then sent for Charles Stewart, who had been
introduced to him as a fit person for managing
prosecutions against wearers of the philabeg. Charles
Stewart, before the arrest of Fassifern, gave Colonel
Crawfurd, at Fort William, a written set of Remarks
on Fassifern's claims, impeaching the authenticity of
those to which Appin and Charles Stewart had sworn,
including the gardener's 90l. But Charles Stewart,
when examined before the Lords, withdrew all this,
and vowed that he had already denied it to the
Colonel. When shown the written statement, he
acknowledged that it was in his hand, but that he
had written it 'to pacify the Colonel, who was then in
a great rage.' For, in early summer, 1752, 'a very
hot inquiry was going on touching the murder of
Glenure.' Relations of Charles Stewart were imprisoned, and Colonel Crawfurd, interrogating Charles
on the claims of Fassifern, told him that *he*, Charles,
'was suspected of some accession to Glenure's murder,
and was to be imprisoned if he did not speak out, and
make discoveries against the claims upon Lochiel's
forfeiture.' Charles 'cannot affirm' that he did *not*
'soothe Col. Crawfurd, who appeared to be in great
passion,' by telling tales against the claims, but rather
suspects that he did. But, if he did, he admits
that he lied, 'in the confusion and terror he was
then in.' So far, the evidence before the Court is
that of a witness who declines to be sworn, and of

a prisoner who withdraws testimony extorted by threats.

The Lord Advocate next quoted a letter to Fassifern, from his Edinburgh agent, Mr. Macfarlane, of December 1751—that is, shortly after Fassifern's release in the affair of the treasure. Mr. Macfarlane obscurely warns him in this letter ' not to be carried, for the sake of a small paultry sum of money into difficulties.' ' Mines were to be sprung,' ' odd appellations are given,' phrases which may, or may not, refer to the business of the French gold.

The Advocate then told how Fassifern, in summer, 1752, a year before his arrest in 1753, got his bag of papers from Mr. Macfarlane and returned it, since when no mortal has seen the incriminated deeds. This, of course, is the crucial point ; but Mr. Macfarlane had himself prepared Fassifern's claim from the very deeds which, having disappeared, are now said to have been recently forged. Mr. Macfarlane can have seen nothing suspicious in them, or he would not have made them the basis of a claim drawn up by himself. His suspicions of 1751 would have revived, and he would have abandoned the case. He still acts daily for Fassifern, but Fassifern has not recovered the documents, nor tried seriously to recover them.

On these grounds bail was again refused.

No decision was arrived at by the Lords of Session till January 1755. By that time all danger from Jacobitism was over. Charles was deserted by

Prussia, by the Earl Marischal, and by his English adherents. The Lords found Fassifern guilty of abstracting his own papers, from the bag in Mr. Macfarlane's custody. These papers it was inferred, were forged. He was sentenced to ten years of banishment, which he passed at Alnwick. Charles Stewart was deprived of his office of notary public. · Some of the Lords were of opinion that there was not a proof of guilt sufficient to infer any punishment. But others were of a different opinion.' In Fassifern's plea he complained of Colonel Crawfurd's frequent examinations of Charles Stewart. and of a present of 10*l.* made by him to that notary.

Innocent or guilty, Fassifern was · uprooted, which is what we ought chiefly to have in view,' to quote Colonel Crawfurd. The gross oppressiveness of the proceedings. the unexplained delays. the series of charges ' dropped out,' the bullying and cajoling of prisoners under examination. the unconcealed political motive. and the rewards of farms which. we learn. were given to the informers, are all characteristic of justice in Scotland after Culloden. The improbability of the charge, against ' a sensible careful man,' must be set against the mystery of the disappearance of the papers. In that disappearance the ' uprooters ' had, of course, no less interest than the accused. After nearly two years *sub squalore carceris,* Fassifern was condemned for suborning the forgery of papers not in evidence. In fact, after all the schemes for his uprooting, he was (in cricketing

phrase) · given out '—several of the Fifteen dissenting
—'for obstructing the field.' What is the legal name
for this offence?

This affair had lingered on from May 1753 to
January 1755 before the Fifteen, the Lords of
Session. It is probable that a jury, disgusted by the
military methods of extorting evidence, would have
made short work of the case, and acquitted Fassifern.
Of this temper in a jury we have a curious contemporary instance. Sir Walter Scott printed for the
Bannatyne Club the trial, in June 1754, of Duncan
Terig, or Clerk, and Alexander Bain Macdonald, for
the murder of Sergeant Davies, of Guise's regiment,
in 1749, on Christie Hill, in Braemar. There was
really no doubt of the guilt of the accused. Scott,
who knew one of their counsel, says that they themselves were convinced of the fact. But two Highland
witnesses told a story of the murdered sergeant's ghost,
which appeared to them in 1750. By making fun of
this apparition, the advocates for the defence, Scott
says, secured an acquittal in face of the evidence.

Probably the jury had another motive—namely,
indignation at military extortion of evidence. A
certain Ensign Small has been mentioned. He seems
to have been an astute and energetic man. We find
him everywhere in the Cumberland Papers. He it
was who, soon after Culloden, arrested the Barisdales
in a cave, and took their swords. In 1749 he arrested
Barisdale on his return from France. He pursued
Lochgarry (after Dr. Cameron's arrest) into England,

and searched the vessels leaving the ports of the East
Coast. We find him in the Islands, mixing with the
people in disguise, and reporting their murmurs and
their curses on the Chiefs and the Prince. In Knoydart he notes that the commons have lost their taste
for a rising. Small was rewarded by a factorship
on the forfeited estates of Cluny and Robertson of
Strowan, and exerted himself to procure the condemnation of the murderers of Sergeant Davies.

Now on June 14, 1754, Mr. Alexander Lockhart,
one of the counsel for the accused, laid a complaint
against Small before the Court of Session. By Small's
instigation, Lockhart said. Terig and Macdonald were
charged with the crime. Small had sought out and
privately examined witnesses, 'giving them an obligation to stand between them and any hazard they
might incur thereby'—such protection was very
necessary. 'He endeavoured to intimidate such as
would not say such strong things as he wished, or
expected.' Lockhart asks 'how far these practices'
(the very practices employed to 'uproot' Fassifern)
'should be tolerated?' Moreover, Small had been
swaggering with a sword, had stopped Lockhart in
the Parliament Close, had insulted, challenged him,
and shaken a stick over his head: 'which, if he
meant to resent, he would be at no loss to find out
where the said James Small lived.'

Small replied that, after doing his best to bring
Clerk and Macdonald to trial, his character had been
blackened by Lockhart before the jury, as having

pursued the accused for private reasons of malice. As an officer and a gentleman, believing in his heart that the accused were guilty (which they undoubtedly were), he had resented the license of Lockhart.

Small was found guilty of contempt, bound over to keep the peace, and obliged to apologise.

Meanwhile General Bland, Governor of Edinburgh Castle, justified Ensign Small in a letter to the English Ministry. Lockhart, the General denounces as a 'famous foul-mouthed Jacobite advocate.' He had 'concerted' his abuse of the Ensign in court 'with his Jacobite fraternity.' The Ensign had very properly 'taken him by the nose, and called him a scoundrell. He took it quietly.' If Lockhart is not warned, his bones will be broken. The General has used his influence with the judges to secure easy terms for the loyal Ensign.[1]

The docile judges, 'the Fifteen,' had accepted evidence extorted by military violence in what was really a political case, that of Fassifern. But it is clear that the jury, in the case of the Sergeant's murder, had resented such intimidation, as denounced by Lockhart, and this resentment, rather than the ghost story, probably procured the acquittal of two undeniable robbers and murderers, Terig, or Clerk, and Macdonald.[2]

Another curious instance of the methods of

[1] June 18, 1754, State Papers.
[2] *Scots Magazine*, June 1754. The details of Fassifern's imprisonment and condemnation are taken from the *Scots Magazine* of 1753-1754.

Government occurs in the case of James Mohr. It was generally suspected that Government connived at his escape from Edinburgh Castle in the disguise of a cobbler (November 16, 1752). The Government, however, broke the lieutenants of the guard, deprived the sergeant of his stripes, and whipped the porter.

But we find a remarkable letter of General Churchill's,[1] saying that 'James Mohr had been taken up on the abduction charge,' and was extremely anxious to make disclosures. That his recent behaviour cannot allow him to be believed unless he is allowed to suppose 'his life is at stake.' That 'should your Grace think proper to employ him, the great difficulty is to bring about his liberation without raising a suspicion of the Cause, *nor can it be so effectually done as by giveing private orders to a Party of the Troops employed in escorting him to favour his escape.'*

If this suggestion was acted on later, if James was allowed to escape from Edinburgh Castle that he might become a spy, as he did, the lieutenants, the sergeant, and the porter were very scurvily treated. The game of justice was not played with much scrupulousness by the English Government.

---

[1] No. 48 S. P. S. From Churchill to Newcastle, Nov. 19, 1751. The story of the ghostly evidence in Sergeant Davies's case will be found in the author's *Book of Dreams and Ghosts.*

IX

A GENTLEMAN OF KNOYDART

THE modern autobiographical romance of adventure has perhaps been overdone. The hero is always very young and very brave; he is mixed up with great affairs; he is a true lover; he marries the heroine, and he leaves his Memoirs (at six shillings) to posterity. Stereotyped as is the method, and mechanical as are most of the novels thus constructed, it is interesting to compare with them a set of genuine Memoirs, which actually are what the novels pretend to be.

Colonel John Macdonell, the author of the Memoirs, was of the Scottos family, a branch of the House of Glengarry. Indeed, in the male line the chiefs of Clan Donald are now represented by the head of the Scottos branch, not to enter on the old controversy as to the chiefship of Clan Ranald. Our Colonel was born in 1728, and was therefore a boy of eighteen in 1746. He had already been conversant with great adventures; he had seen Rome and his King, had been thrice wounded in one engagement of the Italian wars, and had relinquished his excellent prospects in the Spanish service to fight

for the White Rose. An emissary between the Duke
of York (not yet Cardinal) and the Prince, the bearer
of a treasure in gold, our hero arrived in the Highlands just after Culloden. Robbed by the wicked
Mackenzies, associated with the last rally of the loyal
clans, betrayed by a cousin to a Hanoverian dungeon,
young Macdonell must needs fall in love, at this
juncture, with his future wife. He insults his
enemies, cows the traitor who denounced him (or
another traitor), marries his lady, retires to Canada,
and, dying in 1810, leaves his Memoirs to his
children.

What more can be asked from a hero? 'Oh,
Colonel Macdonell and Mr. Robert Louis Stevenson,
which of you imitated the other?' the critic is
tempted to exclaim. But, if the real Colonel John
'does it more natural,' the fictitious David Balfour
'does it with the better grace.' The good Colonel
never, of course, discourses to us about his contend-
ing emotions, or dilates, like Mr. Balfour, on the
various trains of casuistry which meet in his simple
soul. He never describes a place, nor a person, not
even when he meets his King, the Duke of York,
or the Duc de Fitzjames ; he only describes action,
vividly enough. He leaves out the love-interest,
with the merest allusion ; and thus, though the
Colonel played a heroic part in romantic occurrences,
he did not write a romance. He arranges his recol-
lections ill, ignoring essential facts, and, later,
dragging them in very awkwardly. His Memoirs

N

are such as an elderly warrior of his period would
naturally pen; they illustrate the chaotic condition
of Highland morals and manners in 1745-54, and
introduce us to figures familiar in the Prince's campaign of Scotland.[1]

Scotus, Scottos, or Scothouse, the estate of the
Colonel's family, lies in the south of Knoydart, and
on the north side of the entrance to Loch Nevis, just
opposite to the Aird of Sleat in Skye.   On the north
of Knoydart, and on the south shore of Loch Hourn,
is Barisdale, the seat of the Colonel's cousin, Col of
Barisdale, the tallest man and the greatest robber,
ruffian, and traitor of Clan Donald.   Universal testimony, from that of the Chevalier Johnstone to the
Whig Manuscript of 1750, applauds the family of
Scottos as brave gentlemen, honest in the midst of ' a
den of thieves' (says our Whig author), loyal when
loyalty had most to tempt or discourage it.   Our
Colonel's father was a younger son of old Scottos.
He resided at Crowlin; concerning his means of life
we learn nothing, but the Colonel was always well
supplied with money in his boyhood.   The clan were
Catholics, and John's father, in 1740, sent the boy,
then aged twelve, to be educated at the Scots College
in Rome.   He was accompanied by a lad of fourteen,
Angus Macdonald, of the Clan Ranald family.   From
Edinburgh they sailed to Boulogne, and in Paris were

---

[1] Written before 1810, the Memoirs are published in the *Canadian
Magazine* of 1828.   Mr. McLennan has founded on these papers his
excellent romance, *Spanish John*.

entertained by Mr. George Innes, head of the Scots
College and brother of Thomas Innes, the first really
critical writer on early Scottish history. From Paris
the pair of boys went, partly by water, partly in a
calèche, to Avignon and Marseilles, whence they
embarked for Toulon. Here they met with the following adventure, which may be given as an example
of the Colonel's style in narrative, though it had no
sequel. Most of his adventures led to nothing, unlike
the course of fiction :—

'One night, as we walked through the streets and
were cracking nuts, my comrade, who was somewhat
roguish, observed a Monsieur with a large powdered
wig, and his hat under his arm, going past us ; he
took a handful of nuts from his pocket and threw
them with all his force at the Frenchman's head,
which unfortunately disordered his wig. Monsieur
turned upon and collared him ; by good luck a
Spaniard was of our party, who instantly ran to the
relief of my comrade and gave the Frenchman a
severe drubbing. We then adjourned to a tavern,
when our Spaniard, calling for a bottle of wine,
brought me to a private room, and after bolting the
door, to my great terror and surprise. drew a stiletto
with his right hand from his left bosom, and made
me to understand by signs that with that weapon he
would have killed the Frenchman, if he had proved
too strong for him. He then took a net purse out of
his pocket wherein there appeared to be about a
hundred Spanish pistoles, and made me an offer of a

part: I made him a low bow, but, not standing in
need of it, would not accept of his liberality, for I
thought I had enough, being always purse-bearer for
myself and companion. My friend made sometimes
free with my pockets, merely to try if I should miss
anything, and was happy to find that I made a discovery of his tricks by immediately missing what he
took in that way. . . . I bought out of our stock
two large folding French knives, by way of carvers.
in case of any sinister accident.'

Such an accident of travel presently occurred.
A Mr. O'Rourk of Tipperary, on his way to study at
Rome, introduced the boys to a certain Mr. Creach,
late of the Irish brigade in Spanish service. Mr.
Creach, finding Master Macdonell alone in his room,
tried to rob him. Macdonell flew at the man; Angus
Macdonald entered; the pair threw Creach on the
ground, and John had his 'carver' out, with a view
to cutting Creach's throat, when O'Rourk interfered
with this wild Celtic justice. Arrived in Rome, the
boys found that the fame of their exploit had pre-
ceded them and done them good service, as they
were reckoned lads of spirit.

John, though the youngest pupil in the lowest
class of the seminary, was advancing rapidly in his
studies when, in the winter of 1743, Prince Charles
rode out of Rome to a hunting-party, and, disguised
as a Spanish courier, continued his course as far as
Antibes. France had invited him, though, when he
arrived, she neglected him. John now conceived

that, in the event of the Prince's landing in England,
'My clan would not be the last to join the young
Charles. . . . This set my brains agoing, which were
not very settled of themselves. I got disgusted with
the life of a student, and thought I would be much
happier in the army.'

John, therefore, contrived to get 'introduced to
King James by noblemen attending on that Prince,
who inquired of me particularly about my grandfather and granduncles [Glengarry and Barisdale,
apparently], with all of whom he had been acquainted
personally in the year 1715,' when Glengarry distinguished himself so brilliantly, avenging the fallen
Clan Ranald, at Sheriffmuir. A recommendation for
John was sent to General Macdonnell (of the Antrim
family), then commanding the Irish of the Spanish
forces in Italy, and, though the Cardinal Protector
demurred to John's change of service, our hero was
equipped with a sword by the Rector of his College.
'Presenting me with the sword, his eyes filled, and
he told me that I should lose that sword by the
enemy, which was verified in seven or eight months
after.' The Rector had the second sight!

Mr. Macdonell, a sage of sixteen, was now horri-
fied by the ethical ideas which he surprised in the
conversation of the young Italian gentlemen who
rode with him to join the Spanish army. They
assured him that his military value depended on his
emancipation from the prudish notions of 'a parcel
of bigots,' but he was destined to refute this theory.

General Macdonnell admitted his young clansman to
his own table, and put him in the way of seeing fire.
He thus describes his first view of that element;
probably his emotions are common to recruits :—

'I'll tell you the truth, I felt myself rather queer,
my heart panting very strong, not with bravery,
I assure you. I thought that every bullet would
finish [me], and thought seriously to run away, a
cursed thought! I dare never see my friends or
nearest relations after such dastardly conduct. My
thoughts were all at once cut short by the word of
command, "Advance quick!" We were at once
within about one hundred paces of the enemy, to
whom we gave so well directed a fire, that their
impetuosity was bridled. The firing on both sides
continued until dark came on, which put a stop to
the work of the evening. The enemy retreated some
distance back, and we rejoined our own army. I
went to Genl. McDonnell, who asked me if I had
smelled powder to-day ; I told him I had plentifully.
" What, Sir," said he, " are you wounded ? " " No,
please your Excellency." " Sir, you will never smell
powder until you are wounded." I got great credit
from the officers commanding the party I belonged
to for my undaunted behaviour during the action,
but they little knew what past within me before it
began.'

The smell of powder was soon in our hero's experience. The Neapolitan general who commanded on
alternate days with the French leader, withdrew his

troops from a strong position on the heights above
Velletri, which was attacked by Prince Lobkwitz
and the famous General Brown, with forty-five
thousand Austrians There was daily fighting, and
General Macdonnell was stopped by his superior
officer while in the very act of driving the Austrians
from the deserted heights, which they, of course, had
occupied. An Austrian surprise cut off Macdonell's
regiment from the main force, and he thus describes
what occurred :

'For my own share I was among the last that
gave way, but when I once turned my back, I
imagined that the enemy all aimed at me alone, and
therefore ran with all my might, and thought there·
was a weight tied to each of my legs, till I had out-
run everyone, and looking behind, saw the whole
coming up. I halted and faced about, every one as
he came up did the same, we soon formed a regular
line, and resolved to revenge our dead comrades and
to fight to the last; but found our situation to be as
bad as before. . . . Reduced to extremity we offered
to capitulate on honourable terms, but could obtain
no condition except surrendering at discretion, rather
than which we resolved to fight while powder and
ball remained among the living or the dead. Our
officers and men fell very fast. I among the rest
got a ball through my thigh which prevented my
standing; I crossed my firelock under my thigh and
shook it, to try if the bone was whole, which finding
to be the case, dropped on one knee and continued

firing. I received another shot, which threw me down ; I made once more an attempt to help my surviving comrades, but received a third wound, which quite disabled me. Loss of blood and no way of stopping it soon reduced my strength, I however, griped my sword to be ready to run through the first enemy that should insult me.

'All our ammunition being spent, not a single cartridge remained amongst the living or the dead, quarters were called for by the few that were yet alive. Many of the wounded were knocked on the head, and I did not escape with impunity. One approached me ; at first I made ready to run him through, but observing five more close to him, I dropt the sword, and was saluted with *Hunts-foot*,[1] accompanied with a cracking of muskets about my head. I was only sensible of three blows and fainted ; I suppose they thought me dead. On coming to myself again, I found my clothes were stripped off, weltering in my blood, and no one alive near me to speak to, twisting and rolling in the dust with pain, and my skin scorched by the sun. In this condition a Croat came up to me with a cocked pistol in his hand, and asked for my purse in bad Italian. I told him that I had no place to hide it in, and if he found it anywhere about me to take it. " Is that an answer for me, you son of a b—ch ? " at same time pointing his pistol straight between my

---

[1] *Hunts-foot* (*sic*), *i.c.* leg of a dog, a term of reproach with the Germans.

The Duke of York and Prince Charles
circa 1733.

eyes. I saw no one near, but the word *quarter* was
scarcely expressed by me, when I saw his pistol-arm
seized by a genteel young man dressed only in his
waistcoat. who said to him, " You rascal, let the man
die as he pleases: you see he has enough. go and
kill some one able to resist." The fellow went off.
Previous to this a Croat. taking my gold-laced hat
and putting it upon his own head. coolly asked me
how he looked in it. He then with his sabre cut off
my queue and took it along with him.'

A civilised scalp!

The Austrians, after all, lost the day. and a
certain Miles Macdonnell rescued our hero, and had
him carried into hospital. Recovering. he returned
to Rome. and was welcomed in a flattering manner
both by his King, who presented him with a sum of
money, and by the young Duke of York. After
seeing some service on the Po, young Macdonell
obtained leave to go to France and join a detachment which was to aid Prince Charles in Scotland.
At Lyons they heard of the Prince's defeat of Hawley
at Falkirk, but at Paris the news was worse, and of
all the Jacobite volunteers (who were Irish) John
Macdonell alone persevered. He urged that, as the
Prince's affairs went ill, ' It was ungenerous not to
give what aid we were capable of, but I could not
prevail on any of them to be of my opinion.' In
fact, it was now plain that France did not mean to
lend any solid assistance to the Cause. The Duke of
York since Christmas had been waiting at Dunkirk

and Boulogne, expecting permission to sail for England with a large force, but delay followed delay. Young Macdonell now went to Boulogne, where he met the Duke, and was introduced by him to the Duc de Fitzjames and to Lally Tollendal. Here the good Colonel's memory deceives him, for he avers that Lally wished to take him to Pondicherry. Now Lally was deep in the Scottish rising, and did not leave France for India till ten years after 1746.[1] Young Macdonell, in these weeks of hope deferred, lived with the Duke of York at Boulogne, Dunkirk, and St. Omer. Finally, he set sail from Dunkirk with several Irish officers on the very day of Culloden, April 16.

Here the Colonel is guilty of an artistic blunder in his narrative. It is plain, from his later statements, that the Duke of York made him the bearer of a letter, and a sum of 1,500*l.* or 2,000*l.* in gold, to Prince Charles. But we do not hear, till later, of the money or the missive. The little company with Macdonell rounded the Orkneys, landed in Loch Broom, and at once heard the fatal news of Culloden. Macdonell's uncle, Scottus, had fallen with twenty of his men, ' and nobody knew what was become of the Prince.' Colonel Macdonell never gives dates, but he must have arrived in Loch Broom between May 8 and May 12, 1746. On May 8, a meeting of chiefs was held at Murlagan, and a tryst appointed at Loch

---

[1] Lally's adventures were romantic, and are only touched on by M. Hamont in his *Lally Tollendal*, pp. 32–5.

Arkaig, in Lochiel's country, for May 15.[1] Our hero
heard something of this at Loch Broom, and determined to join the rallied clans. He first went to
Laggy, at the head of Little Loch Broom, where he
found Colin Dearg Mackenzie of Laggy, with several
other Mackenzie gentlemen, and sixty of the clan.
'We thought ourselves as safe [he and his friend,
Lynch, an Irish officer,] as in the heart of France.'

Now began the purely personal romance of the
Colonel. The Mackenzies entertained him and Captain Lynch at dinner in a dark and crowded room ;
he noticed that men gathered suspiciously behind
him, and he remembered that they had remarked on
the weight of his portmanteau. He therefore rose
more than once from table to inspect that valise, but,
while the company were drinking the Prince's health,
Colin Dearg walked out. Absent, too, was the portmanteau, when the guests left the table, but Colin
explained that he had packed it on the back of our
Colonel's horse. There, indeed, it was, but when the
Colonel stopped at Dundonell, and opened his valise
in search of a pair of shoes, a canvas bag containing
1,000l. was missing. A gentleman of the Mackenzie
clan had slashed open the portmanteau and stolen the
money of the Prince whose health they were drinking ! It was the affair of the Loch Arkaig hoard on
a smaller scale. The situation of our injured hero
was the more awkward, as Dundonell, where he

---

[1] Mackenzie's *History of the Camerons*; see documents on pp.
233–44.

found himself, was the estate of a Mr. Mackenzie, nephew to the thief, Colin Dearg. Mr. Mackenzie was absent ; Mrs. Mackenzie was at home, but in bed. However, she saw Macdonell, who told her what had occurred, and entrusted to her another bag of five hundred guineas : 'If killed, I bequeath it to your ladyship. God be with you! I wish you a good morning.' Accompanied by Lynch, Macdonell now returned to Laggy. He dared not use force against Colin Dearg, for, if he fell, Colin would win his own pardon by producing a letter from the Duke of York to Charles, which our hero was carrying, though he now mentions it for the first time. Accused by Macdonell of taking the money, Colin Dearg denied all knowledge of it, and, as he was attended by a tail of armed clansmen, Macdonell had no resource but in retreat.

He breakfasted at Dundonell with 'the most amiable lady,' took up the 500 guineas, and, after fatiguing marches, reached Loch Arkaig. On the shores of the remote and lonely loch our Colonel met, and recognised, his gigantic kinsman, the truculent Col of Barisdale. Col said that Lochiel and Murray of Broughton were at Achnacarry; he himself and Lochgarry were mustering men, 'to try what terms could be got from the Duke of Cumberland.' This must have been on May 14. At Achnacarry the wounded Lochiel received our hero kindly, and Mr. Murray of Broughton took charge of the remaining 500 guineas and the letter from the Duke of York to the Prince. Lest any one should think that the Colonel is romancing, there exists documentary evidence to corroborate his tale. The unhappy Murray of Broughton, in his accounts of the Prince's money after Culloden, writes: ' From a French officer who had landed upon the East Coast, £1,000. N.B.—This French officer was charged with 2,000 guineas, but said he had 1,000 taken from him as he passed through the Mackenzies' country, and gave in an account of deductions from the other thousand.' Murray adds that he has charged himself with 1,000*l*., ' tho' he still thinks he did not receive quite so much.' He must have received the 500*l*. (perhaps in *louis d'or*, which he reckons as guineas), and some loose cash. Murray was writing from memory, so was Colonel Macdonell. Murray calls him a French officer, and really he was in French service. There cannot have been two such officers who, at the same time, were robbed of 1,000*l*. by the Mackenzies, and reported the loss just after Culloden.'

Macdonell slept at Achnacarry and was wakened by the pipes playing *Coyya na si*. News had just arrived of an attempted surprise by Cumberland, whose forces were actually in sight; Barisdale was accused of having concerted the surprise, but the story is improbable. Eight hundred Camerons and Macdonalds now retreated by the west end of Loch Arkaig, and our hero, with Captain Lynch, made for

---

¹ Murray of Broughton in Chambers's *Rebellion of* 1745; edition of 1869, p. 515.

Knoydart. Lynch later returned to French service, carrying Macdonell's report to the Duke of York, and soon fell at the battle of Lafeldt, where the Scots and Irish nearly captured Cumberland. As for Macdonell, 'I had put on a resolution,' he says, 'never to leave Scotland while Prince Charles was in the country.' The death of Macdonell's father, and the infirmity of old Scottos, also made his presence at home necessary to his family. So, he says, 'I waved the sure prospect I had of advancing myself both to riches and honour,' in the service of Spain.

Knoydart, during the winter of 1746-47, must have been in a state of anarchy. Old Glengarry, accused by Barisdale, was a prisoner in Edinburgh Castle; Young Glengarry was in the Tower. Col Barisdale and his son were captives in France, on a charge of treason to King James. Lochgarry had fled to France with the Prince. Old Scottos was decrepit. No rents were paid; the lands had been wasted by the English; clansmen were seizing farms at will.[1] In these melancholy circumstances our Colonel marched alone into the Mackenzie country, to hunt for the money stolen by Colin Dearg. Then this odd adventure befell him :—

'I went to take a solitary turn and met a well-dressed man in Highland clothes also taking the morning air. After civil salutations to each other, I entered into discourse with him about former transactions in that country. He of himself began to tell

[1] Letter-Book of Alastair Ruadh, MS.

me about French officers that came to Lochbroom—
how the 1,000 guineas had been cut out of one of
their portmanteaus by Colin Dearg, Major Wm.
McKenzie of Kilcoy,[1] and Lieutenant Murdoch
McKenzie from Dingwall—all officers of Lord Cromartie's regiment, being all equally concerned ; and
how not only those who acted the scene, but all the
people in that part of the country, had been despised
and ridiculed for their mean and dastardly behaviour ;
but that had his (McKenzie's, who was speaking to
me) advice been taken, there should never have been a
word about the matter. The following dialogue then
ensued :—*Question.* "And pray, Sir, what did you
advise ? " *Answer.* "To cut off both their heads, a
very sure way indeed ! " *Q.* "What were they, or
of what country ? " *A.* "The oldest, and a stout-like
man, was Irish. The youngest was very strong-like,
was a Macdonell of the family of Glengarry." *Q.*
" How was the money divided ? " *A.* " Colin Dearg
got 300 guineas, William Kilcoy got 300 guineas,
and Lieutenant Murdoch McKenzie got 300 guineas."
Q. "What became of the other hundred ? " *A.*
" Two men who stood behind the Irish Captain with
drawn dirks ready to kill him, had he observed Colin
Dearg cutting open the portmanteau, got 25 guineas
each ; and I and another man, prepared in like
manner for the young Captain Macdonell, got 25

[1] William, fourth son of Donald the fifth of Kilcoy. He married
Jean, daughter of Mackenzie of Davochmaluag, and died without
issue. *History of the Mackenzies*, p. 585.

guineas each." *Q.* "You tell the truth, you are sure?" *A.* "As I shall answer, I do." *Q.* "Do you know to whom you are speaking?" *A.* "To a friend and one of my own name." "No, you d—d rascal," seizing him suddenly by the breast with my left hand, at the same instant twitching out my dirk with the right, and throwing him upon his back, "*I am that very Macdonell.*" I own I was within an ace of running him through the heart, but some sudden reflection struck me—my being alone, and in a place where I was in a manner a stranger, among people which I had reason to distrust, I left the fellow upon his back, and re-entered the house (Torridon) in some hurry. My landlord, Mr. McKenzie of Torridon, met me in the entry, asked where I had been. I answered, "Taking a turn." "Have you met anything to vex you?" "No," I returned smiling. "Sir," says he, "I ask pardon, you went out with an innocent and harmless countenance, and you came in with a fierceness in your aspect past all description." "Mr. McKenzie," said I, "none of your scrutinizing remarks; let us have our morning!" "With all my heart," he replied. Soon after, being a little composed, I related to him my morning adventure. He remarked that the man was a stranger to him, and had been a soldier in Lord Cromartie's regiment. That very day I quitted that part of the country and returned home, where I continued sometime.'

The *some time* must cover the years from 1747 to the autumn of 1749. Old Glengarry was released at

that date from Edinburgh Castle. To him, at Invergarry, Colonel John told the story of his wrongs, and
from his chief he obtained an escort of five men.
With these at his heels, he marched to Dundonell,
and told Mr. Mackenzie that he desired a meeting
with Colin Dearg. Colin came, but his escort con-
sisted of some thirty-five men armed with dirks and
clubs. The Colonel, however, was determined to
beard his enemy, and devised the following tactics.
He himself would sit between Colin Dearg and Dundonell : two of his five men would slip out and guard
the door with drawn swords ; meanwhile the Colonel
would insult the Mackenzies. If they raised a hand
he would pistol Colin and dirk his host, Dundonell ;
his three retainers would fire the house, and the
Macdonells would escape in the confusion or perish
with their foes. It was a very pretty sketch for a
camisado.

'After a short pause Dundonell mentioned the
cause of our present meeting *in as becoming a manner
as the subject would admit of*; to which an evasive
answer was returned by his uncle, Colin Dearg, pre-
tending to deny the fact. I then took him up, and
proved that he himself was the very man who with
his own hands had taken the gold out of my portmanteau, after cutting it open with some sharp
instrument. This I said openly in the hearing of all
present. To which I got no other reply than that
" the money was gone and could not be accounted
for." I returned that " If the cash was squandered

O

the reward due to such actions was yet extant"—
and being asked what that was, I answered, "The
gallows." At this expression the whole got up standing, and seeing them all looking towards me, I drew
my dirk and side pistol, and presenting one to my
right and the other to my left, swore that if any
motion was made against my life, I would despatch
Dundonell and his uncle, who seeing me ready to put
my threat in execution, begged of their people for the
love of God to be quiet, which was directly obeyed.
In the meantime my men had taken immediate possession of the outside of the door and were prepared to
act according to my orders. I called to them to stay
where they were, but none of the people in the house
knew what they had gone out for.'

The money was gone, no man dared to touch our
hero, and he and Dundonell went peacefully home
together! Our hero had dominated and insulted the
Mackenzies and was obliged to be satisfied with that
result.

In the following years (1751-54) Knoydart and
Lochaber were perfectly demoralised. The hidden
treasure of Loch Arkaig had set Macdonalds against
Camerons; cousins were betraying cousins, and
brothers were blackmailing brothers. The details
(much veiled in this work) are to be found in the
Duke of Cumberland's MSS. at Windsor Castle. The
murder of Campbell of Glenure by Allan Breck, or
by Sergeant Mohr Cameron, and the reports of Pickle,
James Mohr, and a set of other spies, had alarmed

the Government with fears of a rising aided by
Prussia. Consequently arrests were frequent and no
man knew whom he could trust. Col of Barisdale, a
double-dyed traitor, was dead in gaol, but his eldest
son was being hunted on island, loch, and mountain.
Now in a letter from an English officer, Captain
Izard, dated September 30, 1751, and preserved at
Windsor, he says: 'Dr. Macdonald, living at Kylles,
and brother of Glengarry, told that young Barisdale
lay at his house the Monday before and proposed
going to the Isle of Skye.'

The giver of this information was not a man
in whom to confide. Our hero, however, confided.
Disguised as a rough serving-man he went fishing for
lythe with 'my relation, Dr. Macdonell of Kylles, an
eminent physician.' An English vessel, the *Porcupine*, under the notorious Captain Fergusson, came in
sight. Dr. Macdonell insisted on taking our hero on
board her, and there, as he sat over his punch, informed the English officers that the servant who
accompanied him was a gentleman. Fergusson
arrested Macdonell at once on suspicion of being
young Barisdale, and he lay for some time a prisoner
in Fort William. Now the Doctor may only have
blabbed in his cups, but, taken with Captain Izard's
report, his behaviour looks very odd. Our hero,
however, does not suspect his relation, the Doctor,
but denounces his cousin, Captain Allan Macdonald
of Knock, in Sleat, as his betrayer, and 'the greatest
spy and informer in all Scotland.' However it be,

the betrayal of Colonel John was apparently a family affair.

A long list of charges, doubtless of Jacobite‑ dealings, was brought against him, and a midshipman on the *Porcupine* assured him that Allan Macdonald of Knock was the informer. So the Colonel was locked up in Fort William, then, or just before, crowded with prisoners, such as Lochiel's uncle Fassifern, his agent, Charles Stuart, Barisdale's second son, and Cameron of Glenevis, with his brother Angus. The date must have been June or July, 1753, for young Barisdale was taken in July, and the Colonel was then a prisoner. Young Barisdale just escaped hanging; Fassifern was exiled; Stuart was accused of the Appin murder; Sergeant Mohr Cameron was betrayed and executed; the traitors were clansmen of the victims, and, though our Colonel says nothing of all this, the facts gave him good cause for anxiety. It is fair to add that no mention of his enemy, Macdonald of Knock, seems to occur in the Cumberland Papers, where so many spies hide their infamy.

Our hero escaped by aid of Mr. Macleod of Ulnish, sheriff-depute of Skye, 'being both my friend and relation as well as the friend of justice.' This gentleman suppressed the only good evidence against the Colonel, which indeed merely proved his wearing the proscribed kilt. After nine months of gaol the Colonel was released and seized the first opportunity to challenge Knock, who would not face him.

So ends the Colonel's adventure. 'I was then in love with your mother,' he says simply, and on this head he says no more. He had ' kept the bird in his bosom,' a treasure lost by many of his kin, and among them, one fears, by Allan of Knock. A certain Ranald Macdonell of [*in*] Scammadale and Crowlin, who, born about 1724, married in May 1815, and died in November of the same year, aged ninety, is said to have 'severely punished that obnoxious person known as Allan of Knock, over whose remains there was placed an inscription not less fulsome than false.'[1] Allan, whether he betrayed the Colonel or not, has obviously a bad name in Knoydart.

The Colonel lived happily on his property till 1773, when he settled in Schoharie County, New York. When the American rebellion broke out he served in the King's Royal Regiment of New York, and, after the final collapse of the British, he retired to Cornwall in Ontario. As General Macdonell wrote of him in 1746, 'He has always behaved as an honourable gentleman and a brave officer, irreproachable in every respect.'

---

[1] *Antiquarian Notes*, by C. Fraser Mackintosh, p. 156.

X

READERS who have followed the adventures of Pickle
the Spy may care to know what were the later fortunes of his inseparable companion, Young Glengarry. These fortunes were not answerable to the
expectations of the Chief. The death of Henry
Pelham, in March 1754, blighted, as we shall learn,
the hopes which Glengarry, like Pickle, had founded
on the promises of the Prime Minister, and left him
a debtor to Government for claims on his lands.
That Young Glengarry, on reaching his estates in
November 1754, behaved with oppressive dishonesty
to his smaller wadsetters, men holding portions of
his land in pawn, we learn from the report of Colonel
Trapaud, who, for some sixty years, was Governor
of Fort Augustus. Early in 1755, we find Glengarry
at Inverness, where he signs a tack, or lease, on January 24. A copy of an undated letter from Pickle
represents Glengarry as 'making a grand tour round
several parts of the Highlands, and having concourse
of people from several clans to wait of him.' Glengarry himself speaks, in a letter to be quoted, about
such a gathering. In 1755, we find General Bland

objecting to Glengarry's journeyings (when Pickle
went to London), and on May 18, 1757, Captain
John Macdonnell, of General Frazer's regiment, de-
parting for America, makes Glengarry his 'factor
and attorney,' also his executor and general legatee.[1]
This Captain Macdonnell was the younger Lochgarry,
who accompanied Pickle in Edinburgh, in September
1754. 'I hope, in case of accident, you'll take care
of Young Lochgary,' writes Pickle.[2] Captain Macdonnell was later Colonel of the 76th, says General
Stewart, and a previous owner of my copy of the
General's book notes in the margin that 'he was
wounded on the Heights of Abraham.' Critics who
think that Glengarry was personated by Pickle will
observe that Young Lochgarry knew both gentlemen
and could not be deceived. He was Pickle's companion in Edinburgh when Pickle had just lost his
father, a Highland chief. In 1757 he makes Glengarry (who had suffered a similar bereavement at
the same time as Pickle), his factor and legatee.
There is, of course, no reason to suppose that Young
Lochgarry had ever heard of such a mysterious per-
sonage as Pickle.

We know nothing else of Glengarry's life from
1755 to 1757, when his manuscript letter book throws
a melancholy light on his closing years. There is a
draft of a letter of 1757 and several drafts of 1758–
1759, in a stitched folio wherein he entered the

---

[1] Laing MSS., Edinburgh University Library.
[2] *Pickle*, p. 282.

brouillons of his correspondence, not always in his own hand. On April 28, 1757, he wrote from London, probably from his rooms in Beaufort Buildings, Strand. He writes to his Edinburgh agent, Mr. Orme, W.S., on a variety of business. His action in settling his estates was much impeded by the retention of his charters and family papers by Sir Everard Falkner (or Faulkner), an English officer. 'I have prevailed,' he says, 'upon Mr. Brado, how (who) is a principal man amongst the Jewes, to endeavour to recover my charters from Sir Everard.' He expects to redeem all the wadsets on his lands, and to compound for a few of the most pressing of his father's debts. But he must have been disappointed, for on his death, in 1761, more of his estate was in the hands of wadsetters than in his own. He must, however, have secured proof of 'my propinquity to those of my predecessors left infeft,' for he was formally inducted into his property before an Inverness jury in 1758. He mentions that, when he left Scotland, 'the appearance of a famine threatened then the whole north,' and 'his friends were buying meal in Buchan.' A wet summer and autumn always meant dearth in the Highlands. He alludes to some military oppression of one of his retainers : 'the attempt is so flagrant that it would not pass unpunished amongst the hotentots.' An unfinished draft appears to be addressed to General Frazer, son of Old Lovat. With him (if it is Frazer) he wants 'to settle family differences *à*

l'aimable.' His correspondent is leaving Scotland
after recruiting.

In June 1758, Glengarry was in correspondence
with persons concerned in the affairs of his sister-in-
law, widow of his brother Æneas, accidentally shot
at Falkirk, in 1746. Æneas must have married very
young; he was not twenty when he died, but he left
a son and a daughter. For some unknown reason
Glengarry was on ill terms with his brother's widow,
as will appear, and she would not permit her children
to visit their uncle. To this business the following
letter refers :

'*To Rory McLeod.*

' (Dated Greenfield, 22nd June, 1758.)

'Dear Sir,—I am favour'd with yours by the last
post, and am not a little surprized to understand
by it that Mr Robison should have wrott either to
Mr Drummond or you that I intended to dispose of
my nephew contrar to the present system of moral
education, all I said to Mr Robison that if I sent
him abroad I could have him educated for nothing,
but that I did not myself aprove of this frugall
method, but that I would advise with Mr Drummond
how to Dispose of him when I would be at Edinburgh,
that if he inclin'd a military life, I might have interest to get him a pair of Colours, but then I would
insist the best *moitié* of his patrimony should be
assigned to his sister, but that what I inclined he

should follow was the law, if he had genius for that profession, and that in that case if Mr Drummond aprovd of it, I would send him for the sake of the language to some country schooll in England. This was all that passed upon honour, and Desired to send over the boy that I might make him acquaint in the country, and should only Detain him two months, I had a Double view in this as I had the countrey about that time all convened, it would have been fifty pounds in his way, and this I told Mr Robison ; and at the same time, as the lassie had no English. I would Keep her all winter with my sister so that in spring she might be presentable, when I would send her for a little time to my sister's Dr Chisolme at Inverness. Mr. Robison approved of all this, particularly of the lassy's coming, and, that he might not be blamed for retaining them, sent them to their Mother's, where the Girle has ever been, and laid the whole blame to her charge. I have still Mr Robison's letter, but he has his views which I am resolved to frustrate. . . . I will shew you my brother's discharge to my father, and I have living witnesses that delivered him Cattle in payment of interest, and part principall, and as one of them is his father's brother, how would go all lengths for him, that there can be no objection to his evidence as Discharges have been burned or Destroyed after the Castle was blown up. . . .

'Your affect. Cousine and humble servant,

'MACKDONELL.'

Burt says that 'to have the English' was the mark, among the Highlanders, of a gentleman's children. Glengarry's niece had as yet no English; her education had doubtless been neglected in the distresses consequent on the Rising. Probably, too, her mother was poor, her husband's portion having been partly paid in cattle. These very cattle may have been among the 20,000 plundered by Cumberland's men after Culloden, as a volunteer writes in his little book of 'A Journey with the Army into Scotland' (1747).

In a letter to Mr. Orme, of unknown date, Glengarry says that his sister-in-law 'is infamous.' On the same affair of the nephew he writes again :—

[No date.]

'Sir,—I have been frequently since my father's death abused in the good opinion conceived in former days of those that ought and were generally believed steadfast friends to this familly, but I must confess I least of all expected it from any of yours, and least of all from yourself personally. I had a letter lately from Robison of Ballnicaird acquainting me that Provost Drummond and you, despairing of the amicable agreement twixt my nephew and me, intended to push matters to the utmost, this was strange proceedings, without ever acquainting me, and in any event a strange procedure between me and my nephew when the opinion of any one or two eminent in the law might in a few moments decide

the whole without further expences, and when they
come to the age to judge for themselves I believe
they will be little oblidged to their present directors,
Mr Drummond only excepted. I sent for my nephew
and niece, their not arriving is laid to your advice,
tho up to that time I little believed it, and from that
Instant foresaw Mr Robison and their infamous
mother's drift. As Mr Drummond is so very good
as take the trouble to look after any so very near
connections, least by others' drift he should be Deceived, I must act the needful to have a near relation
of the father's side subjoined with him to take care
of the whole, and their Education, and bring their
Mother and Mr Robison to account for their inter-
missions with his effects and moveables, most of
which he received as payment, and at his Death
were very considerable, there are still living witnesses
that can prove this, and I have which I believe may
be in my Agent's custody, his discharge or Bond
for 6000 merks, pay'd by his father of his bond of
patrimony. Should this stand in law, as it ought in
equity, and Justice, I will refer any differences of
this kind to any named by Mr Drummond, and
another by me.

'. . . Acquaintance, friendship, and blood connection might expect a friendly demand, not by a
Sheriff Officier.

'But as the world has taken a turn, and that
men of business are not to mind such punctilios, I
have nothing to say but that I hope it may not be

long when a blood relation and connection with this
family may be claimed both as an honour and protection, it was so formerly. and may be still the same.'

(He adds that he wishes proceedings stayed still
he comes to Edinburgh, and refers to his 'late violent
indisposition.')

'Your sincere friend and affect. Cousine.'

This undated letter is probably of 1758. though
early in 1759 Glengarry had another very severe
illness, from which it may be doubted if he ever
entirely recovered. He writes to Mr. Orme, 'I am
drinking goat-whey and milk. that is my diet . . . I
shall be soon upon my leggs, and see you soon.'

The following is an important letter, undated in
the draft. to the Chief of the Macleods :—

[Undated. Really of June 21, 1758.

'Dear Macleod,—I thought to have had the
pleasure some months ago of drinking a glass with
you at White House. But a Severe fitt of sickness
of which I am now getting the better prevented me.
I have settled my affairs in the country as well as
my present situation and the circumstances of my
tenants could admitt, but as their whole [property]
was once destroyed, and that they have not recovered
yet quite in their stock I was oblidged to give them
a longer delay than I expected.'

He therefore asks Macleod to 'go conjunct with
me in security for borrowing 400l.'—an invitation

which Macleod declined. If Macleod will not help him, 'I cannot be active in making aplication to be discharged of the claims the Government has against my estate, *which I was once made sure of*, but that *vanished with those then at the helme.*'

Such a promise, broken on the change of the hand at the helm, is several times referred to—by Pickle. He writes to the Duke of Newcastle, 'he bitterly complains that nothing has been done for him, of what was promis'd him in the strongest terms, and which he believes had been strickly performed had your most worthy Brother (Henry Pelham) his great friend and Patron, survived till now.'[1]

Among the many odd coincidences between Pickle and Glengarry, this is not the least curious. Both the spy and the chief entertained great expectations from Government, and both confess that these hopes 'vanished with those then at the helme,' obviously, that is, with Henry Pelham's death.

Glengarry goes on, in his letter to Macleod, '*but to be explicit on this*' (namely, on his 'being made sure' of the abandonment of Government's claims on his estate) 'and the confusion my father and the late unluckie troubles left this estate would draw to tow great lenth, I will therefore reffer it till meeting.' He ends with compliments 'to Lady Macleod, and the two lovely little Misses.'

---

[1] February 19, 1760, *Pickle*, p. 312: also p. 266, April 8, 1754: 'Since the loss of my worthy great friend [Henry Pelham] on whose word I wholly relay'd, everything comes far short of my expectations.'

It would have been pleasant to hear Glengarry
when, over a bottle, he was 'explicit' on the reasons
for which Henry Pelham promised to abate the demands on his estate. Government knew that Glengarry was in the affair of Loch Arkaig. They
arrested his accomplices in 1751, but left him free.
Government knew, by their spies, that Glengarry
frequented the Earl Marischal in Paris in 1752, and
that, in 1753, he was perpetually running over, as
a Jacobite agent, to Paris. But they then arrested
Glenevis and Fassifern, while they promised to abate
their claims on Glengarry's estate! To explain all
this to Macleod 'over a magnum,' as Glengarry
elsewhere convivially remarks, could not be an easy
task. His letter, in the draft, is undated, but on the
same page is a letter to his solicitor, Mr. Orme, W.S.,
dated 'Greenfield, 21 June, 1758.' In this letter
he speaks of that just cited as having been sent 'by
this very post.' Macleod was in Edinburgh, but
left before Glengarry's appeal could reach him.
Now, without the 400l. the Chief could not go to
town. He therefore wrote again to Macleod, repeat-
ing his supplication, and being 'explicit' indeed as
to his former patron in the Government, though not
as to the reasons for his patronage.

'An absolute discharge of the heavie claim the
Government has against me I was once promised,
but those that was then at the helme *are no more.*'

The only person of those 'then at the helme'
who was now, in 1758, 'no more' was precisely

Henry Pelham. He died in March 1754. Pickle
was his 'man.' Pickle had received promises from
him which were never fulfilled. So, oddly enough,
had Glengarry! We know what Pickle's services to
Henry Pelham had been; we can guess at those of
Glengarry. But after Henry Pelham's death—in fact.
at the very time of his death—Prince Charles's party
broke up for ever in England, and the Earl Marischal quarrelled irreconcilably with the Prince. The
services of Pickle were therefore no longer needed.
Pelham's engagements with him were not kept, and
the promise to Glengarry, by a coincidence, was also
broken by the faithless English Government.

People who maintain that Glengarry was not
Pickle may be asked to produce a theory which will
account for the singular series of coincidences in the
fortunes of the Chief and the spy. Even in this new
coincidence alone, it will be interesting to see how
they explain the circumstance that Glengarry, like
Pickle, found his expectations blasted, and the
promises made to him unfulfilled, in consequence of
the death of Pickle's employer, the brother of the
Duke of Newcastle. What possible claim could a
professed Jacobite agent, known for such to Government, as young Glengarry was, have on the good
offices of the First Lord of the Treasury? It has
been fondly suggested that Pickle was an unknown
miscreant, personating Glengarry. That will be
shown to be physically impossible ; but, granting the
hypothesis, why was Glengarry, no less than Pickle,

favoured by Henry Pelham? No other person can be meant by the phrase 'those at the helme,' now 'no more.' Newcastle, indeed, was out of office in 1756, if 'no more' is explained as ' out of office.' But when Glengarry wrote to Macleod in 1758 Newcastle was again at the Treasury.

Macleod would not back Glengarry's bill for 400*l*. His agents advised him against this measure. In February 1760 Pickle, who was anxious to go to London, asked the Duke of Newcastle to send him a bill, payable at sight, ' for whatever little sum is judged proper for the present.' The Duke's answer, with the bill payable at sight for the little sum to defray Pickle's travelling expenses, is to be directed by his Grace

'To Alexander Mackdonell of Glengary by
Foraugustus.'

Apparently. then, Pickle had some means of getting at Glengarry's correspondence. The two gentlemen spell 'Fort Augustus' in the same singular way. On September 11, 1758, Glengarry wrote to Mr. Orme's subordinate :—

' Will you dow me the favour to order me the " Calledonian Mercury " regullarly every post to the care of Mr. William Fraser, merchant at forAugustus ? '

The almost unvarying uniformity in bad spelling which marks Pickle and Glengarry will be commented on later.

P

The last years of Glengarry were disturbed by the legal results of an early piece of domestic slyness. His father, old Glengarry, commonly described as a weak, indolent man, married, first, a lady named Mackenzie, of the Hilton family. As his eldest son was not of age in January 1745 the marriage may have been in 1723 or 1724. After bearing a second son, Æneas, and apparently a daughter, Isobel, Lady Glengarry died (1727). In a deed of 1728 we find Old Glengarry already remarried to a daughter of Gordon of Glenbucket, who in 1724 was nearly murdered by evicted Macphersons. The stepmother of Young Glengarry was a managing woman, and 'factrix' of her husband's estates. Now, in 1738 Old Glengarry pawned or 'wadsetted' his lands of Cullachy to his kinsman Lochgarry. The wadsetter paid 2,000 merks in money and gave bills for the rest. But in January 1745, when Alastair was in Scotland on furlough from his French regiment, Old Glengarry formally 'disponed' his estates to his eldest son. Doubtless this was done with an eye to the chances of a rising; in any case, the transaction was kept a secret from Glengarry's wife and factrix.

Hence arose trouble, for the pawned estate of Cullachy had been redeemed. Lochgarry had been paid his 2,000 merks, or they were set off against another debt, but his bills were not returned to him. They lay in Lady Glengarry's custody, and she could not be asked for them without revealing the secret transference of the whole property to Young Glen-

garry in 1745. He therefore gave Lochgarry a
written promise that the bills should never be used
against him. But Lochgarry being attainted, after
1745, and exiled, his possessions were forfeited to the
Crown. Government therefore demanded, in 1758,
that Glengarry should redeem from them Lochgarry's
wadset of Cullachy. He pleaded that it was already
redeemed before 1745, but of this he could bring no
evidence. He writes to his Agent on August 2,
1758, that he is not certain of the year of the wadset
(really 1738), as he was not then in the kingdom ; he
was in France. 'Lochgarry being more in debt to
the familly than the [amount of the] mortgage, he
delivered up his contract of wadsett, which I thought
was all the seremony necessary ; and the signature
being tore from it was laid, according to custom,
among the family papers, which were carried off,
and are now in Sir Everard Falconer's custody.' He
knows little of estate affairs, ' as I was always abroad.'
His rental of 1744 was burned with the house of his
factor, Donald McDonell, Younger of Scotus.

After the Rebellion, he did not meddle in matters
of the property, till his father's death (1754). ' The
tenants could hardly pay what would subsist him.'

' Every tenant took possession of what farme he
pleased.' In 1746 ' Mrs. Mc.Donell of Lochgary being
destitute of all suport, having a numerous family of
young children, came from Badenoch, took possession of Cullachy, and there lived untill she followed
her Husband abroad.'

'The lands of Cullachie was only set till lately
from year to year, the tenants were frequently
removed, I know of no written rentall, it is not
customary . . . Discharges were not formerly required, nor were they necssary.'

Glengarry explains all this to his Agent on
January 6, 1759 :—

'When I got disposition to my Father's estate I
was then under age, at this time Lady Glengarry,
how [who] then had so much to Say with her husband,
the Disposition Grant was concealed from her, and
as the Bill granted by Lochgarry was in her Custody,
had they demanded it would have Discovered the
Scheme in my favours, I granted my Obligatory to
Lochgery that these Bills should never make against
him.'

The sense can be puzzled out of the anacoloutha.
On February 3, 1759, he repeats his story :—

'I will only observe that the reason of the bills
not being cancelled or retired by Lockgerry, was that
they were then in Lady Glengarry's custody, and
that the disposition of my Father's estate in my
favour was keept secret from her, which would have
been discovered had Lochgerry demanded his bills,
and this occasioned my giving him my obligation
they should never make against him.'

The whole affair is a specimen of the informal
manner in which Highland business was done. The
frequency of 'removals' of tenants also throws doubt
on the theory that Evictions were a novelty intro-

duced by the Commissioners of Forfeited Estates.
The anarchy after Culloden is shown by the squatting
of tenants on whatever farms they chose to select.
The Judges could not be induced to accept Glengarry's account of the redemption of Cullachy, as he
had no documentary evidence, and Cullachy appears,
after the Chief's death, among his mortgaged lands.[1]

The latest of the drafts in Glengarry's Letter
Book are of December 1758, January 1759. He
appears much aggrieved by Colonel Trapaud,
Governor of Fort Augustus, for the following cause:
his ground-steward had been claimed, unjustly it
seems, as a deserter from the army. A party of
soldiers then acted in the manner described in the
following draft, which has no date or address :—

' The party in the dead of night was posted round
my hutt, of which I was ignorant untill my servants
were stopped from going from door to door. Alarmed
at this, I suspected some straglers were come to break
open some valts in the old Castle, which was formerly
Done.'

The indignant chief drafts the following remonstrance to Colonel Trapaud :—

' I never thought to have reason to write you
in so cooll a strain. My own Behaviour, not to
mention the pollitess showen to you by my friends
in Generall since you lived in this countrey claimd
a more Gentle return, and as our Actions are always
above Board It depends upon yourself that the same

[1] *Antiquarian Notes*, p. 123.

Harmony Should allways subsist, and I will be very happie still to remain,

Sir,

Your sincere friend and Humble servant.'

Trapaud's behaviour, Glengarry writes, is ' picking,' and Pickle also spells *pique* ' pick.' The worst of it is that Glengarry ' is lick to lose the use of his eyes,' for at the time of this assault in his ' hutt' he was exceedingly ill. ' I am now writting,' he says to Colonel Lambert (January 6, 1759) 'in this confus'd stile with only the fowrth part of one eye open, beeing near losing my life with a plague of a distemper, which, when recovered, seised my eyes.' On January 15, 1759, he tells Captain Forbes that he can hardly see. On February 24, 1759, he expresses a civil surprise at Macleod's refusal to back his bill for 400*l.* On February 3, he was still ' hardly able to crall,' but intended to go south; his sister Bell was going to Edinburgh. Macleod's persistent refusal probably made the journey to London impossible, where Glengarry expected ' to be off or on with the Government claim against my estate.'

There are no later drafts in the Letter Book, but Pickle, at all events, had the use of *his* eyes when he wrote to the Duke of Newcastle on February 19, 1760,[1] offering to raise a regiment. Glengarry, six weeks later, urged the same proposal through the Duke of Atholl.

On April 21, 1761, Glengarry made his will. He

<hr>

[1] *Pickle,* pp. 312-314.

recommends his sister and sole executrix to seal up
his cabinet, which is not to be opened 'till the
friends of the family meet.' The Macdonnells of
Greenfield, Leek, and Cullachy are then · to see all
the political and useless letters among my papers
burnt and destroyed, as the preservation of them
can answer no purpose.'

Mr. Fraser Mackintosh, who publishes these
extracts, adds, · why Glengarry who lived several
months after the execution of his will, did not himself
destroy the papers above alluded to, can be conjectured by people for themselves—all that need be
said here is that their destruction was a pity, and
the reason given unsatisfactory.' [1] His affairs · were
found to be in a deplorable state.' It may be
conjectured that Glengarry clung to his papers,
which must have been compromising enough. If
his malady again affected his eyes, he might be
unable to select the documents which it was wiser to
destroy. Nor could he well endure to entrust ' my
sister Bell' with the task of selection. She must not
know her brother's guilt. That secret must have
oozed out, for it has left traces in tradition.[2]

Thus closed miserably a singular career. Im-
poverished, dying in a ' hutt,' beside the ruins of his
feudal castle, distrusted, not even permitted to see
his young nephew and heir, Glengarry reaped the
harvest sown by his mysterious attendant, Pickle.

---

[1] *Antiquarian Notes*, pp. 120, 121.

[2] The tradition of Glengarry's treachery has reached me both from
Scotland and America, under dread secrecy!

OF all the companions of Pickle, the most inseparable
was Glengarry. Now, since the appearance of 'Pickle
the Spy,' the author has been denounced before the
Gaelic Society! Amidst 'applause' a Celtic gentleman, the news-sheets say, accused me of bringing a
charge of an odious nature, *without any proofs*. Of
course, if I have no proofs, nobody who thinks so
need argue against what I, myself, regard as a chain
of irrefragable circumstantial evidence. Nor am I
aware that any arguments, beyond clamour, have
been advanced, in favour of Glengarry's innocence,
except those which I shall presently examine. But
first I must meet the charge of wresting facts to suit
my 'prepossessions.'

I had no prepossessions: how should I? If I
knew so much as that there was any young Glengarry,
before I read the Pickle letters, it was the limit of
my information. These documents were pointed out
to me, several years ago, by Sir E. Maunde Thompson.
when I was in search of a manuscript to print for
the Roxburghe Club. I began to read them, where
they are to be found, scattered through five or six
volumes of the Pelham Papers, in the British Museum.

They are not all in sequence in one volume, nor in
chronological order. On a first hasty examination,
nothing appeared to indicate their author. I therefore had transcripts made of the Pickle Letters, and,
after reading them, arranged them chronologically,
being helped, where dates failed, by their allusions to
public events : such as the death of Frederick, Prince
of Wales, the death of Henry Pelham, and so forth.

On a first glance at the originals, I had no hope
of detecting the spy called Pickle. He might be a
servant, secretary, or retainer of any Jacobite family.
But indications as to his identity kept occurring,
when once the papers were sorted, and the hunting
instinct awoke in the reader, the fever of the chase.
Pickle was apparently no · paltry vidette,' for he
was in close relations with the Prime Minister, Henry
Pelham, and, later, with the Duke of Newcastle.
Now a lacquey may, as Sir Charles Hanbury
Williams's dispatches show, report to an Ambassador,
but a Prime Minister is less easy of access. Next,
Pickle was, or had succeeded in persuading Pelham
that he was, a person of the first importance in the
Highlands. A critic has replied that, of course, a
spy would pretend to be important, and, naturally,
would be accepted as such. Ministers are scarcely
so gullible. They do not accept a casual stranger's
identity without inquiry.

Presently it appeared, from a letter of the Court
Trusty, or Secret Service man, Bruce,[1] who attended

[1] In 1749 a Mr. Bruce was appointed to survey the forfeited and

Pickle in Edinburgh, that he now, by his father's death, was head of a great clan. Pickle's father's death occurred in September 1754. Now, on examination, it appeared that Old Glengarry, and no other Chief, died on September 1, 1754, in Edinburgh, where we find Pickle, with Young Lochgarry, in mid September. Pickle, writes Bruce, the Court Trusty (signing 'Cromwell') is adulated by military society in Edinburgh, where he stays for at least a month. He is to be observed, when he goes North, by the Governor of Fort Augustus, near which lie Glengarry's lands. The Governor (Trapaud) writes unfavourably of the new Glengarry (December 13, 1754), and Pickle writes that he will, if not permitted the use of arms, prevent officers from shooting over his lands.

Pickle then is, or affects to be, a young Chief, just come, by his father's death at Edinburgh, in September, into estates near Fort Augustus. He is also, or pretends to be, the chief of the Macdonnells, for he says (April 1754),' there could be no rising in Scotland without the Macdonnells : he is sure that he shall have the *first* notice of anything of the kind ; and he is sure that the Young Pretender would do nothing without him.' Finally (as stated on p. 209), writing to the Duke of Newcastle (Feb. 19, 1760), he speaks of

unforfeited estates of the Highlands, including Glengarry's. Pickle speaks of employing ' Cromwell ' (Bruce) to draw up for him a judicial rent roll. The two Bruces, the surveyor and the Court Trusty, are obviously the same man, and he is probably the writer of the tract, *The Highlands in* 1750. (MS. 104. King's Library.)

Pickle in the third person, says that he is ready to raise a Highland regiment (which only a Chief could do), and ends, ' Direction ' (of reply) ' To Alexander Mackdonnell, of Glengary, by Forangustus.' Before I read that line, I had said to a Highland friend, · The traitor is a Macdonald.' · Not Clanranald, I hope,' he answered, and then Pickle's last letter gave me the clue to Glengarry.

Thus there was, and could be, no ' prepossession ' on my part. The circumstances all pointed direct to Glengarry, or to a personator of his, and to no one else. Thus it became a · working hypothesis ' that Pickle either was, or was personating, Glengarry : a Chief on terms of perfect intimacy with Prince Charles. He was, or affected to be, a Macdonnell, a Chief, with lands near Fort Augustus, to which he succeeded by his father's death in September 1754, the date of the death of Old Glengarry.

Taking Pickle's identity, natural or feigned, with Young Glengarry, as a working hypothesis, it became necessary to trace the career of that chief. At every stage, in every detail and date, after 1750, whatever was true of Young Glengarry was found to be true of Pickle. Every gleam of light that revealed the long forgotten incidents of Young Glengarry's career, after 1750, fell also on the sinister features of Pickle. My hypothesis thus ' colligated ' all the facts. New facts from MSS. came into view after my book was published ; my hypothesis colligated these also. Everything fell into its place : everything

coincided in the identification of Pickle with Young
Glengarry.

To upset the evidence of a long series of
coincidences, all pointing in the same direction, some
hypothesis other than the hypothesis that Pickle is
Glengarry must be advanced. Only one alternative
suggestion has been ventured, as far as I am aware
—namely, that Glengarry was *personated* throughout,
for ten years, by some unknown 'inward' or close
intimate, calling himself 'Pickle.' That hypothesis
I shall prove to be not only morally but physically
impossible, to demand a physical and moral miracle.
We are left, then, with the equation, Pickle=
Glengarry.[1]

To the *a priori* objection, that it is morally incon-
ceivable that a Highland Chief, of character hitherto
unsuspected, should sink so low, I need hardly reply.
Too many Chiefs, from the death of Malcolm MacHeth,
had been in the same *galère*. Young Glengarry, moreover, *was* suspected by several independent witnesses.
We have also read the story of Barisdale, Glengarry's
cousin. *A priori* improbability there is none. We
therefore proceed to examine the career of Young
Glengarry, and to show how his comings and goings,
his entrances and exits, the changes in his fortunes, his
unconsidered private letters, his spelling, and his
handwriting, all combine to identify him with the
author of the Pickle Correspondence.

---

[1] It is needless to consider the theory that Pickle was James Mohr
Macgregor, who died in 1754.

About the early years of Alastair Ruadh Macdonnell of Glengarry it is unnecessary to write at great length. Born apparently about 1725, for he was not of age in the beginning of 1745, Young Glengarry had one brother of the full blood, Æneas, accidentally shot at Falkirk in 1746. He had also a sister, Isobel. Before 1728 his mother died. Wodrow says that she was imprisoned by her husband on an islet, and died of hunger (1727). Young Glengarry now received a stepmother, a daughter of Gordon of Glenbucket. He does not seem to have been attached to this lady, who bore two sons to Old Glengarry. According to Murray of Broughton, Young Glengarry 'was most barbarously used by his father and mother-in-law' (p. 441). Alastair, at all events, was sent to France as early as 1738, where he was not likely to learn English orthography. His own, though pretty consistent in its blunders, is of the kind which Captain Burt found prevailing in the Highlands.

Alastair's boyhood was probably unluxurious. Burt tells the following curious anecdote on this head. After 1715, the Castle of Invergarry, which had been adorned by the father of the Glengarry of Shirramuir, was gutted by the English soldiery. It was refurnished and made inhabitable by the agent of a Liverpool Company, who smelted iron in the district. Glengarry, meanwhile, 'inhabited a miserable hut of turf, as he does to this day' (1735 ?). To this manager, a Quaker, a number of gentlemen

of the clan paid a visit. After receiving them hospi-
tably, the Quaker observed that they would always
be welcome in 'my house.'

'God d—n you, Sir, your house! I thought it
had been Glengarry's house.' They then assaulted
the Quaker, who was rescued by his workmen.[1]
Alastair was better lodged in France, where, in
1743, he got a Company in the Royal Scots. In
1744 he was with Pickle's friend, the exiled Earl
Marischal, at Dunkirk, meaning to start with the
futile French expedition from Gravelines.

How that expedition was 'muddled away' we
have told in the essay on the Earl Marischal. At
this time the Earl in France, and Murray of Broughton in Scotland, gravely distrusted James's agents in
France, Sempil and Balhaldie. Now Balhaldie was a
connection of Lochiel, and was aware that Murray
held him in suspicion. He, therefore, after the
collapse of the expedition of 1744, sent over to
Lochiel Young Glengarry, 'freighted with heavy
complaints' against Murray. Lochiel next, in the
spring of 1745, brought Murray and Young Glengarry together. The young Chief told Murray that
Balhaldie accused him of bidding the Prince come to
Scotland, with or without French assistance, and
'seat himself on the throne, and leave the King at
Rome' (which was precisely what James desired and
Charles repudiated).[2] Glengarry was therefore to warn

[1] Burt, i. 265-267.

[2] Murray of Broughton's *Memorials*, p. 107. James's letter to
Louis XV., p. 508.

the party against Murray. Murray told Glengarry
the real facts—namely, that Balhaldie was too imaginative, and Glengarry seemed quite satisfied. Indeed,
he produced a letter to the same effect as regards
Balhaldie from Æneas Macdonald, the banker, and,
later, the informer.

Glengarry and Murray presently met at that
strange tavern gathering in Edinburgh, where, out
of the company, Traquair, Lovat, Glengarry, Murray,
Macleod, and Lochiel, Lochiel alone preserved his
honour. Glengarry then went to the Highlands
with letters for Sir Alexander Macdonald of Sleat
and other gentlemen. In January 1745 Glengarry
had induced his father secretly to dispone to him his
lands, an action which became a serious trouble to
him later. In May 1745 Murray sent him with
despatches to the Prince in France, and with reasons
why Charles should not come unless accompanied
by a French force. Late in 1745 Young Glengarry
was taken at sea, and lodged in the Tower.

Charles, meanwhile, was loyal enough to his imprisoned adherent. On November 4, 1746, Charles
wrote to d'Argenson, 'there are three prisoners in
London, sir, in whom I take a warm interest. These
are Sir Hector Maclean, Glengarry, and my secretary, Mr. Murray of Broughton. All three hold
French commissions, the first was born at Calais. . . .
I implore you, sir, to take every means to secure
their exchange, and will regard it as a personal
obligation.'

These gentlemen, however, were not naturalised French subjects, like Nicholas Wogan, who, after fighting when a boy at Preston in 1715, and after losing an arm at Fontenoy, took part in the campaign of 1745, and later saw Cumberland's back at Laffeldt fight. Nicholas may have been exchanged, in 1746, as a French prisoner ; for Murray and Glengarry this plea was unavailing. The Prince, however, did his best for both men, and ill they rewarded him.[1]

Glengarry told Bishop Forbes the same story in 1752. He was the bearer of a letter from the Chiefs, imploring the Prince not to come over without arms, money, and auxiliary forces.[2] But he could not find Charles, who was incognito, 'lurking for a spring.' Towards the end of 1745 Alastair was captured, as we saw, while conveying a piquet of the Royal Scots to join the Prince. He pined in the Tower, he says, for twenty-two months, and was then released. His fortunes were frowning. His father lay in Edinburgh Castle, a written information having been laid against him by a number of the gentlemen of his clan who had been out in the Rising. His lands and cattle had been destroyed and driven away by the English soldiery. Men squatted on what farm they chose, and could only pay rent enough to 'subsist' his father. The French Government made demands on him for money advanced to him while

---

[1] Charles knew of Murray's 'rascality' by April 10, 1747. Letter of the Prince to James. Stuart Papers, *Memorials*, p. 398.

[2] *Lyon in Mourning*, iii. 119. The anecdote is also given by Robert Chambers in *Jacobite Memorials*.

in the Tower, and stopped his pay. His grant from the Scots Fund (1,800 livres) was inadequate. The Prince could not procure for him a regiment. In these gloomy circumstances Alastair took a step which nobody can blame in itself. He attempted to reconcile himself to the English Government. The following letter is from a friend sincerely anxious for his success :— [1]

(State Papers, Domestic, Scotland, Bundle 38 (1747), No. 6.)

' Roterdam, Oct. 17, 1747.

' Sir,—I take this opportunity of my worthy friend an officer of the Royals of informing you how I have had severall letters on the following Subject from Mr. Macdonell Junior of Glengary who desires me to charge you with this letter. He has frequently and seriously reflected on the many good Advices given him by you and Maj. White when he was Prisoner at the Tower, to abandon that party and the service of France. I am thorrowly convinced that he is determined so to do if it is agreeable to the Ministry, and that he will give the Duke of Argyle and them all the assurances that a man of honour can give of his behaving as a peaceable Subject, if they will allow him to wait upon them in London. Let me beg of you for God's sake to persuade these great men to accept of this young Gentleman's offer, by which at once you'll detach him from that party that has given

---

[1] This letter was published, from my transcript, by Mr. A. H. Millar, in the *Scottish Review* for April 1897.

birth to all the Calamitys that both his Clan and
Country has suffered this age past: as I shall be
some months here before my affair is Negociated
you'll have time to send me answer, which I pray
God may be favourable. Please write me as soon
as you can. I am with my Compliments to your
family,

> ' Sir, your most obedt. oblidged humble
> ' Sert.
> ' WILL : BAILLIE.

' P.S.—The young man depends very much on the
Duke of Argyle's interest.

'To Major Macdonald at London.'

On September 20, 1748, Glengarry wrote from
Amiens, telling James that he ' waited an opportunity
of going safely to Britain,' on his private affairs. In
December he asked James to procure for him the
colonelcy vacant by the death of Lochiel. Young
Lochiel, a boy, had been appointed. James could do
nothing, and was too poor to send money. But, on
Glengarry's request, he dispatched ' a duplicate of
your grandfather's warrant to be a peer '—Lord
Macdonnell and Aros. Glengarry often signs ' Mackdonell,' without Christian name.[1]

On June 8, 1749, Glengarry explained his circumstances to Cardinal York and to Lismore, James's
agent at Versailles. ' I shall be obliged to leave this

---

[1] Stuart Papers. Browne, iv. 100, iv. 22, 23, 51.

country, if not relieved.' Presently he went to London, with Leslie, a priest suspected of treachery by the Jacobites.[1] Leslie says, ' Glengarry did not intend to appear publicly' in London, 'but to have advice of some counsellors about an act of the Privy Council against his returning to Great Britain.' He was so poor that Leslie pledged for him, to Clanranald, a watch of Mrs. Murray's of Broughton, wife of the notorious traitor. He had already 'sold his sword and shoe-buckles.' This must have been the very nadir of his fortunes, and four years later Campbell of Lochnell told Mrs. Archibald Cameron that now, in 1748 or 1749—the lady could not remember which—Glengarry offered his service, 'in any shape they thought proper,' to the English Government and Henry Pelham.[2] Without pausing to discuss the value of Mrs. Cameron's evidence (given on January 25, 1754) we return to what is actually known of Glengarry in 1749. He had left London, probably little the better for his visit. On September 23, 1749, Glengarry wrote to Lismore from Boulogne. He has been in London, by advice of his friends, 'ces Messieurs croyant que je ne ferai point de difficulté de me conformer aux intentions du Gouvernement, mais étant toujours determiné de ne me point égare[r] des principes de mes Ancêtres, ne du devoir que je dois a mon Roy je ⌈de?⌉ me lui tenir, je puis retire ⌈retirais?⌉.' If not relieved, he must return to England.[3] We know what his protestations of

[1] Browne, iv. 98 102.   [2] *Ibid.* iv. 118.   [3] *Ibid.* iv. 64.

loyalty were worth. We do not know what occurred to Glengarry, in London, at this time.

Starving in July or August 1749, Glengarry appears (according to Æneas Macdonald, the banker) to 'have plenty of cash' at the end of the year (December). In October his father had been released from Edinburgh Castle, a point of no evidential importance, as several other gentlemen were also simultaneously set free. His estates were not forfeited, though remonstrances on this head were addressed to the English Government. They exist in the State Papers.

Before Æneas Macdonald met Glengarry in December, and earlier in the winter of 1749, Young Glengarry and Archy Cameron went North, and helped themselves to the Treasure of Cluny, the gold of Loch Arkaig.[1] On January 16, 1750, Glengarry reported his journey to Edgar, and accused Archibald Cameron of taking 6,000 louis d'or, and damping all hearts in the Highlands.[2] Cameron, on his side, appears to have accused Glengarry of obtaining the money by forging a letter from James. James, writing to Charles about Cameron's charge, leaves a blank for the name (March 17, 1750). But Æneas Macdonald supplies the name of Young Glengarry (October 12, 1751).

That Young Glengarry was concerned in the loot-

---

[1] Newton to Waters, March 18, 1750, *Pickle*, p. 93; Lord Elcho's Diary; Glengarry to Prince Charles, admitting the fact, 1751; Browne, iv. 79; 'Cluny's Treasure,' *supra*.

[2] Browne, iv. 66.

ing of the treasure in winter, 1749, is certain from
his own admission to Charles, corroborated by the
confession of Cameron of Glenevis to Colonel Crawfurd, in October 1751. In that confession appears the
earliest charge of treachery against Glengarry, who,
Cameron vows, must have betrayed him (p. 153). At
about the same time (November 30, 1751, February 14,
1752) Holker (of Ogilvie's French Scots Regiment)
and Blair anonymously warned young Edgar against
Glengarry. He is a friend of Leslie, ' an arrant rogue,'
and is ' known to be in great intimacy with Murray '—
of Broughton, the traitor, an acquaintance which is
proved by Murray's own ' Memorials,' already cited.
Even if we discount Mrs. Cameron's story, with those
of Archy Cameron and Glenevis, as Camerons were
at feud with Macdonnells, we have no reason to suspect hostile animus in Young Edgar, Blair and Holker.[1]
They remark (February 14, 1752) that 'Mr. Macdonald
of Glengarrie says that he is charged with the affaires
of his Majesty,' in London.

Now, what was, in 1751 the real situation of
Young Glengarry ? He had left Rome in September
1750. In January 1751 he was in Paris, and wrote
to Edgar, asking for money. He was confined to bed
by a severe cold.[2] At an uncertain date, probably
April 1751, he was residing publicly in London, for
he thence announced to Charles his approaching
marriage ' with a lady of a very Honourable and
loyall familie in England,' after which he will repay

---

[1] *Pickle*, p. 161.   [2] Stuart Papers, Windsor Castle.

his share of the Loch Arkaig gold. On this head he
has satisfied James. He discloses the embezzlements
of Cluny![1] On July 15, 1751. he wrote from London
to James, and to Edgar, with political and loyal
observations. Yet, in 1751. Glenevis believed, for
very good reasons, that Glengarry was already an
informer. If the suspicions of Glenevis were correct, Glengarry was an informer in 1751, the date
assigned by Pickle to the beginning of his own
service is about 1750.

Thus. in 1751, Glengarry was tolerated in London
by the English Government, though still professing
loyalty to James. As late as October 1754 he had
not 'qualified' or taken the oaths. He must, therefore, have made his peace with England—otherwise!
He had resigned his French commission. Moreover,
while his accomplices in the Loch Arkaig affair,
the Camerons, were arrested, Glengarry, the 'un-
qualified,' was allowed to go about London, and
travel to France and Scotland, though the English
Ministry knew that he was at least as guilty as
Glenevis and Downan.

The inferences are obvious. Government had a
motive for sparing Glengarry. Again, quite apart
from the Pickle letters, Glengarry is assuredly betraying one or the other party. To James he poses
as an active conspirator. To the English Government
he poses as, at least, 'one peaceable subject,' for they
allow him to live, and love, in London, and to go where

[1] *Pickle*, p. 162.

he pleases. He was in Edinburgh in April, 1752, and dined with Bishop Forbes. Later, he seems to have gone to Lochaber, which Government knew, from an Informer.

We now come to the Elibank Plot, to kidnap the Royal Family. It flickered from November 1752 to summer, 1753. Glengarry, writing from Arras on April 5, 1753, gives Edgar, James's secretary, a veiled account of the affair. 'The day was fixt,' on, or for, November 10, 1752, but the English shuffled, and did not act. 'The concert in Novr. was,' says Glengarry, 'that I was to remain in London, as I had above four hundred Brave Highlanders ready at my call, and, after matters had broke out there to sett off directly for Scotland, as no raising would be made amongst the Clans without my presence.'[1] He then alludes to 'my leate illness at Paris,' which has left him 'still very weake'—a phrase used at the same time by Pickle.

Now the Pickle letters begin on November 2, 1752, and Pickle speaks of himself, to his English employers, in precisely the same terms as Glengarry uses about himself when writing to Edgar. Pickle says that, among his Jacobite friends, he explains his supplies of English money as remittances from ' Baron Kenady.' Now, in Lord Advocate Craigie's letters of 1745,[2] we read · in most things Young Glengarry is advised and directed by Baron Kennedy,' a Baron of the Scottish Exchequer. Thus, if Pickle is Glengarry,

[1] *Pickle*, p. 180.   [2] Jesse's *Pretenders*, Appendix.

he would naturally represent his chief adviser, Baron
Kennedy, as the source of his supplies. He announces
(Boulogne, November 2, 1752) 'you'l soon hear of
a hurly burly,' and he must make a long journey,
first to Paris, then South, as he writes on November 4
to Henry Pelham.[1] The hurly burly is the Elibank
Plot. 'I will see my friend' (Henry Pelham) 'or that
can happen.' To Pelham he says. 'I will lay before
you *in person* all I can learn.' Pelham knew Pickle
personally, and could not be deceived as to his identity, as to his being a Chief, as he represented himself. In December 1752 Pickle. in London, informed
against Archibald Cameron and Lochgarry, whom
Charles had sent to Scotland, also against Fassifern
and Glenevegh (Glenevis) as agents for Charles with
the Southern Jacobites. Pickle has seen Charles, and,
in town, Lord Elibank, who 'surprised me to the
greatest degree by telling me that all was put off
for some time.' He has promised Charles 'to write
nothing to Rome,' which Glengarry actually did, in
April 1753. In later letters to his English employers,
Pickle speaks much of a severe illness, at Paris,
which 'nearly tripped up his hiells,' and left him,
like Glengarry at the same date, 'very weake.' He
had caught a cold, with a relapse at the masked
ball of the Lundi Gras, where he met the Prince.
'They now believe Pickle could have a number of
Highlanders even in London to follow him.' 'Nothing can be transacted in the Highlands without his

[1] *Pickle*, pp. 170–175.

knowledge, as his Clan must begin the play.'[1] The scheme is a night attack on the Palace of St. James's. Pickle has often discussed it with his friend, the Earl Marischal, Frederick's ambassador to the French Court.[2]

Here, then, are the following points shared in common by Pickle and Glengarry. (1.) Both in November 1752 are engaged in a deep Jacobite Plot (2.) Both are expected to lead a force of Highlanders, 'even in London.' (3.) No rising can take place among the Clans without each of them. (4.) Both are in correspondence with Rome. (5.) Both suffer from a severe illness at the same time, and are left very 'weake' (6.) Both are friends of Baron Kennedy. (7.) Both frequently visit the Earl Marischal in Paris.

That Glengarry visited the Earl in 1753 I cannot prove by independent evidence. But I can show, by independent evidence, that he, as well as (by his own statement) Pickle, did so at an approximate date. Glengarry had known the Earl since 1744. Here is another spy's undated testimony (1752-1754) to Glengarry's familiarity with the Earl Marischal in Paris, about this date, when Pickle haunts the old exile.[3]

'Macdonald of Glengarry, goes by the first of these names, lives at a *Baigneur's* in the *Rue Gueneguaud*, and keeps one Servant out of Livery, and two in

---

[1] *Pickle*, pp. 191-194.   [2] *Ibid.* p. 190.
[3] MSS. 33,050; f. A25.

Livery. When he first came to Paris he kept a *Carosse de Remise* by the month, but now only hires one occasionally to make his visits, which are chiefly to

Lord Ogilvie

Mr. Ratcliffe

Mrs. Carryl of Sussex

Mrs. Hamilton (Lord Abercorn's Cousin who has changed her Religion and lives with Mrs. Carryl)

The 3 Messrs. Hayes (who are cousins and lodge at the *Hotel de Transylvanie, Rue Conde*)

Macloud ⎱ at Roisins, a Coffee House in the
Fitzgerald ⎰ Rue Vaugirard

Lord Pittenweemys, the Earl of Kelly's Son, at the *Hotel d'Angleterre, Rue Tarrane*

Sir James Cockburn, at the *Caffe de la Paix*, in the *Rue Tarane*.

Lord Hallardy ⎫
Mr. Gordon ⎪ at a *Baigneur's* on the Estra-
Mr. Mercer ⎬ pade where they keep them-
L. Cromarty ⎭ selves conceal'd,

Frequently to the Jesuits' College.

'*And never fails going to Lord Marshal*, whose Coach is often lent him when he has none of his own.

'N.B.—Tuesday 9th. Janry. Macdonald waited in his own Coach from ten o'clock at night till past eleven, in the *Rue Dauphine*, when a Person took him up in a Chariot, who, by the description, is

believed to be Lord Marshal. It is about that time
that the Pretender's Son is suppos'd to have been in
Paris.'

Thus Glengarry undeniably frequented the old
Earl Marischal. no less than Pickle did, and the English Government knew it. Yet they did not arrest
him. as they arrested Glenevis, Downan, Fassiferu.
Archy Cameron, and tried to arrest Lochgarry, on all
of whom Pickle had informed. Moreover Glengarry,
in Paris. is not starving. but has a servant out of
livery, and two in livery. keeps or hires a carriage. or
uses that of the Earl Marischal.

I respectfully submit that these seven common
notes of Pickle and of Glengarry cannot possibly be
explained. except on one of two hypotheses. Either
Pickle is Glengarry, or he is audaciously personating
Glengarry. not only by letter. but bodily. For he
promises to visit Henry Pelham ·in person,' and
Henry Pelham. with the English officials and police.
cannot but have known the aspect of Glengarry, a
man who. for twenty-two months, was an important
state prisoner in the Tower, and had, later. lived
openly in London, though. as we shall see, under
surveillance.

ˑ That point I prove thus : on August 12. 1753.
Charles. in hiding at Liège, and elsewhere in the
Netherlands. desired, as he notes in a draft, an in-
terview 'with G.' [1] In August. or September. 1753.
Pickle sent in accounts of his interview with Charles,

---

[1] *Pickle*, p. 210.

in whose company he had travelled from Ternan to Paris. The Prince asked Pickle to allow arms to be landed on his estate, which Pickle refused, 'nobody knowing as yet in what manner the forfeited estates would be settled.'[1] Pickle himself is now in England.

Now we know, from a report in the State Papers, that, in 1753, the English Government received intelligence from a spy on Glengarry. 'Mr. McDonald of Glengarry has been several times in France within these three weeks, and is suspected to be an agent for the Young Pretender, who, it is believed, has been lately in Paris, incog. N.B.—The abovementioned Mr. McDonald lodges at the second House on the right hand side of the way in Beaufort Buildings, in the Strand, and is a young, fair, fullmade man.'[2]

Thus, just when Charles wishes to meet 'G,' Glengarry is coming and going from France to England, suspected by a spy to be a Jacobite agent, while Pickle is reporting to the English Government on his own simultaneous journeys and interviews with the Prince. Yet the English Government, though independently informed of Glengarry's movements, and his familiarity with the Earl Marischal (whom they know to be intriguing for the Jacobites with Prussia), arrest Clanranald, arrest Fassifern, but never touch Glengarry!

This is not the limit of their favours. Far from

---

[1] *Pickle*, p. 219.   [2] State Papers, Scotland, Bundle 44, No. 67·

incommoding Glengarry, Henry Pelham promises
that Government will remit all their large claims on
his estate. For this, as least, we have Glengarry's
written word, as has been shown already in ' The
Last Days of Glengarry.' [1]

The Celtic believers in Glengarry's innocence may
explain why, when Pelham was arresting Jacobites all
over Scotland, in 1753, he not only allowed Glengarry,
who had not ' qualified,' and against whom he had
copious information, to go free, but also ' promised an
absolute discharge of the heavie claims the Government
has against me.' He made similar promises to Pickle,
who complains of their non-fulfilment. And, on the
hypothesis of Glengarry's guilt, his motive is now
transparent. In addition to payments of ready money,
sorely needed, his estates escaped forfeiture, *and he
was promised remission of the fines.* These facts, of
course, were unknown before I had access to Glengarry's MS. Letter Book. My hypothesis colligates
the new facts as well as the old, which is the note of
a good working hypothesis.

To the seven common points between Pickle and
Glengarry, in 1752–53, we now add an eighth : both
have been disappointed by Henry Pelham's promises,
broken after his death. Such coincidences cannot be
fortuitous, and Glengarry's friends must explain why
he, a known Jacobite agent, was so endeared to Henry
Pelham.

At this time, the autumn of 1753, James Mohr

---

[1] Glengarry's Letter Book, MS., p. 207, *supra.*

Macgregor made his absurd 'revelations,' about an
Irish plot to invade Scotland. He, his chief, Balhaldie, and a Mr. Trant, were particularly concerned.
Government had also news, from Pickle, Count
Kaunitz, and other sources, of Frederick's tampering
with the Jacobites, through the Earl Marischal, the
friend both of Pickle and of Glengarry. It would
have been natural to arrest and examine Glengarry,
who, as Government knew, was a familiar friend of
the Earl Marischal. In place of doing that—they
consulted Pickle! The Duke of Newcastle wrote a
paper of Memoranda, proving his agitation, and making a note that Henry Pelham should collogue with
'the person from whom he sometimes receives information.' [1] That person was Pickle.

Here are Pickle's answers!

(*Private intelligences concerning some particular*
persons.)

'He says Mr. Trent told him there was a Collection already made for the Pretender of about £40,000,
and that his friends here said he should [not] want
for money, tho' it were £200,000.

'Mr. Trent and he were very familiar formerly,
but as he is here grown a great man, he does not see
so much of him. Trent is not gone, but is expected
to go every day. This Mr. Trent is son of Olive Trent
[once mistress of the Regent d'Orleans, and complained of by Bolingbroke].

[1] Add MSS. 32,955, f.83.

'He does not know, nor believe, any one has come from Lord Marshal hither lately with authority. He is sure no Arms have come to Scotland this year, if there had, he must have known it. [James Mohr said arms had come.] He says Sullivan's Brother has been twice at Rome lately, but does not know his errand.

' Bohaldie [James Mohr's Chief] was an Agent of the Pretender with the late Lord Temple (Sempil?), but the Irish got him turnd off, and he is sure Lord Marshal would never trust him, because he will never believe him. [James Mohr had alleged that the Earl was engaged with Balhaldie.]

' *MacGregor was a Spy of both sides, and will never be trusted.*

' When he [Macgregor] escaped to Bulloigne he was very poor, but Lord Strathallan etc took com passion upon him, and he knows the Old Pretender sent him £20.'

This report damaged poor James Mohr; he was dismissed, and, in a few months, died a destitute exile. General Stewart of Garth claims our sympathy for James, who ' rejected an employment which he considered dishonourable in itself, and detrimental to the good of his country.'[1] Alas! his employers rejected James !

We now reach the crucial point of the hypothesis that Pickle *personated* Glengarry. 'Whoever Pickle was, it was clearly his intention to personate Glen-

---

[1] *Highlanders*, ii. xvi. Appendix.

garry,' says Mr. A. H. Millar.[1] Now on this point, I need scarcely recapitulate what is said at the beginning of this chapter. On September 14, 1754, we find the bereaved Pickle, an orphan now, but also a Chief, by his father's death, in Edinburgh with Young Lochgarry, who cannot but have known Young Glengarry, his Chief. For this presence of the orphan in Edinburgh, we have not only his written word, but that of Bruce ('Cromwell'), the 'Court Trusty' who accompanied him. We have his testimony to Pickle's enhanced pride. He it is who tells us how 'the Army people make up to Pickle, thinking to make something of him,' how General Bland (unconscious of guile) suspects *him*, as a friend of Pickle's; how Pickle is going North, to his estates, and how the Governor of Fort Augustus, hard by, is ' to try his hand upon Pickle.'[2]

All this Pickle himself confirms, in two letters of one of which only the briefest analysis has hitherto been given.[3] But these dull confirmatory letters may be relegated to an appendix. Briefly, we learn from his letters how Pickle has hurried to Edinburgh, for some reason of his own, on the news of a death which coincides with that of Old Glengarry. Coincidently, too, Pickle's family affairs are in great disorder. He writes again from Edinburgh (October 10, 1754), and this letter is in his feigned hand.[4] In his second epistle from Edinburgh Pickle confirms

---

[1] *Scottish Review*, April, 1897, p. 223.
[2] *Pickle*, p. 283.   [3] *Ibid.* p. 284.   [4] See Appendix.

all that Bruce, the Court Trusty, has said about his
approaching journey North, whence Colonel Trapand,
Governor of Fort Augustus, gives a bad account of
Glengarry as swindling his wadsetters.[1] Pickle also
confirms Bruce's account of the jealousy of General
Bland.

That Young Glengarry, as well as Pickle, was a
week's distance from town after his father's death
(September 1, 1754) I now confirm by the following
letter to himself, where he is supposed to be interested
in Old Lochgarry. It is probably from the Major
Macdonald who, while he was a prisoner in 1747,
persuaded him to conform to the English Government.

'London : Sept. 12, 1754.

'My dear Cuss.—I have duely received the
Honour of yours of 3d current. I must own that
the melancholly news [Old Glengarry's death] gave
me an inexpressible shock, the only thing that
abates my greife is that my dear late friend is so
well represented in your dear person. I pray that
all the powers above may combine to make you
shine even above your noble Ancestors. I hope
that Hevon will long preserve and prosper you for
the protection of a poor name that seems at present
in a very tottering and abject condition; No doubt
this accident will naturally retard your coming to
this place [London] yet I can't think otherwise than

---

[1] December 13, 1754. *Pickle*, p. 285.

R

that your interest calls you hither has soon you may have settled your domestique concerns.

'I have a line from Samer [probably St. Omer] by which I understand that the whole Coy [Corps?] seem'd determined to get ride of Loch[garry] at all events surely he's a most incorrigible man, and if a certain person [the Prince] does not interpose he must fall a sacrafice to his enemies' resentment and to his own folly. Mrs. Macdonald and the young folks join in compliments, our friendes of Crevan street salute you, and I ever am, My dear Cous,

'Yours whilst J. M.

'London: Sept. 12, 1754.

'I did not receive your note dated wednesday till Thursday 12 o'clock.' [1]

Thus, all Pickle's movements at this solemn hour of Old Glengarry's decease tally with those of Young Glengarry. Pickle is adulated by the army people, and goes North to his estates near Fort Augustus, whence the Governor reports on—Glengarry.

Can Pickle, then, while Glengarry is in Scotland, after his father's death, be posing in Edinburgh as himself a young, newly orphaned chief, going to his lands near Fort Augustus; personating Glengarry, in fact—for no other Chief had just lost his father?

Mr. Millar says: 'Whoever Pickle was, it was clearly his intention to personate Glengarry. . . .

---

[1] This letter, with a draft of Glengarry's reply, written on the back, is in the possession of General Macdonald, the owner of Glengarry's Letter Book.

It is hardly possible to imagine that an impostor
could have deceived the Edinburgh folks, to whom
Glengarry must have been well known,' and whom,
hurrying to his father's funeral, and to arrange his
affairs, he must just have visited, for Old Glengarry
died in Edinburgh. I venture to call such an im-
personation a physical impossibility, prolonged, as it
was, for some six weeks. It is *physically impossible*
that, both in London and Edinburgh, many men who
knew Young Glengarry should have supposed another
person—Pickle—to be that hero. Yet, if the personation was played off, it was not discovered, then or
later; for Pickle continued to be the informer, and
to be the shadow of Glengarry. As soon as it is
admitted that Pickle is feigning to be Glengarry, the
case for that Chief's innocence is given up. The
personation, among people who knew Glengarry inti-
mately well, is *impossible*.

Pickle's day of usefulness had gone by. On
April 24, 1755, an official gave in a report of a
conversation with the Chief, 'the head of a great
Clan of his name,' who wanted money.[1] In April
1756 Pickle again came to London, and dunned the
Duke of Newcastle: 'not the smalest article has
been perform'd, of what was expected and at first
promised. I am certain my first friend' (Pelham)
'mentioned me to the King. . . .'[2] In an undated
letter he speaks of being on an 'utstation' in the
Highlands, and talks of Glengarry in the third

---

[1] *Pickle*, pp. 288 289.　　　[2] Add. MSS. 32,864, f. 137.

person.[1] He tells of Glengarry's greatness, of Jacobite overtures to him, and repeats his usual fond demands.

In 1758, 1759, we know, from his own letters, that Glengarry was eager to go to London, to make terms about the fines on his estate. But Macleod would not back his bill for 400l. On February 19, 1760, Pickle wrote the last letter to Newcastle extant in the Pelham Papers. He speaks of Pickle in the third person, but he writes in Pickle's hand. Pickle wants to give information ; Pickle wishes to raise a regiment (and so did Glengarry), if he gets ' the Rank of full Colonel, the nomenation of his Officers, and suitable levie money : ' also ' a bill payable at sight ' for travelling expenses. He ends, ' Mack mention of *Pickle*. His Majesty will remember Mr. Pelham did, upon former affairs of great consequence. Direction—*To Alexander Mackdonell of Glengary, by Foraugustus* '[2]

A reply from Newcastle directed to Glengarry would be opened by Glengarry, and then, if Glengarry did not write Pickle's epistle of February 19, 1760, where is Pickle? Mr. Millar suggests that, ' if Pickle were a traitor in Glengarry's family, he must have been in a position to intercept the reply to this letter, or the whole plot would have been exposed.' This is a romantic hypothesis. There is no trace of any gentleman (such as Pickle was) eternally in attendance on Glengarry. And why did

---

[1] *Pickle*, pp. 290-291.   [2] *Ibid.* pp. 312 314.

the hypothetical traitor offer to raise a regiment,
which only Glengarry could do? There is no con-
ceivable motive for writing such a letter on the part
of any one but Glengarry, who was terribly pressed
for money, and could raise a regiment. Besides,
the physical impossibility of Pickle's supposed personation has already been demonstrated. Glengarry,
who had long been in very bad health, died on
December 23, 1761. The nature of his will has been
explained.

The internal evidence of identity in the authorship of Pickle's and Glengarry's letters remains to be
considered. Both write the same shambling style.
In an age of bad spelling both have a long list of
blunders in common. I give a few :—

1. aquent	acquaint.	
2. estime	esteem.	
3. tow .	two.	
4. dow .	. . do.	
5. sow .	so.	
6. triflle	trifle.	
7. (jant / (chant	jaunt.	
8. (utquarters . / (utstation .	out quarters. / out station.	
9. pick .	. . pique.	
10. (Foraugustus / (forAugustus	. Fort Augustus.	
11. how .	who.	

12. lick   .   .   like.
13. supplay   .   supply.
14. relay .   . rely.
15. puish   . . push.

Of these, 1, 2, 3, 4, 5, 6, 12, 13, 14 occur, sporadically, in other Scotch writers of the age, as in the Gask Correspondence. Pickle combines them all. But I have not elsewhere met 7, 8, 9, 10, 15. ' How ' for ' who ' (11) I have met in Macleod of Raasay's letters in the ' Lyon in Mourning,' and in one letter of 1725, while 'howse ' for ' whose ' occurs in a Scotch epistle in the Cumberland MSS. The *accumulation* of these fifteen mis-spellings is the common note of the orthography of Pickle and of Glengarry. It constitutes a note of identity of authorship.

But, believers in personation may say, ' Pickle had carefully studied and adroitly copied Glengarry's orthography, as, *ex hypothesi*, he wished to pass for that Chief.'

Then why did he not also imitate Glengarry's handwriting ?

Glengarry wrote two hands ; one is a sprawling scrawl, sloped much to the right, in his rough drafts of letters, preserved in his Letter Book ; the other is merely the same hand written smaller, closer, not so sloped, in his letters, for example, to James and Edgar. The Windsor Letters, the neater and more careful, I could not compare with those of Pickle at the British Museum. But I took Glengarry's Letter Book, or folio of scrawled drafts, thither, and Mr. Millar (author of the criticism in the *Scottish Review*) kindly compared the two sets of documents, he having much experience in such studies. I append what is essential in his report, contributed to the *Dundee Advertiser* of April 28, 1897.

'Mr. Lang has come into possession of much new evidence upon the subject. Amongst other documents he has the Letter-book in which Glengarry frequently copied his letters with his own hand and signed them. This book comes from an unchallengeable source. By Mr. Lang's invitation I had to-day the pleasure of comparing the handwriting of Glengarry in this book with the Pickle letters in the British Museum. At the first glance one would say that the manuscripts are so unlike superficially that they were not both written by the same person. Glengarry wrote a wide, sprawling hand, with a very distinct slope towards the right. The Pickle letters are all written in the vertical style, and the lines are small and neat. When examined more closely, however, there is a striking similarity in the details. Having selected Pickle letters that contained similar words to those in the Letter-book, I have made a careful comparison of them minutely. It is beyond question that whoever Pickle was he wrote in a feigned handwriting to prevent identification should any letter miscarry. If Glengarry wished to feign another hand than his own, the most obvious

way of effecting his purpose would be to change the
sloping style into the upright style. When Pickle
wished to disguise his hand he used the upright
style. There are several letters which Glengarry
wrote in a very peculiar manner. The capital letter
" T," for instance, was distinctly Glengarrian. But
the capital "T" written repeatedly by Pickle is
absolutely identical with that used in the Glengarry
book. Such words as "most," "humble," "Sir,"
" I," and "Tho'" are precisely the same in form in
both cases, the only difference being the change of
the slope. There is only one curious fact which
comes out after careful examination. When Glengarry is writing adjectives that begin with the letter
" d" he generally uses a capital. Pickle never does
this, but uses the small "d" instead, yet that small
" d" is exactly similar in form to the same letter
written by Glengarry. This is certainly minute
criticism, and might not be sufficient alone to esta-
blish the case against Glengarry; but when the
other fact is borne in mind, that Pickle and Glengarry make the same errors in the spelling of uncommon words, the confirmatory proof is very
strong. It is not likely that any letter exists in
which Glengarry fully acknowledges his treachery,
and the main evidence must therefore be circumstantial. If Mr. Lang had now to begin writing his
book with all the additional evidence before him
which he has obtained since its publication, he would
probably find few who would dissent from his con-

clusion that Pickle the Spy was no other than
Alastair Macdonnell of Glengarry. There may be
coincidences in events in the lives of two men; but
it is incredible that Pickle, when disguising his handwriting, should fall into the same formation of many
of the letters which was peculiar to Macdonnell of
Glengarry. Though begun upon a mere surmise by
Mr. Lang, extended research seems to confirm his
notion as to the identity of these two personages.
It is not a pleasant conclusion for any one who
believes that all the Highlanders engaged in the
Rising of 1745 were indomitable and patriotic
heroes. There were blacklegs in the army of Prince
Charles Edward, as there are in every movement of
the kind; but there were also noble characters prepared to shed their blood and sacrifice their prospects in support of what they believed to be the
rightful cause. Glengarry, apparently, must now
take his place among the execrated traitors.—I am,
&c.   'A. H. MILLAR.
'London : April 26, 1897.'

I am no expert in handwriting, and I offer no
opinion, except that Pickle's confessedly feigned hand
is more like Glengarry's careful hand, in the Stuart
Papers, than like his sloping scrawl, meant only for
his own eyes (and these nearly blind) in his Letter
Book. The Duke of Atholl has compared letters from
Glengarry, in his possession, with those of Pickle, and
has arrived at the same conclusion as Mr. Millar.
Pickle's hand is Glengarry's, disguised.

Such is my chain of evidence towards proving
the personal identity of Pickle and Glengarry. Both
men, it is hardly worth while to add, had been
officers in French service. I am aware of not one
discrepant feature to discredit the identity which
Pickle practically asserts, when he declares himself
(corroborated by Bruce) to have become, by his
father's death, Chief of the Macdonnells, just when
Old Glengarry died, and Young Glengarry succeeded
to the headship of the clan. To sum up the whole
case :

Young Glengarry's conduct, as far as we know,
is stainless, till, after endeavouring to 'conform' in
October 1747, he presently poses as a religiously
faithful subject, or devotee, of James in January
1748. He is starving in London, which he visits in
July 1749, his father being soon after released from
Edinburgh Castle. Young Glengarry, in the winter
of 1749, visits Cluny at Dalwhinnie, in company
with Glenevis, Lochgarry, and Angus MacIan. Glengarry obtains, by his own admission, a share of the
treasure, and then formally charges Archy Cameron
with looting 6,000 *louis d'or*. Archy accuses him of
forgery ; they carry their quarrel before James in
Rome. Early in 1751 Glengarry, though he is not
known to have taken the oaths, is allowed to reside in
London, and announces his approaching marriage
with an English lady. But Glengarry is already
suspected, and he knows it ; for when Leslie, the
priest, is charged with treason by the Jacobites,

Glengarry says that the blow is aimed at *him*. Nothing is proved against Leslie, but stories of Glengarry's intimacy with Murray the traitor, and the spy Samuel Cameron, called Crookshanks, are anonymously brought by Blair and Holker. In October 1751 Samuel's brother, Glenevis and Downan, arrested for their share with Glengarry in the matter of the French gold, accuse Glengarry of informing against them. They lie in gaol in Fort William; Glengarry (though the Government know him to be their accomplice) lives freely in London, and travels where he pleases.

In November 1752, April 1753, we have the affair of the Elibank Plot. On one side is Pickle, who is to lead Highlanders in London; Pickle, without whom his clan, and the North, can do nothing; Pickle, a friend of Prince Charles, and a correspondent of the exiled King in Rome; Pickle, who is ' very weake ' after a serious illness in Paris (February–March, 1753); Pickle, the constant associate of the Earl Marischal; and on the other side is Glengarry, who claims every one of these notes for himself. Both Pickle and Glengarry are friends of Baron Kennedy's. Glengarry is known to Government to be a trafficker with France, and with the dreaded envoy of Prussia, the Earl Marischal, but Government consults Pickle in place of arresting Glengarry. Pickle has had great promises made to him by his employer, Henry Pelham, so has Glengarry. Both complain of the breach of these promises after

Pelham's death. Pickle comes and goes to Prince Charles in France in August 1753. Glengarry is accused, to Government, of visiting France at the same time as a Jacobite agent. Jacobites are being arrested all over the country, but not a finger is laid on Glengarry.

Pickle and Glengarry both leave London for Edinburgh on the news of Old Glengarry's death, both are then bereaved young chiefs going to their northern estates near Fort Augustus. In this capacity Pickle, for some six weeks, is the centre of military attention in Edinburgh. Pickle wishes Bruce to assist him in drawing up a judicial rent-roll. Bruce surveys the lands of Glengarry. Pickle now, like Glengarry, remains in the North, where both are magnates, but both are poor. Pickle offers to raise a Highland regiment, and asks the Duke of Newcastle to direct his answer to Glengarry. The spelling of Pickle and Glengarry is identical in a score of peculiarities, and Pickle's handwriting is that of Glengarry in a simple disguise.

What makes Pickle's design to raise a regiment especially interesting is the fact, now to be proved, that *Glengarry entertained the same wish at the same moment.* He wrote to the Duke of Atholl to that effect, on April 5, 1760, and his letters are printed in the Duke of Atholl's ' Chronicles of the Atholl and Tullibardine Families ' (iii. 476–477). Thus Pickle and Glengarry were inseparable to the last.

Whoever is unconvinced by this array of circumstantial evidence against Glengarry must, at least, suggest an alternative hypothesis which will colligate the facts. The hypothesis of a personation of Glengarry by Pickle has been proved absurd and impossible. Recent research, after the publication of 'Pickle the Spy,' has added to the original evidence proof of Glengarry's insincerity as a Jacobite; the Glenevis affair; the promises made to Glengarry, as to Pickle, by Henry Pelham; the identification of 'Cromwell' (Bruce); the relations of Glengarry with Pickle's friend, Baron Kennedy; a few new similarities of Pickle-Glengarry spelling; the identity of their handwriting; and their simultaneous desire to raise a regiment. All these facts confirm the previous conclusion. A false hypothesis is not apt to be strongly confirmed by facts unknown when it was framed, nor would a jury regard the charge against Glengarry as 'without any proof in the world.' To say so, as has been audaciously done, is to illustrate prejudice, not to enlighten criticism. In truth, the game was up as soon as the person calling himself Pickle offered to raise a clan regiment, and asked the Duke of Newcastle to reply to Glengarry. More than one interpretation of that fact there could not logically be. But what is logic? A Lowland pedantry !

XII

OLD TIMES AND NEW

SOME years ago, when fishing in Loch Awe, I found a boatman, out of Badenoch, who was a charming companion. It may be the experience of others also that an English keeper usually confines his conversation, at least with strangers, to the business in hand, whereas a Scottish or Highland attendant will talk about Darwinism, Mr. Herbert Spencer, history, legend, psychical research, religion, everything. The boatman had a store of legends, and one day we fell to conversing on the old times, in the Highlands, and the new. He voted for the old. Among the advantages, he mentioned the game : and then, with sparkling eyes, the plunder ! Property, of old, had been *les vaches d'autrui*, the cattle of Lowlanders and of other clans.

Often, since that day, one has reflected on the old times and the new. The old were not wholly what is supposed. Thus Mr. Mackenzie, in his ‘History of the Camerons,’ contrasts the manly sport of the past with the modern driving up of deer to be shot down by ‘ drawing-room ’ gunners. Stalking is more common now, but the drawing-room way was

the old way! 'The tenants drive everything before
them, while the laird and his friends are waiting
with their guns to shoot the deer.' So writes Burt,
between 1726 and 1740. 'When the chief would
have a deer only for his household,' he does not stalk
it himself; 'the gamekeeper and one or two others
are sent into the hills, . . . where they often lie
night after night to wait an opportunity of providing
venison for the family.' [1]

I have seen in the Highlands heart-breaking
destitution. I have seen an old shivering woman
gathering nettles for food near Tobermory. On one
side of a river I have seen scantily clad girls hanging
about listless, in the rain, beside hovels more like
the nests of birds than human habitations. On the
other side of the water were comfortable cottages
and thriving crops. The former was the Protestant,
the latter the Catholic side of the stream, which the
Reformation did not cross. In the bleak cold of
June, on Haladale, I have said, 'Who would stay
here that could go away?' The gillie observed
that he had been in America, running the blockade,
but he vastly preferred Haladale. He numbered his
horses and kine; he was a man of substance. But,
poverty for poverty, give me nettles and shell-fish in
the North, before fried fish (and too little of that) in
the New Cut.

Moved by the extreme wretchedness in which
some Highland cotters seem to live, by the cry of

[1] *Letters from the Highlands*, ii. 70 (1818).

'congested districts,' by the laments of the evicted,
and by the belief in 'good old times' behind the
Forty-five, a Lowland observer naturally asks himself
if the old times were really so good? In one respect,
and that essential, they bear the palm : the people,
as a rule, loved and revered their Chiefs, and the
Chiefs adopted at least the airs of popularity among
the people. Even Young Glengarry, not a model
Chief, resented the oppression of tenants falsely
accused, as he maintained, of being deserters.[1] Moreover, the poor did not live, generally speaking, in
view of the luxurious rich. Clanranald and Glengarry had castles which must have been built at the
expense of the undefined 'services' of their people
long ago ; but the warrior Glengarry of Killiecrankie
discouraged refinement and delicacy of living. The
smaller lairds lived plainly, even poorly. Occasional
feasts were given to the Clan. Every man 'was
treated as a blood relation.' Consequently, if destitution existed, it did not provoke social hatred and
discontent. This, at least, is quite certain.

On the other hand, the presence of extreme
poverty, of famines, by no means rare, of exactions
which Lowlanders considered tyrannical, and the
occurrence of evictions, before 1745, seem equally
well established. Ignorance was one safeguard
against discontent, and in the absence of schools, in
the rarity of the Presbyterian clergy, with their
innate democratic ideas, ignorance flourished. Over-

----

[1] Glengarry's Letter Book, MS. (1758-9).

population was encouraged, by minute subdivision
of lands, for the purpose of increasing the Chief's
military following. Thus poverty was artificially
fostered, and, with it, idleness and habits of plunder
and of tippling.

This little picture of a Highland home is given in
a book of 1747 :¹ 'I have seen in their Huts, when
I have been walking, and forced to retreat thither
for Shelter from the Rain, their Children, sometimes
many in a Hut, full of the Small Pox and [at ?] their
Heighth, they having been lying and walking about
in the Wet and Dirt, the Rain at the same time
beating through the Thatch with Violence ; so that I
used to get from one End of the House to the other
to keep dry ; but it was all in vain, the Rain soon
following me. These children at the same time
seemed hearty, drinking Whey and Butter-milk, Wet
and Cold with the Inclemency of the weather, and
yet so well !'

This sketch was drawn somewhere in the country
between Inverness and Fort William, after Culloden.

The raising of the early Highland regiments
(1756–62) relieved the population, but also diffused
knowledge, while the Chiefs' power, as sanctioned by
law, was destroyed. The soldiers, who had seen the
New World, whether gentry and officers or privates,
did not incline to stay at home when rents were
raised. They emigrated to America, almost by

---

¹ *A Journey through part of England and Scotland, Along with
the Army, &c.* By a Volunteer. Osborne, London : 1747, p. 176.

clans, in years of famine, as in 1782. The Chiefs were alarmed and indignant; they were also needy. They screwed up rents, introduced sheep, moved populations to the coast, or evicted them. Voluntary emigration (the wisest policy) was succeeded by the removal of clansmen who were reluctant to go, or who could not afford to go, their poor goods not being marketable. Many even sold themselves into voluntary slavery for their passage fare.

Some chiefs became opulent for a generation; their families were ruined by their following of George, Prince Regent; their estates fell into English hands, and forests were made at the expense of new evictions.

This is a brief and gloomy account of what followed Culloden. An example may be given in the case of the great Glengarry family.

On the death of Glengarry, in 1761, his affairs were found, as was natural, in a lamentable condition. To study them and the later changes on his estate is to gain a view into the heart of Highland grievances. Fortunately materials for this examination exist, and have been published by Mr. Fraser Mackintosh in his ' Antiquarian Notes' (1897).

Perhaps it may be best to begin by giving a brief account of the way in which such estates as Glengarry's were usually occupied by the clansmen. The Chief let to tacksmen, or leaseholders, gentlemen of his clan, part of the lands which he did not hold in his own hand. Part of his ' tack,' again, the tacks-

man cultivated; part he let out to cotters, · under
which general term may be included various local
denominations of *crofters*, mailers, &c. . . . Frequently they have the command only of a small
share of their own time to cultivate the land allowed
them for maintaining their families. Sometimes the
Tacksman allows a portion of his own tillage field
for his cotter; sometimes a small separate croft is
laid off for him, and he is likewise allowed, in
general, to pasture a cow, or perhaps two.' [1]

'The Tacks,' says Dr. Johnson, 'were long considered as hereditary,' but, in his time, strangers
would make larger offers, and the hereditary tacksman was apt to be dispossessed, with cotters,
crofters, and all. As to the tyrannical and oppressive
conduct of the tacksmen, much will be reported
later. According to Young Barisdale's plea (1754),
Old Barisdale held possession, from Glengarry,
without a line of written paper. The tacksmen, in
war, were officers of the Clan regiment, and led, or
drove, the tenants to the field.

Apart from tacksmen and their cotters, were
' small tenants' holding direct from the Chief. They
usually occupied, in townships, a farm in common :
the shares may once have been equal, but, by 1738,
one man might hold a fourth, another but a fifteenth.
They dwelt in a hamlet near the arable crofts, of
which the division might vary from year to year.
They had also grazing, and, money being very scarce,

[1] Lord Selkirk, *State of the Highlands*, p. 42 (1805).

their chief wealth was their cattle. Interest and part principal of his patrimony were paid, in cattle, to Glengarry's younger brother Æneas.[1] Cotters, who acted as labourers, were scattered among the little communities of small tenants. Rents were mostly paid in kind, and in ' services,' little money passed.

Another system was that of ' wadsets.' A chief simply *pawned* a farm to a clansman, say Glengarry to Lochgarry, for a certain period, and for a certain sum of money. When he repaid the money, he recovered the farm. The wadsetter might build and improve, but no money was returned on redemption. The wadsetter sublet to tenants of either class, and either he or the Chief might make the better thing of the bargain. There were many poor wadsetters on a small scale. Colonel Trapaud accuses Glengarry of bullying his small wadsetters in Knoydart out of their wadsetts, and making them ' accept of common interest.'[2] ' The principal wadsetters refused, on which he ordered them out of his presence.'

Such was the system of a Highland estate; of its working more will be said later. On Glengarry's death, his heir was his nephew, Duncan, a minor: Glengarry and the boy's mother had been on the worst terms. In actual money, Glengarry's rents, at the day of his death, were but 330*l.* yearly. The rent ' uplifted' by his wadsetters was larger. There were heavy debts, both on the estate and personal:

---

[1] Glengarry's Letter Book, MS.
[2] November–December, 1754. *Pickle*, p. 285.

the amount of the claims of Government I have
nowhere found stated. Trustees ruled for the heir,
who, however, must have been of age when Morar
was sold to the Master of Lovat (Simon of the
Forty-five) in 1768. This cleared the personal debts.
In 1772, the new Glengarry wedded Miss Marjory
Grant, eldest daughter of Sir Ludovick Grant of
Dalvey. Mr. Fraser Mackintosh says that 'regardless
of sufferings, she strove with success to clear off the
debts, to raise the rents, and generally to aggrandise
the position of the Glengarry family.'

The wadsetts were paid off: the wadsetters must
now be tenants, on increased rents, or go. Most of
them emigrated to the New England States. Bad
years came : the small tenants fell into arrears. In
1782, a year of famine, arrived the first sheep farmer
from the Border. In 1785, fifty-five tenants were
warned and removed, · say 300 souls.' In 1786, 500
people emigrated under their priest, a Macdonnell
of the Scothouse or Scotos family. They settled in
Canada. They had fled from famine, as much as
from increased rents.

Duncan Macdonnell died in 1788; his son was
Sir Walter Scott's Glengarry, ' the last of the Chiefs,'
in costume and demeanour, but, it seems, a great
evictor. The French war made Highland recruits
desirable, and emigration slackened, but there was
an exodus in 1802, the settlers peopling Glengarry
County in Ontario ; sentiment apart, a very happy
change.

We have seen Alastair's free rent in 1761; it was
330*l.* in money. In 1802 the rental was 5,090*l.*!
The eccentric history of Scott's friend, Glengarry
(for whom he wrote a Death Song) is well known.
He was accidentally killed in 1828, and Glengarry
was sold some years later. It has changed hands
twice, since the first sale, and, says Mr. Fraser
Mackintosh, 'It is a fact not less painful than pre-
posterous that at the present day (1894), some dozen
crofters (all remaining) cannot get sufficient land
out of the tens of thousands of acres at Knoydart,
to maintain them, without the intervention of the
Crofters Commission.'[1]   Yet in 1753, Lochgarry,
perhaps in a sanguine way, reckoned the Macdonald
claymores, 'by Young Glengarry's concurrence only,'
at 2,600.[2]

   This is a typical specimen of the fortunes of a
large Highland estate, compromised in the Rising of
1745.   There are, of course, happier examples; but,
in this instance, we see every stage of the revolution-
ary changes in the condition of the Highland people.

   Now an Englishman, or a Lowlander. asks himself,
did the good old times contain the germs of these
social maladies, exhibiting themselves in other forms,
under other conditions?   To this conclusion we
appear to be forced by the evidence.   If Chiefs
were callous and selfish after the Forty-five, if the
land could not, or did not, support the people
properly after Culloden, these misfortunes, moral

[1] *Antiquarian Notes*, pp. 120-134.   [2] *Pickle*, p. 217.

and material, existed before the starving and ill-arrayed clansmen died on the English bayonets. There had been no reason to expect better treatment than the Clans have actually received, from several of the powerful families. Extreme destitution had prevailed; evictions had occurred, and had sometimes been bitterly avenged. There had been 'Agrarian outrages' before Culloden, attacks on men, and mutilation of cattle.

Our evidence, as to the state of the Highlands, comes from various sources. We have Lowland, English, and Anglified witnesses. The Duke of Argyll cites a Highlander, Forbes of Culloden, but he was a Whig, and President of the Court of Session. Yet there was no juster, more fair, or more wise and tolerant man in the North. We have Captain Burt, author of 'Letters from Scotland,' written between the Rebellions of 1715 and 1745. Some modern Highlanders call him their foe : he certainly looks with English eyes, but he tries to be fair, and is far from unsympathetic. His tenderness for the poor is remarkable. We have the Gartmore MSS. (circ. 1748), which is Whiggish, and 'MS. 104,' in the King's Library. It is, apparently, of 1749 50. All these witnesses agree as to the oppression of the people, their involuntary idleness, their dependence on tacksmen, chamberlains and factors, their destitution, while their liability to raised rents and evictions are, by some of these witnesses, insisted upon. But all are writing from the Whig point of view ; their desire to improve the popular condition is part of their desire to reduce the power of the Jacobite Chiefs.

On the other side is General Stewart of Garth, enthusiastically Highland, anxious to keep up population for military purposes, as well as from honourable sympathy, and decidedly inclined to overlook the poverty, plundering, enforced idleness. tippling, and blackmail of the good old times. We have also Mr. Fraser Mackintosh, who, while he delights to tell a story against Cluny, for example, maintains that there were no evictions before 1745. Unluckily, we have no authoritative treatise from the Jacobite and 'old times' side, written between 1747 and 1790. The best evidence might be found in Gaelic poetry, which, in general, proves one important point.

Whatever the material condition of the Highland people, whatever their lack, in many parishes, of elementary education, they possessed, in legends, *Märchen*, traditional poems, and the living art of popular song, a native culture—rich, dignified. and imaginative—which newspapers merely destroy. This great element of happiness, where it survives, is the bequest of the good old times.

Such is our evidence; and now, having described its nature, we may turn to the details.

A considerable portion of the people were terribly destitute. We have heard what the biographer of Young Barisdale says, about a diet of shellfish from March to August, about the faces that never wear a smile. Franck, writing in 1654–1660, tells us how, when Monk held Scotland, the Strathnaver crofters bled their cows in winter, and fed on blood mixed with oatmeal.[1] Burt and Knox testify to the same practice, a century later and more. 'This immoderate bleeding reduces the cattle to so low a plight that in the morning they cannot rise from the ground, and several of the inhabitants join together to help up each other's cows.'[2] 'The gentry may be said to be a handsome people, but the commonalty much otherwise; one would hardly think, by their faces, they were of the same species, or, at least, of the same country, which plainly proceeds from their bad food . . .'[3]

The old times were not so good; the peasants, who protected and concealed him, could not give Lord Pitsligo salt to his porridge: 'Salt is dear.' But people who have seen nothing better are not discontented. The gentry—not chiefs, but tacksmen—as we have said, did not live luxuriously. Examples may be given. 'Although they have been attended at dinner by five or six servants, they have often dined upon oat-meal varied several ways, pickled herrings, or other such cheap and indifferent diet . . . Their houses are *sometimes* built with stone and lime' (like Barisdale's palace), but other houses of the gentry 'are built in the manner of the huts.' Burt

---

[1] *Northern Memoirs*. This author does not speak of drinking the blood of the *living* cow. See *op. cit.* p. 209, and note, p. 372. This correction applies to p. 283.

[2] Burt, ii. p. 31.   [3] *Ibid.* p. 26.

mentions one such house, with beasts dwelling under the roof of the owner, or tacksman. For many years Old Glengarry dwelt in a hut, his castle being occupied by an English commercial gentleman. The laird's children were ' dirty and half naked '—this is on hearsay—and it was a common proverb that ' a gentleman's bairns are known by their speaking English.' Glengarry's niece, daughter of Æneas, shot at Falkirk, ' had no English,' when she could not have been under thirteen years of age.[1]

Thus there was no very great gulf, in some cases, between gentry and peasantry, where comfort was concerned. The difference of appearance between them, as between beings ' of a different species.' is the less intelligible. But herrings and game are more nutritious than nettles, cows' blood, and shell-fish, especially where all are scarce.

As to rents, payments to chief or tacksman, how did things fare? Conservatives, like Dr. Johnson and Sir Walter Scott, have written about the chiefs ' degenerating from patriarchal rulers to rapacious landlords.' The Duke of Argyll, on the contrary, speaks of the sub-tenants, in the good old times, as ' holding at the will of the lease-holders or tacksmen, and complaining bitterly of the oppressions under which they laboured.' This is on the evidence of Sheriff Campbell of Stonefield, speaking of Mull, Morven, and Tyree, in 1732.[2] ' It was only begin-

---

[1] Glengarry's Letter Book, MS.
[2] *Scotland as it was and as it is*, p. 245.

ning to be felt by these poor people that even a bare subsistence could not be secured when plunder had been stopped, and before industry had begun.' What were the 'oppressions,' not including, of course, such exceptional outrages as those of Barisdale? Well, Burt tells us that a tenant's improvements, in 1730–1740, meant an instant rise of rent. 'What would the tenant be the gainer of it' (enclosures and improvements on his farm), 'but to have his rent raised, or his farm divided with some other?'[1] The division would serve to recruit another swordsman for the Chief. The writer of a MS. of 1747, in the possession of Graham of Gartmore,[2] says, 'The practice of letting many farms to one man' (the tacksman, say Lochgarry or Barisdale), 'who, again subsetts them to a much greater number than these can maintain, and at a much higher rent than they can afford to pay, obliges these poor people to purchase their rents and expences by theifts and robberys.'[3]

In the good old days, something like the iniquitous Truck System existed, we learn from the same authority, on some Highland estates. 'Some of the substantial Tacksmen play the merchant, and supply the common people . . . As the poor ignorant people have neither knowledge of the value of their purchase, nor money to pay for it, they deliver to these dealers

---

[1] Burt, ii. 51.

[2] The Gartmore MS. is denounced as full of ignorant Lowland prejudice, by General Stewart of Garth.

[3] Burt, Appendix, ii. 357.

(the tacksmen) 'cattle in the beginning of May for what they have received; by which traffick the poor wretched people are cheated out of their effects for one half of their value.' This is a mournful aspect of the good old times. The MS. 104 confirms the statements, and describes the thriftless agricultural methods.

Each of these (the tacksmen) · possesses some very poor people under him, perhaps five or six on a farm, to whom he lets out the skirts of his possession, these people are generally the soberest and honestest of the whole. Their food all summer is milk and whey mixed together without any bread, the little butter or cheese they are able to make is reserved for winter provision, they sleep away the greatest part of the summer, and when the little Barley they sow becomes ripe, the women pull it as they do flax, and dry it on a large wicker machine over the fire. Then burn the straw, and grind the corn upon Quearns or hand mills. In the end of Harvest, and During the winter they have some Flesh, Butter, and cheese, with great scarcity of Bread. All their business is to take care of the few Cattle they have. In spring, which is their only season in which they work, their whole food is bread and gruel without so much as salt to season it.

'About twenty years ago Lochiel erected two or three Water Mills, but by reason of the great distance of many of the people from them, and their natural Laziness, with the prejudice in favour of the old

Custom of burning the straw, they were made very
little use of. The custom has been given up some
time except by the Camerons and Macdonalds, some
McLeans, and some of the people of Skye.'

It is not safe, of course, to argue from a report
about the state of the people in one part of the
Highlands to a conclusion about their condition
everywhere. A river may divide comfort from
destitution. And it is certain that reports by Lowlanders, Englishmen, or Highlanders, like the famous
Forbes of Culloden, who practically defeated the
Rising of 1745, will not please some Highland
reasoners.[1]

Forbes reported in 1737 on the Duke of Argyll's
lands in Morven, Mull, and Tyree. He speaks of
the 'tyranny' and 'unmerciful exactions' of the
tacksmen, large leaseholders who sub-let to smaller
tenants. Hence the lands lie waste, and 'above one
hundred families have been reduced to beggary and
driven out of the island.' This is precisely the
modern complaint against the bad new times, a
complaint with which we all sympathise. Tacksmen,
according to Culloden, were as bad as factors.

---

[1] We have another statement by Culloden : 'From Perth to Inverness, and thence to the Western Sea, including the Western Islands, . . .
no part is in any degree cultivated, except some spots here and there
in straths or glens, by the sides of rivers, brooks, or lakes, and on the
sea-coast. The grounds that are cultivated yield small quantities of
mean corns not sufficient to feed the inhabitants, who depend for their
nourishment on milk, butter, cheese, &c., the product of their cattle. . . .
Their habitations are the most miserable huts that ever were seen.'
Culloden Papers, p. 298.

Culloden, therefore, suggested the granting to the
sub-tenants of nineteen years' leases if they would
'offer frankly for their farms such rent as fairly and
honestly they could bear.' Such leases he had
power to offer, and did offer. 'No takers!' Culloden was surprised, but he need not have been. The
weight of the tacksmen would be against him, also
the conservatism of the people. A fixed rent was a
new crude hard thing: a system of shuffling along,
above all as the general policy was to find room for
swordsmen—was an old endurable thing. Culloden,
however, persuaded some sub-tenants to offer. On
the tacksmen he put pressure. He had with him
some tacksmen from the mainland, better acquainted
with farming methods. *They* offered for the insular
tacksmen's farms, whereon the insular tacksmen
also offered. Fixed now were rents, and fixed the
duration of tenancy.

One Culloden lease to a kind of village com-
munity of six people in portions of land of different
sizes is dated April 18, 1739, from Stoney Hill.[1]
The lease of 1739 is for nineteen years, 'and that in
full satisfaction of all casualitys, and other prestations
and services whatsomever,' except for services in
repairing harbours, mending highways, or repairing
miln-leads, for the general benefite of the Island

---

[1] This is the house near Musselburgh, which the wicked Colonel
Charteris lent to Culloden, who had defended him from a charge of
rape. In one room (when I was a boy) you saw in the centre a great
black blotch, and black marks as of footsteps tiptoeing out to the door.
A gruesome room !

(Mull). The tenants were to pay cesses, ministers'
stipends, schoolmasters' salaries, &c., 'freeing and
relieving the Duke' from these burdens. Failure of
rent meant removal, and made the lease null and
void ; the tenants having leave, however, to take
over the share of a defaulter or choose a substitute
for him.

What the sub-tenants gain is freedom from a
tacksman, secure possession while they pay, and
freedom from all but the stated customary services
and 'casualities.' One of these was military service
in a Jacobite rising. A tenant in Mull could not now
lose his holding if his tacksman ordered him to join
the Prince and he refused. As to the other 'services.'
the Duke of Argyll regards them as indefinite and
oppressive. He selects examples from Sinclair's
paper for the Board of Agriculture in 1795. Rent
was mainly paid in kind, chickens, cattle, grain, *plus*
' tilling, dunging, sowing, and harrowing a part of an
extensive farm in the proprietor's' (or tacksman's)
' possession.' Peats, thatching, weeding, cartage.
harvesting, and so forth, were exacted, with implements, eggs, butter, cheese, a tithe of fish and oil,
woollen yarn, and so forth. These services might
easily be made oppressive, and did not conduce to
improvement in agriculture.

The exact weight and money value of these
services must have varied widely. The author of
MS. 104 proposes that, in future, all services shall be
definitely stated in writing when a tenant takes a

farm. 'Extravagant services are still required' (*circ.* 1750) 'and performed, which the landlord would be ashamed to commit to writing.' He also, like Culloden, advocates the compulsory granting of leases for not less than twenty years. But he has already said that the people, accustomed to hereditary entry on farms from father to son, refuse to take written leases.

As to 'services,' Mr. Fraser Mackintosh, on the other side, tells us how the Lochiels, in exile, 'regularly received part of the rent.' That he only sent 100*l.* to Lochiel's children in France, and made the tenants work on his lands instead of on the county roads, is a charge made by Colonel Crawfurd against Lochiel's brother, Fassifern.[1] Mr. Fraser Mackintosh comments on the loyalty of Lochiel's tenants, but adds ' in former times rent in the form of money was a minor easy consideration, the real burden or tax being services'—especially ' the almost intolerable burden' of war. Thus the exile of the Chief became ' really no hardship to the people,' enabling them ' to pay a double (money) rent now and then with comparative ease.' [2]

Thus, in this author's opinion, ' the real burden or tax' was 'services,' not money rent. Happily he gives a case of commutation of services for money on Glengarry's estate. The commutation was ' apparently quite disproportionate and oppressive. For instance, in the case of Dugald Cameron, late cow-

[1] Cumberland Papers, 1753.   [2] *Antiquarian Notes*, p. 207.

herd to Glengarry, afterwards tenant of Boline, while
his rent was 11*l*. 4*s*. 3*d*., the converted services
amounted to 3*l*. 2*s*. 8*d*.' Well, if services were ' the
real burden,' where is the 'oppressive dispropor-
tion'?[1] This seems absurd.

If it be agreed that 'services' were the main
part of rent, how oppressive a hostile tacksman, say
Barisdale, might make them is easily conceived.[2]
Whatever we may think of the advantages of a
definite Culloden rent, it is pretty plain that the
people did not like it. But the old kind of rent and
services was of scarce any value to a probably non-
resident proprietor, who could get high returns on
the new system from large farmers or graziers. He
did not want hens and cheese, and had now no use
for claymores. The consequences were raised rents,
emigration, evictions, the Highland grievances.

But were there no evictions, and removals, and
forced migrations in the good old times?

Mr. Fraser Mackintosh says, 'The Commissioners
on the Forfeited Estates, or, more properly, their
Factors, were the first evictors in the Highlands, and
they were guilty of favouritism to such a degree in

---

[1] *Antiquarian Notes*; compare pp. 126 and 207.
[2] Here is a formal rent from Burt (ii. 56) :—
      Donald Mac Oil vic ille Challum.
      Money £3. 10. 4. Scots £0. 5. 10¼.
      Butter 3 lb. 2 oz.
      Oatmeal 2 bushels 1 Peck 3 Lip.
      Sheep ¼ and ₁₄.
Other tenants paid in shares the rest of the sheep. Then there would
be 'services,' engaging Donald's time and labour.

T

favour of strangers, that many of the tenants emigrated voluntarily.'

Indeed, Glenure was shot, by Allan Breck or
another, because, as factor for the forfeited estates
of Lochiel and Ardsheil, he had evicted Cameron or
Stewart tenants, and preferred Campbells. But Mr.
Fraser Mackintosh ought to know that the Commissioners were *not* the first evictors. Who drove a
hundred families from Mull and Tyree about 1738,
as Culloden tells us? Who 'removed' James Stewart
of the Glens before Campbell of Glenure did? Why
Ardsheil, whose bastard brother he was. Who
evicted some and threatened to evict all Macphersons from the Duke of Gordon's lands in Badenoch
in 1724? Why the Duke and his factor, Gordon of
Glenbucket.

The story is told in a letter of Cluny to the Earl
Marischal.[1] The Macphersons held lands in Badenoch 'as feuars, woodsellers, or kindly tenents to
the Duke of Gordon.' He however 'vexes and reduces us by perpetuall lawsuits,' and '*has taken it
into his head to root us intearly out of our own country.*'
He therefore feued most of his Badenoch lands to
Glenbucket 'for the half of its value, or, I may say,
a third, meerly out of design to take it out of the
hands of the Macphersons.' Glenbucket, 'in order
to begin the work of extirpating us, has turned out
the tenants of six farms.' Their high offers of rent

---

[1] 'Cluny, May 10, 1724.' *Stuart Papers*, p. 113, Appendix,
pp. 100-105

were refused, so they dirked Glenbucket, 'in a most
barbarous manner.' The operation can scarcely be
performed in a gentle fashion. 'They very luckily
missed their aim by the favour of a buff belt he had
about him,' also by the favour of a claymore that
was lying convenient. The Duke now threatened to
'extirpate' or evict 'the whole name of Macpherson,'
which he proceeded to do 'with a body of a thousand
men, foot and horse.' All parties were Jacobites,
and King James settled *hæc certamina tanta*. He
had no objections to eviction. He writes to the
Duke of Gordon, 'I am far from blaming you for
any steps you may have taken which are authorised
by the law of the land, but there are only a few
offenders, and, politically, the *eviction* disunites loyal
clans.'[1]

Indeed the more one thinks of Mr. Fraser
Mackintosh's assertion that the Commissioners were
the first evictors in the Highlands, the more grotesque
does it appear. We turn to the manuscript 'Letter
of a Gentleman' whose sympathies are with 'the
wretched commons,' not with the Chiefs.[2] 'The
gentlemen of the name of Mackenzie,' says our
author, 'are frugal and industrious. . . . They have
screwed up their rents to an extravagant height,
which they vitiously term improving their estates,
without putting the tenants upon a proper way of
improving the ground, to enable them to pay that

---

[1] James to the Duke of Gordon, August 27, 1724.
[2] British Museum. The King's Library, 104.

rent, which makes the common people little better than slaves and beggars.'

No 'screw' but eviction could be used by these Mackenzie landlords, frugal and industrious.

Here is a case among the Camerons from the same MS. :—

'To shew the present disposition of that Clan,' described as 'lazy, silent, sly, and enterprizing people.' 'I will relate an instance of their barbarity which happened since the year 1725. The possessor of a farm belonging to the Duke of Gordon, of the tribe of the Macmartins, about three miles to the North of Fort William, demanded an abatement of the usual rent, which the Duke refusing, he left the farm, boasting that no man would dare to succeed in it. For some years it was untenanted, till at last the Duke prevailed on Mr. Skeldoich, who was then minister of the parish, who could not find a place to reside in, to take this farm. The former possessor lay still till the minister had plentifully stocked the farm with cattle and built a house on it, then, with some other rogues, finding that the cattle were carefully watched, went to the place where the calves were kept, and with their durks cut off their heads, and cut the skins so that they would not be of any use.'

They also destroyed the Duke's salmon nets on the Lochy. Later, watching till the minister chanced to be away from home, 'they pulled down part of his house, and fired several shots towards the place where his wife lay.' The worthy clergyman then thought it time to move into Fort William. Our author adds that cadets of Highland houses have possessed farms ' for ages' without leases, and when they are not able to pay their rents, *and are turned out*, they look upon the person who takes the farm after them as usurping their right. These people have often refused to take a written lease, thinking that, by so doing, they gave up the right of possession.

All this, written about 1749, is hardly congruous with Mr. Fraser Mackintosh's bold statement that the Commissioners of Forfeited Estates were the first evictors in the Highlands. We learn that, ' by reason of the great poverty and slavery of the commons,' on the Mackenzie estates, out of the clan levy of 3,000 men, ' a third are but dross.' Let us add that the Campbells evicted the Macdonalds from Kintyre, by cutting their throats ; that every defeated clan was likely to be, more or less, evicted; and that all the Macgregors were evicted. These were operations of clan warfare, though not much more enjoyable for that. But when a sub-tenant held from a tacksman, on a ' precarious tenure,' does Mr. Fraser Mackintosh maintain that he was never evicted ? Why did Robin Oig shoot Macfarlane at the plough tail? He did so simply for the old agrarian reason.

In Prestongrange's speech for the Crown, at the disgraceful trial which ended in the judicial murder

of James Stewart of the Glens, he says that 'a delusion in a peculiar manner prevailing in the Highlands,' is that 'a cause of mortal enmity arises if a
man should be removed by another from his farm or
possession which he hath no manner of title to hold
or retain.'[1] 'The delusion,' he says, 'prevails elsewhere,' but is 'in a particular manner prevalent in
the Highlands.'

How could a popular delusion of this kind come
into existence if the Commissioners of Forfeited
Estates were 'the first evictors in the Highlands'?
Demonstrably they were nothing of the kind. There
were evictions in the good old times.

On the other hand, evictions had probably not
been much practised with a view to obtaining higher
rents or making improvements, but for other reasons.
Claymores, not money, had been in request from
tenants before 1745.

Once more, according to Burt, a Lowland
authority, the Chief 'must free the necessitous from
their arrears of rent, and maintain such who, by
accidents, are fallen to a total decay.' Far from
throwing a lot of small farms into a large one, or a
sheep-walk, 'if, by increase of the tribe, small farms
are wanting for the support of such addition, he
splits others into lesser portions, because all must
somehow be provided for.'[2]

This policy is the precise reverse of the Culloden
lease, which terminates, *ipso facto*, when rent falls into

---

[1] *Scots Magazine*, 1753. p. 498.   [2] Burt, ii. 5, 6.

arrears. A Chief, bound by consanguinity to treat
all his tenants as gentlemen, might practise shooting
at them, like Clanranald with his famous piece, 'the
Cuckoo,' but certainly was not apt to evict often for
arrears of rent. He lived at home, he built a great
castle like Glengarry's (probably by aid of 'services'),
he fed on the sheep, kine, butter, milk, of his tenants,
but he shook them by the hand, perhaps forgave
arrears, held clan feasts, and was a god on earth.
When he raised rents, united farms in one hand, did
not shake that of every clansman, but rather evicted
them, discontent was natural, inevitable. Holders
of land, proud free men, must emigrate, or become
labourers or artisans in towns. Who does not sympathise with their emotions?

On the other side, the Chief must subdivide and
subdivide, in the good old times, 'because all must
somehow be provided for.' But all could not be
and were not ·provided for.' We have seen the
pictures of cruel exquisite poverty from Franck in
1654, to the Gartmore MS. in 1747, and the Culloden
Report in 1738, and the 'Life of Barisdale' in
1754, and Burt's Letters of about 1735. It seems
reasonable to suppose that all arable lands were
eagerly cultivated as far as the implements and
skill of the people availed to cultivate them. It was
the interest of the chiefs to increase their bands of
warriors and the sentiment, if not the interest, of the
clansmen urged them to stay on the land.

But the land could not maintain them! The

younger gentry pushed their fortunes abroad as men
of the sword or in commerce. But the commons
were often at the starving point ; we hear of famines.
Glengarry writes of a great scarcity, when meal had
to be bought in the Lowlands. Burt tells of no meal
in Inverness. ‘A house, grass for a cow or two,’ and
‘as much land as will sow a boll of oats,’ rocky land.
needing spade culture, was a cottar's ‘only wages
of his whole labour and service.’ says the Gartmore
MS. The author reckons that there is not in the
Highlands employment for more than half the
population, even when land has been remorselessly
sub-divided. Many earned a harvest wage in the
Lowlands. Others ‘sorned’ on their kindred. Armies
of tramps were supported by the generosity of the
poor ; nay, Lowland beggars came North, allured by
the open hands of the Highlanders. Whisky shops
were everywhere ; here men sauntered and drank.
Plunder was habitual ; a captain of a ‘Watch’ like
Barisdale was at once thief and thief-taker. ‘They
live like lairds. and die like loons,’ says Franck.
speaking not of all the Highlands (as Macaulay
quotes him), but chiefly of Lochaber. ‘Upon this
fund’—blackmail—the Captain ‘employed one half
the thieves to recover lost cattle, and the other half
of them to steal.’ Lochiel laboured to reform his
clan in this respect. The exactions of tacksmen,
‘sub-letting farms to a much greater number than
they can maintain, and at a much higher rent than
they can pay, obliges these poor people to purchase

their rents and expences by theifts and robberys.'
of cattle ; for the Highland honesty about portable
property is extolled by Burt.

As to the moral iniquity of cattle robbing, all
morality is local, and a man who does not sin against
the local standard is no extreme criminal. The Macdonalds held a simple creed of communism. 'They
say that the Cattle are God's creatures, made for the
use of man, for which the earth yields grass and
herbs in plenty, without the labour of man, and that
therefore they Ought to be common '—that is, ought
to belong to the Macdonalds.[1] The same ideas had
prevailed on the Border :

> If every man had his ain cow,
> A richt poor clan Buccleugh's wad be.

Dr. Carlyle shows that Border cattle thieves,
though not encouraged by the gentry, were a
powerful class about 1740.

This is not a picture of a golden age, and Bailie
Nicol Jarvie, in ' Rob Roy,' sums up this theory of
what the age was really like. But, if we turn to
Stewart of Garth,[2] we find the real condition of the
Highlands in times past revealed in a rosy haze.
Blackmail is only extorted from *Lowlanders*, as if
Barisdale had Lowland neighbours![3] The game and
fish were ' free to all '—a palpable error as regards
salmon, at all events, while one doubts if every clansman was made free of Cluny's forest. We do not read
of grouse and venison in cotters' huts. ' Cottagers

---

[1] MS. 104.   [2] *Sketches*, 1822.   [3] *Ibid.* i. 40.

and tradesmen were discouraged from marrying.'[1]
Yet the surplus population was very large. A young
amorous Highlander set himself up for marriage
by 'thigging'—that is. by begging among friends
for cows, sheep. and seed-corn.[2] They did not discourage him. 'The extinction of the respectable
race of tacksmen . . . is a serious loss to the people.'[3]
Mr. Fraser Mackintosh, however. speaking of Skye,
says, 'large tacksmen . . . could be relied on to
assist (each other) or keep aloof, if the oppressed
were below their class or set.'[4] The author of MS.
104 would reduce the power of tacksmen by making
all tenants leaseholders for terms not under twenty
years, and would pay off all wadsetts on forfeited
estates. 'because the gentlemen who had them were
great oppressors of the Poor, and most of them,
though they did not themselves take arms. were very
active in forcing the people into the late Rebellion.'

An association had been made by Sutherland
farmers in General Stewart's time to suppress sheep-
stealing. He objects to the new social state which
made this association necessary. Previously ' crimes
had been so few that, from 1747 to 1810, there
was only one capital conviction for theft.' This may
have been so in Sutherland. and the MS. Letter
already cited makes it probable. 'The Mackays of
Lord Reay's country,' though previously reckoned
'the wickedest clan,' now 'abhor thieving.' But

[1] *Op. cit.* i. 84, 85.   [2] Burt, ii. 107.
[3] *Sketches*, i. 135, *not*   [4] *Antiquarian Notes*, p. 284.

'the common people who dwell along the East
Coast are next to the Caithness people for poverty,
slavery, and dwarfish stature, while the people
further up the country towards Strathnaver' (where
Franck found them bleeding their cattle for food)
'live better.' A third of the Earl of Sutherland's
levy 'are mean, despicable creatures.' Thus one
county showed very different conditions; however,
like the Mackenzies, the Sutherland men 'abhor
thieving.' Elsewhere in the Highlands, hangings for
theft occupy a good deal of the old *Scots Magazine*.
Many pretty men 'died for the law,' as every one
knows.

General Stewart, objecting to the new farmers' association, seems not to have observed that blackmail
and 'Highland Watches' were old-fashioned 'associa-
tions for protecting property.' Complaints are made
by him of ' cutting down farms into lots,' as if the old
Chiefs had not infinitely subdivided the soil.[1] The
old extreme poverty is left out of notice by General
Stewart, with the old tippling, loafing, 'sorning,'
thieving, 'thigging' habits. Much land could be
and was cultivated, he says, which is now pasture,
the harvest only failing 'in cold and wet autumns.'[2]
These not being unknown in the Highlands, but, on
the other hand, very common, famines followed often,
notably in 1782.

If the Lowlanders, the English, and the Anglified
Highlanders, like Culloden, paint too gloomy a

---

[1] *Sketches*, i. 150.   [2] *Ibid*. ii. Appendix, xliv.

picture of the good old times, General Stewart may be regarded as erring in the opposite direction. His charge against the new Chiefs and landlords is the callous hurry with which they seized their pecuniary advantage, 'which proved ruinous to their ancient tenants.'[1] This is also Scott's opinion, in his *Quarterly Review* article of 1816. He, too, a Tory of the Tories, condemns the heartless greed of evicting landlords.[2] General Stewart records cases of delicate consideration and honourable sagacity on the side of the landlords. But often we find either a well-meaning hurry to make sweeping 'improvements,' and benefit people in a way they detest and do not understand (as by giving them leases), or a mere hasty desire to save such a ruined estate as war had left to Glengarry, by raising rents, causing, with the aid of frequent famine years, wholesale emigration. This policy was, indeed, far unlike what Burt reports: 'the poverty of the tenants has rendered it customary for the Chief, or Laird, to free some of them every year from all arrears of rent; this is supposed, upon an average, to be about one year in five of the whole estate.'

These habits vanished with the change in the Highlands; the old 'arts of popularity' were no longer practised by the Chiefs : clan affection became clan hatred. If we may believe a tithe of our Whig or Lowland information, it should have done so long before 1745. Cattle, sheep, red-deer, grouse, now

---

[1] *Sketches*, i. 189.
[2] See also the Introduction to *The Legend of Montrose*.

occupy the place of the swords of the North; the banker, brewer, or upholsterer shoots the Chief's game, or misses it.

Truly money is the root of all evil. When specie was scarce in the North, a guinea a thing seldom seen, the fatal treasure of Loch Arkaig produced, or evoked, the moral consequences of hatred, malice, treachery and slander. Twenty years later the lack of money hardened the hearts of Chiefs (which had not been so very soft before). Clansmen had to emigrate, and they were wisest who sailed first from a land of famine. Their descendants, or some of them, dwell happily in a realm of forests, hills, and streams, deer and salmon, still retaining Highland courtesy, Highland speech, Highland courage, and Highland hospitality. They seem to have chosen the better part, and to be more fortunate than their cousins in the new times, or their fathers in the old days that were not really golden.

On the whole, a distressed Highlander need not, it seems, conceive that the old times were free from distress, or that Chiefs were really always humane. They acted in accordance with their immediate interests. They kept rents low when it paid to have a following, and they screwed rents up when money was more desirable than men. The two policies might be contemporary; this among Mackenzies, that among Macdonalds. Ensign Small reported [1] that, among the Macdonalds, 'the gentry

---

[1] Cumberland Papers, 1753.

are fond of a rising, the commoners hate it.' The
author of MS. 104 represents the Macdonalds as
'cursing their Prince and their Chiefs.'

The world, to its disadvantage, allows interest to
override sentiment, which we only find here and
there, as in the noble words of Lochiel. When he
arrived with Prince Charles in France, in the autumn
of 1746, he was, of course, very poor. The Prince,
according to Young Glengarry, in a conversation
with Bishop Forbes, was obliged to give Lochiel a
full security for his estates before the Chief would
raise his clan. Consequently Charles felt bound, said
Glengarry, to secure a French regiment first of all
for Lochiel. This, in Lochiel, would have been a
singular piece of caution! But let us hear his own
words, in a letter to King James.[1] 'I told H.R.H. that
Lord Ogilby or others might incline to make a figure
in France; but my ambition was to serve the Crown,
and serve my Country, or perish with itt. H.R.H. say'd
he was doing all he could' (to return with forces to
Scotland), 'but persisted in his resolution to procure
me a Regiment. If it is obtained, I shall accept it
out of respect to the Prince, but I hope Yr. M. will
approve of the resolution I have taken *to share in the
fate of the people I have undone*, and, if they must be
sacrificed, to fall along with them. It is the only
way I can free myself from the reproach of their
blood, and shew the disinterested zeal with which

---

[1] January 16, 1747.

I have lived, and shall dye, Your Majesty's most
humble, most Obedient, and most faithfull subject
and servant,

'DONALD CAMERON.[1]'

There speaks a man who makes real the ideal of
the Clan system. But the ideal, though a hundred
times illustrated in the conduct of the commons,
has left less conspicuous examples in the behaviour
of some Chiefs. 'My brother-in-law, Major Grant,
pretended that the man,' (a recruit) 'I sent from
this country, I *sold*, which is false,' says Old Lovat
to Cluny.[2] Major Grant, his brother-in-law, knew
Old Lovat. He, like Barisdale, was an example of
the kind of chief who, till after 1745, was not impossible. He throve wickedly on the survival of a kind
of society, the tribal society with its usages, which
was in no sense exclusively Celtic, but originally prevalent all over Europe. In parts of the Highlands
tribal society outlived its day, and gave to Lovat
the opportunities which he abused.

[1] Browne, iii. p. 477.
[2] March 26, 1740. *Gleanings from Cluny Charter Chest*, p. 4.

APPENDIX

..

I.—*PICKLE'S LETTERS*

THESE two letters of Pickle's, not published in full in
Pickle the Spy, illustrate ' The Case against Glengarry ' in
this volume. In the letter dated Edinburgh, 14th September, 1754, we find that, immediately on hearing of his
father's death, the writer sent a note to Gwynne Vaughan,
an English official, and went to Edinburgh, writing from
Newcastle on his way North. His ' family affairs are in
confusion.' Now Old Glengarry died in Edinburgh, on
September 1, 1754, and, as has been elsewhere shown,
Young Glengarry at once repaired to the North. No
reader of these letters can doubt that their writer is, or is
feigning to be, Young Glengarry. Now no such pretence
could possibly succeed in Edinburgh, where Young Glengarry, a man eminently well known, happened to be at the
moment. For the rest, the letters are mainly concerned
with the Informer's proposed terms of payment, now that
his ' situation is greatly altered,' by the death of his father,
obviously Old Glengarry. Further comment seems needless,
the evidence being beyond suspicion, and capable of but
one interpretation.

Dr. Sir,—I have receivd the pleasur of yours of 20
Septr, but have been of late so hurried that I had no time
to return a proper answer. I thought I was pritty pointed
in my last in regard to a certain stipulation, but as by
yours I imagen I was not so well understood, I beg leave to
be now more explicite. I waited patiently four years (since

1750) without making the least demand, but for Journy expences, which fell so farc short that I spent all my owne ready Mony, and ran in debt eight hundred £st. Now, Sir, I expect that your friend will pay this sume by way of gratification, which will make me free of all debt contracted during my several trips, for I expect to be considered for what is past, as well as for times coming : I *had had his worthy Brother's*[1] *paroll for this as well as a promise of his countenance, and protection, in all my other claimes. as I will not varrie the least in my demand, notwithstanding my situation is greatly altered*, I will only mention £ five hundred St. yearly, twice regularly payd by Grandpapa, for I won't absolutely have to dow with any other. If Mr. *Kenady* (Duke of Newcastle) whose friendship I have a right to Claim, in vertue of his Brother's promise, will obtain this for me, there is nothing honourable he can think of, but I am able to perform. Only I beg he be not prejudic'd by that swarm of Videts that dally infest him. The Services I can be of are pritty well known, and as I am embark'd I am determin'd to percevere, but then I expect that Mr. Kenady (D. of N.) will fulfill his worthy Brother's promise to me, which was to clear me of the Debts contracted in my new way of lief, when that is done, and a certain thing yearly fixt, Mr. *Kenady* shall dispose of me in what shape he pleases. Young Swift (Lochgarry) is arrived, and upon his waiting of *20* (Genl. Bland) was not recevd as was promis'd he should. When I waited of him, he did not receve me as I expected, haughtly refusd the use of a fulsie without I should qualifie. I smiling answr'd, if that was the case, I had then a right without his permission, but that he could not take it amiss that I debar'd all under his comand the pleasure of hunting upon my grounds, or of any firing, which they can't have without my permission, so that I thought favours were reciprocall. *20* (Genl.

---

[1] Henry Pelham's.

Bland) and his Club pretends to be well inform'd of the
minutest transaction in the Grand Monark's Cabinet, *O
rare pollitirians, Poor 21 (Bruce) is greatly to be pityed, for
my old friends are mad at my consulting him in all my affairs,
and 20 (Bland) and some about him spoke very injurious of
him to me*. I think this ought to be put to rights. *I go
North in a few days*, I hope to prevail on *21* (Bruce) to
follow in order to assist me in making a Judicial rent roll.[1]
My stay will not exceed a month, and his not a fortnight,
so that if you expect me up, write under *21* (Bruce's)
cover, and I shall obey your comands. But Mr. *Kenady*
(D. of N.), your friend, must enable me to go about it in a
proper manner, and I am sure I will performe the business
to his entire satisfaction. Young Swift, (Lochgarry) has
verbally communicated to me most of *Miss Philips* (Young
Pretender's) amours. She has turn'd adrift all, or most
of her former companions and galants. (This refers to
the rupture between Prince Charles and his English
adherents.) My presence is much wanted, and ardently
wished for by hir, and hir present conductors. But I cant
hear any thing materiall till old *Swift* (Lochgarry) return
from hir. What I mentiond concerning *Black Cattel* is fact,
but I hate repetitions, and at any rate must deffer further
particulars till my return from the North. I will expect the
pleasure of hearing to satisfaction and pointedly from you
—I will beg the continuance of your good Offices, and will
conclude by making offer of my Compts. to Mr. *Kenady*
and assures him that all now depends upon himself, as
Every thing is in his option.

I ever remain, Dear Grandpapa

Your most obedient and most oblidged humble Servt.

ALEX GUTHRY.

Edinbr. 10. Octr. 1754.

---

[1] One Bruce did survey the Forfeited Estates and others.

(Pickle to G.V.) (Gwynne Vaughan)

Add. 32,736. f. 525.   Edinbr. 14 Septr. 1754.

Dr. Sir,—I am vastly uneasy not to receive the least
answer to either of my letters from Newcastle, or that which
I wrote immediately upon my Father's death ;[1] but, as I
have the greatest confidence in your friendship, I perswade
myself that nothing prevents my receiving apointed answer
to every article in both my last, but the multiplicity of
weighty Affairs daily crouding upon the Duke of Newcastle ;
therefore without any suspicion or diffidence I am determined to continue firm to our Concert, untill you acquaint
me if he agrees to my Proposals, which if he does, he may
safely rely upon everything in my power, and I think I
can't give stronger proof of my sincerity than by this offer,
*in the confusion of my Family affairs, which in its present
situation, demands all my attention.* I have heard fully from
Lochgary, who acquaints me that the Young Pretender's
affairs take a very good turn, and that he has lately sent
two expresses to Lochgary earnestly intreating a meeting
with Pickle, and upon Lochgary's acquainting him of the
great distance Pickle was off, he commanded Lochgary to
a rendezvous, and he set out to meet me the 4th. Instant,
and is actually now with me.

I shall very soon have a particular account of the
present plan of operation.   I have now the ball at my foot,
and may give it what tune I please, as I am to be allowed
largely, if I fairly enter in co-partnership.   The French
King is in a very peaceable humour, but very ready to
take fire if the Jacobites renew their address, which the
Young Pretender assures him of, and he will the readier
bestirr himself, as the English Jacobites hourly torment
him.   Troops, Scotch and Irish, are daily offered to be

[1] At Edinburgh, Sept. 1, died Old Glengarry.

smuggled over : *but I have positively yet refused to admit any.*
The King of Spain has lately promised to add greatly to
the Young Pretender's patrimony, and English Contributors
are not wanting on their parts.

I suspect that my letters of late to my friends abroad
are stopt, pray enquire, for I think it very unfair dealings.
I am in a few weeks to go north to put some order to my
affairs. I should have been put to the greatest incon-
veniency if *21* (Bruce) had not lent his friendly assistance ;
but as I have been greatly out of pocket by the Jants I
took for Mr. Pelham, I shan't be in condition to continue
trade, if I am not soon enabled to pay off the Debts then contracted. I have said on former occasions so much upon this
head to no effect that I must now be more explicit, and I
beg your friendly assistance in properly representing it to
the Duke of Newcastle. If he thinks that my services, of
which I have given convincing proofs, will answer to his
advancing directly eight hundred Pounds, which is the
least that can clear the Debts of my former Jants, and fix
me to the Certain payment yearly of Five hundred at two
several terms, he may command anything in my power
upon all occasions. I am sorry to be forced to this
explanation, in which I always expected to be prevented.
I am so far from thinking this extravagant, that I am
perswaded it will save them as many thousands, by dis-
carding that swarm of Videts, which never was in the
least trusted. If the Duke of Newcastle's Constituent
(the King) was acquainted with this, I dare say he would
esteem the demand reasonable, considering what he throws
away upon others of no interest or power on either side.
I beg you'll acquaint me with the soonest of the Duke of
Newcastle's answer, and assure him of my ready obedience
to his commands. I have referred to *21* to enlarge further
upon this, and other subjects I have been conversing with
him some days ago, *as he can inform you of my great hurry*

and confusion for this fortnight past,[1] which will be all the apology I will make for this hurried scrawl, and I beg you'll be fully convinced of the great esteem etc. etc. etc.

P.S.   Pray let me not be denied the Arms I wanted, and I hope in case of accidents, you'll take care of young Lochgary.   I am just this instant informed that *Mr. Nordly* has left the King of France for the summer season, and is residing now in England, but can't learn in what particular place—*21* is supposed to be the Watchman: whose letter will explain what he hints of Lochgary.

Mr. Nordly is not deciphered yet.

(Copy of Pickle's letter to G. V. (Gwynne Vaughan) deciphered.   R. Oct. 16th, 1754.)

II.—MACLEOD

' The Rebels had an implacable Illwill and Malice against Him (Macleod) as they alledged, and many of them believed, that he not only deserted, but betrayed their Cause: what truth there is in this I will not take upon me to determine.' So says the writer of the MS. 104, ' The Highlands of Scotland in 1750.'

' Surely never did man so basely betray as did Macleod, whom I shall leave for the present to the racks and tortures of a guilty conscience, and the just and severe judgement of every good man.'   Thus writes Murray of Broughton, after narrating how Macleod gave a written promise to aid Prince Charles whenever he landed.   What he *did* was to send information to Forbes of Culloden, ' it is certain that the pretended Prince of Wales is come

---

[1] On account of Old Glengarry's death.

into the coast of South Uist and Barra.' He begs that his name as informant may be kept secret.[1]

Macleod can thus avoid the charge of betraying the Cause, only by disproof of Murray's allegation that he gave a written promise to rise. But this allegation is confirmed by family tradition. ' Miss Macleod of Macleod, Dunvegan Castle, remembers having seen in the family charter-chest an interesting correspondence between His Royal Highness and Macleod, in which Norman " invited the Prince to come over, several months before he arrived," but the letters have since disappeared, and the family knows nothing as to where they have gone to.'[2]

On the showing of Miss Macleod, as reported by Mr. Mackenzie, in the passage just cited, Murray might well cry ' never did man betray so basely as did Macleod.' Despite his written promise to Prince Charles, Macleod was the first to send information against ' the pretended Prince of Wales.' After Prestonpans, ' it would appear,' writes Mr. Mackenzie, ' that Macleod was taking lessons in duplicity from Simon,' Lord Lovat. Macleod scarcely needed instruction in treachery; but, if Mr. Mackenzie is right, he now meant to send Young Macleod with the clan to join the Prince, while he stayed at home, and said that he could not help it.[3] This domestic arrangement was not carried into effect.

Macleod was born in 1706, and inherited the family lands with 60,000l. He died in 1772, leaving 50,000l. of debt. He is still spoken of in the traditional history of his family as An Droch Dhuine, or ' the Wicked Man,' partly because of his extravagance, partly ' for his cruel treatment of his first wife and Lady Grange.'[4]

[1] Dunvegan, August 3, 1745. Culloden Papers, p. 204.
[2] History of the Macleods. By Alexander Mackenzie, F.S.A., p. 129. Inverness, 1889.
[3] Ibid. p. 133.   [4] Ibid. p. 149.

When we add his treachery to the Prince, we see in Macleod a character far from exemplary. His grandson speaks of him as 'always a most beneficent and beloved chieftain, whose necessities had lately induced him to raise his rents.' . . . . 'The Jacobites treated him as an apostate, and the successful party did not reward his loyalty.'[1] He reaped as he had sown.

---

[1] Mackenzie, pp. 150, 151.

INDEX

X

PRINTED BY
SPOTTISWOODE AND CO., NEW-STREET SQUARE
LONDON